I0524030

NEXT LEVEL
hot

How To Set The World On Fire Series:

Book 1:
How To Set The World On Fire

Book 2:
Money Jane

Book 3:
Next Level Hot

NEXT LEVEL
hot

T.K. RIGGINS

Next Level Hot

Published in 2019 in accordance with Franchise Publishing.

Cover design by: Edge of Water Designs, edgeofwater.com
Interior Formatting: Spica Book Design, spicabookdesign.com

Issued in print and electronic formats.
ISBN 978-0-9959002-4-0 (Book)
ISBN 978-0-9959002-5-7 (E-book)

Franchise Publishing
Vancouver, British Columbia

Printed in USA

For my young fam:
You can be anything you want.

Table of Contents

Prologue

Zuke couldn't stop his hands from trembling. The darkness, the rivers of lava, and the smell of burnt animal flesh all fed upon his fears. He wanted to escape this living nightmare.

"Look, a scorpion." Mardious pointed to their left.

Richard, the leader of their elite team, spun around. "Quiet," he said. The warrior jabbed his index finger towards the sky and tapped his helmet. He shook his head in disgust, then turned back to focus on leading the group deeper into the heart of Skyland.

Zuke glanced at the ground where Mardious was pointing and searched for the little beast. He had to peer closely to see the black, cunning creature; it blended well with the rocky terrain. He nodded at his wizard colleague, who smiled back politely.

They moved ahead with the rest of the task force, but Zuke knew that Mardious was up to something. He might have disliked Richard and the rest of the warriors, but Mardious absolutely hated them.

Mardious blamed warriors for everything he'd lost in life, and had trouble taking orders from any of them. Although they were on the same team, Mardious could only pretend to be content for so long.

Mardious flicked his fingertips in a little dance, as if he were playing an imaginary piano. It was how he focused his power.

Zuke's head started to swivel. The two warriors behind him stolidly marched forwards. The sky above was too dark to notice anything. The caverns that lined the path on either side of them were even darker.

He stared at the ground and tried to concentrate. He tugged on the cuffs of his golden leather gloves. They were given to him by his mother, and he used them to focus his power. He was about to use his own magic to feel what Mardious was up to, but then he noticed something scurry up the path.

The scorpion that Mardious had pointed out sped past Zuke, and the next few warriors in their group. It only slowed once it reached their leader, where it marched just behind Richard's left foot.

Zuke wondered if Mardious was going to try and hurt Richard. The scorpion's claws seemed too small to do much damage. Its stinger would be more effective, but how deep would it reach? Would it penetrate through a boot, or would the scorpion have to climb higher?

Before there was any trouble, Zuke reached out and clutched Mardious' arm.

Mardious froze. He turned his head slightly, but didn't make eye contact with Zuke. He was like a puppy that had been caught doing something it knew was wrong. Even though Zuke couldn't see Mardious' dark brown eyes, he knew how sad they'd look.

Mardious fluttered his fingers, and the scorpion moved away from the path.

Zuke let go of his arm, and they continued on in silence.

The path Richard led them along was specially marked on his map with a different colour of ink. The area was a garden of cavernous hillsides and small active volcanoes, which made it uncomfortably warm, but well-lit. The jagged terrain made their trek difficult, but it also gave them plenty of places to rest or hide, if necessary. There were only two occasions where they thought they spotted a dragon flying above them, but luckily one hadn't noticed them yet.

Richard raised his closed fist, and everyone stopped. They had arrived.

Across a stream of lava was a level field of brittle shale. A single cave stood in the very centre of the area. The entrance was broad enough for a giant, and although Zuke couldn't see in, he could sense how close they were to their target.

Richard turned to the group, drew his sword, and hunched over. They all huddled together as he used his weapon to sketch an outline of the territory in the loose, rocky path.

"Once we get to the cave entrance, we'll search for the mark of The Chosen," he said. He pointed to each of the warriors, and they all nodded in agreement. "Once we find it, I'll be able to mark the spot where the relic is buried, and we'll all dig together."

"Dragoon," the warriors rumbled. Zuke saw Mardious shudder. They both hated the trademark salute of the Guardians.

Richard marked a spot on each side of the cave entrance. "I want you two to be our eyes," he said, pointing to Mardious and Zuke. "If you give us the signal, we all take cover until the danger passes. We'll only engage as a last resort."

The two wizards nodded. Zuke felt nervous again. He wasn't confident in their plan for a dragon encounter, but they had no other options. He could only hope it would work; they couldn't afford to make a mistake.

The group carefully made their way across the narrow stone bridge over the lava stream. Once on the other side, they picked up the pace and raced across the field.

Even though the warriors were twice the age of the wizards, they were much faster, and Mardious and Zuke quickly fell behind. Zuke's lungs searched desperately for air, and the taste of metal crept onto his tongue. He tried to focus on his breathing instead of wondering what was lurking in the darkness. Before he had time to worry, the run was over.

Zuke took his position on the left side of the cave entrance, while Mardious stood on the right. Zuke hunched over as he tried to breathe, but he still couldn't help but look up to the overcast sky. The clouds obscured any sign of starlight, which made the night feel eerie. He gripped the rocks behind him, and imagined himself as a fly on the wall. It wasn't as comforting an idea as he'd thought.

"Clear," he heard one of the warriors say.

"Clear," echoed another.

"There are some bones here. They still have meat on them," Richard said.

Zuke looked back, and shifted to see around a couple boulders. Richard was holding a bone as tall as he was. Zuke had expected to see raw flesh hanging from it, but the meat was cooked. In fact, it looked well done.

A roar from above made Zuke jump. He searched the sky, but there was only darkness. He looked over at Mardious, who also moved his head frantically. Their eyes met, and they both shrugged.

"Found it," said another warrior.

Zuke glanced back again. Richard whispered something to the other warriors, and then stood tall. He counted out twelve steps from the cavern wall, and then checked his original position. He took six wide steps to his left, and pointed at the ground.

One of the group members rushed over and dropped a sac, spilling six shovels to the dirt. Each of the warriors grabbed one and broke ground. They worked hard and fast, and dust flew everywhere.

Zuke checked the sky again, but there was still nothing there. He pushed his nervousness aside and let the excitement creep in. They were getting closer. He tugged at the cuffs of his golden gloves and couldn't help but smile. One day, perhaps one day soon, he would wield ultimate power.

A loud clang echoed through the cave. Zuke whipped his head back just as Richard dropped his shovel and started clawing at the ground. A white glow shone from the hole, and Zuke could see the edge of an etched white stone. It was beautiful and magical.

Mesmerized by the luminous relic, he left his post to move closer to the warriors. They dug harder as more of the ancient artefact was exposed. Zuke wanted to grab a shovel, to help them uncover it faster.

Then he felt the earth shake.

Mardious came rushing past him. "Hide," he said nervously.

Beyond the cave entrance stood a golden, three-headed dragon. Its wings were spread out so wide they blocked all the light from the volcanic surroundings. Two of the dragon's heads looked off to the sides, but the centre one sniffed the air curiously.

Zuke stared at the dragon's massive claws, where a giant hog was caught in its clutches. The hog's eyes were glassy and staring, and its tongue dangled limply. There was blood everywhere.

He started trembling again.

A hand grabbed Zuke's arm and yanked him towards a boulder at the back of the cave. Richard shoved Zuke into his team's hiding position. "Do something," he whispered.

Zuke stared back into the team leader's angry eyes, and then faced the rest of the group. The warriors looked worried, but Mardious seemed confident. It gave him courage. He gave Mardious a nod to signal the first phase of their contingency plan.

Since Mardious was better at controlling animals, the plan was for him to use his magic to connect with the dragon. He closed his eyes and fluttered his fingers. He swayed back and forth, bobbed his head up and down, and focused on his power.

After a few seconds, Mardious opened his eyes and smiled. "I think it's gone," he whispered.

Richard carefully looked around the boulder, and then ducked back quickly. His eyebrows furrowed. "Try again," he said.

Zuke turned and took a peek. The dragon had entered the cave, and was sniffing around carefully. It knew something was wrong.

He turned to Mardious in shock, and could see the panic set in for his wizard partner.

"I can't do it," Mardious whispered.

Richard shoved Zuke. "Your turn, Beardy."

Although Mardious and Zuke did look similar, Richard acted like he could only distinguish between the two of them by Zuke's ability to grow facial hair. But Zuke understood how all wizards might look the same to Richard, because all warriors looked the same to him.

Zuke stretched out his arms, pulled on the cuffs of his golden leather gloves, and relaxed. He peered around the boulder again and went to work.

He closed his eyes and slowed his breathing. If Mardious couldn't connect with the dragon, Zuke knew he wouldn't be able to. Part of their plan relied on being able to use the dragon, but it seemed like they had underestimated the beast. Animal control didn't work on intelligent animals, and he was surprised that the dragon fit into that category. Their only course of action now was to distract the dragon so that they could regroup and plan their next move.

He didn't know what dragons felt threatened by, but another creature in the area seemed plausible. He imagined the scorpion they had seen earlier. He remembered its dark colour, the slender but dangerous tail, and how it scurried along the ground. It was important to remember every detail if he was to create an illusion of it.

After a few moments, a loud screech sounded from the cave entrance. He peeked his eyes open to find the dragon roaring. Its back was to the group, because its focus was now on a new enemy. A giant scorpion stood outside the cave entrance, snapping its claws menacingly.

All three heads of the dragon swam through the air like sea serpents, trying to study the scorpion from a different angle. The central head leant back and blew fire towards the threat, but it missed; Zuke had moved his illusion back and away from the cave entrance, out of the dragon's range.

The dragon chased after the scorpion, into the open field of shale. Zuke stepped forwards so he could keep an eye on the distracted beast. The rest of the group could now refocus and work on a plan of escape.

"Nice work," Richard said, but Zuke was still concentrating on his illusion and tried to ignore him. "Grab your shovels, we're almost done."

"Dragoon," the warriors responded. They returned to the glowing white rock and continued digging.

"Are you crazy?" Mardious said. "We don't have enough time. We need to get out of here before that thing comes back."

"Get back to your post," Richard commanded. He continued throwing dirt everywhere with his reckless shovelling.

Zuke was now at the front of the cave. He felt like a puppeteer, getting the dragon to chase the scorpion around like a hound chased a rabbit. The hunter was always close to catching its prey, but the hunted remained just out of reach.

A loud clang echoed through the cave. One of the warriors had hit the white stone too hard.

The dragon stopped moving. All three heads turned towards the den curiously, although one of them kept an eye on the scorpion. Zuke moved his illusion back and forth to taunt the dragon, but never close enough to make contact.

"It knows," Zuke shouted.

The dragon started barking; each head took a turn as the others listened. Zuke hadn't thought dragons could communicate with each other, but it looked like this one was having a conversation with itself.

The dragon kicked rocks towards the scorpion instead of continuing the chase. The stones flew through it and bounced on the ground beneath. The illusion disappeared.

Zuke brought his arms down and stared straight ahead. The dragon was now glaring at the cave. The middle head leant back, and then came forwards to let out a crippling roar. The two others joined in to create a threatening cacophony.

Zuke turned and saw Mardious staring at him. They didn't need to say anything. They retreated past the digging warriors and hid behind the boulder. They peered back around the edge as the dragon charged towards the cave. Instead of hiding, the warriors stood strong.

"Get—"

Mardious grabbed Zuke's arm and shook his head; their pleas didn't matter. If the warriors wanted to challenge the dragon on their own, they wouldn't listen to anything they had to say.

Four warriors held their shields strong, while the other two grabbed bows. They all huddled together to guard the precious white treasure, waiting for their opportunity to strike.

The dragon slowed its pace as it reached the cave entrance. Its heads moved low, and all six eyes stared straight ahead. It growled, analyzing its enemy.

"Hold," said Richard.

The middle head lifted high as the other heads slithered around maniacally.

"Hold!" Richard said louder.

The dragon stopped moving. The middle head opened its jaws. An orange glow formed in the back of its mouth.

"Now!" Richard commanded.

The two archers fired arrows at the dragon in rapid succession. The dragon closed its eyes and mouth, and then barked at itself again. It didn't seem overly concerned with the warriors' attack; none of the arrows had penetrated its scales. The warriors were outmatched.

The front four lowered their shields, drew their swords, and rushed the dragon.

They had only taken a few steps before the dragon decided to go on the offensive. Its right head leant down, opened its mouth, and blew a stream of fire across the incoming platoon.

While the warriors were distracted by the fire on that side, using their shields to deflect it, the dragon head on the other side came rushing in. Its sharp teeth grabbed the closest attacker and threw him against the wall. His painful scream was cut short by his impact with the cavern.

Zuke turned away and hid once more behind the boulder. He tried to clear his head as more screams echoed throughout the cave, but only one thing ran through his mind. "We're dead," he said. He clutched Mardious' arm.

Mardious shook Zuke's hand away. "Get ready to move." He closed his eyes, stretched his neck, and tilted his head from side to side. His fingers went to work on their imaginary piano.

Zuke felt the rush of air around his feet as Mardious focused his power on the dusty ground. The dirt and shale that the warriors had thrown around like savages was now broken up and easier to control. He used it to cover the lower half of the cave in a small, black cloud of dust. Screams still rang off the walls. Mardious grabbed Zuke's hand and led him from behind the boulder.

They stayed close to the wall as they swiftly worked their way to the entrance. They couldn't see the dragon through the dust cover, but more importantly the dragon couldn't see them. Before they knew it, they were back in the open terrain of Skyland.

Mardious let go of Zuke's arm, and they ran as fast as they could.

Zuke felt the burn in his lungs instantly, but his legs were as strong as a warrior's in that moment. He noticed that Mardious was running just as fast. Fear fuelled the both of them.

He heard a roar from the cave. He didn't want to, but he looked back. Richard had emerged from the darkness, and was now retreating just as the wizards had. No one else followed. Soon after, another roar sounded from behind the cloud of dust.

Zuke focused on the stream of lava that marked the finish line in their desperate race from danger. He tried to search for somewhere beyond the bridge to hide, but didn't see anything. They'd have to get lucky and find cover as soon as they could.

He heard panting from his right, and checked on Mardious. He was starting to struggle, falling behind in their race towards freedom.

Zuke slowed down a little to try and encourage his friend. "C'mon," he said. "We're almost there."

"I ... can't ..." Mardious couldn't get any other words out.

"There's a small cave just beyond the bridge." Richard had caught up to run beside Zuke. He didn't look tired at all, although there was now a bleeding gash down his arm. "The dragon won't be able to reach us in there."

Another roar sounded from behind them. Zuke looked back, and saw the dragon emerge. He locked eyes with the central head, and thought he saw it bare its fangs in a smile. It barked a few orders to itself and spread its wings out wide.

Zuke tried to focus on the bridge, but they were too far away. The dragon was about to take flight, meaning they were all doomed. He looked to his right at Mardious, who was trying to give an extra ounce of effort. He looked to his left at Richard, and saw a confidence that was unwavering.

He knew that the only way they'd be able to escape was if one of them made a sacrifice. One of them had to distract the dragon so the others could make it. An illusion wouldn't work this time: he hadn't the concentration, and the dragon already knew that trick. One of them had to be a hero.

Zuke closed his eyes and took a deep breath. He felt his heart pound a little faster. He knew what he had to do; he knew what it took to survive. He was the only one who could do what was needed.

He swivelled to his left and shoved Richard with everything he had.

Richard went tumbling to the ground, but Mardious and Zuke kept on running. Zuke focussed on the bridge with a relieved smile. He heard another roar, and then a thundering crash as the dragon pounced on the fallen warrior. A faint scream was the bittersweet sound of victory.

Mardious and Zuke made it over the lava and to the cave entrance that was their refuge. Mardious went in first, but Zuke looked back to check on the dragon. He was just in time to see it rise into the air with a great flap of its wings, away from the corpse it had torn apart.

Zuke looked up to the sky. He thought he saw other shadows moving about. The three-headed dragon's cries must have alerted the other beasts in the area. He didn't want to wait for any to come to its aid.

"Over here," Mardious said. He grabbed Zuke's arm and dragged him deeper into the cavern. They found a small nook on the right side, and both sank to the ground.

The dragon landed with a crash in front of the cave, and then barked to itself. Its low rumblings were amplified as they echoed off the walls.

A second later, the wall to Zuke's left glowed orange, and a burst of fire went rushing past the two wizards. They remained comfortable in their nook, finally out of danger.

Zuke saw Mardious rub the scar on his hand. They had been so close to finding another piece of the puzzle, but they had ultimately failed again. "I'm sorry," he whispered. He knew how much it meant to Mardious to have their plan succeed.

"You did all you could," Mardious said. "Next time, we'll be better."

The dragon screamed again, as if furious at their escape. Another pulse of flame shot past them, followed by two more. It was so hot Zuke had to turn away from the blaze. He hated fire.

He sighed. "Next time we'll be better," he agreed. He knew they had been lucky; if they were to do this again, they would need a better plan. They needed to be smarter. They needed to assemble a team with more skill. They needed to find a weapon that could slay dragons.

CHAPTER 1

Grind Won't Stop

Kase stuck three fingers out, but Curtis clenched his fist. Kase had lost again.

"Warrior always beats wizard." Curtis softly tapped Kase's hand. "Are you even going to challenge me, Two Times?"

Kase was getting restless. It wasn't that the stakes were high; it was that he was tired of losing to Curtis and listening to his superior's annoying remarks. It reminded him of his Uncle Eowin's teasing, and not in a good way.

"On three," Kase said. He tried to focus. He closed his hand tight. Curtis had chosen warrior twice, but would he dare do so a third time? They both pumped their fists once, then again. He had to make a decision quickly.

On the third pump, Kase laid his fingers straight, palm down. He slumped over in defeat.

"Wizard beats scholar." Curtis slid his three fingers into Kase's outstretched hand. "I win!"

"This sucks," Kase muttered. He handed Curtis his apple half-heartedly.

"Respect the game." Curtis patted Kase on the back, took his bounty, and then leant against the wall. He pulled out his sage mirror, and tapped its face. "I still don't believe you can't beat me in a round of Warrior-Scholar-Wizard, but you won the Quest Series twice. Guess it's a good thing you didn't have to compete with me."

Kase rolled his eyes and stared out at the street. Even though they had taken a few minutes to play their quick match, everything still looked the same.

"The Quest Series is a team competition," Kase retorted. "The Liberati would have dominated any group you put together." Just as they had last year. He could still remember the looks on the other teams' faces when the Grand Master had posted the points total from their scavenger hunt. Between their feather jackpot and Lenia's new teleportation trick, they had collected over twice what the other teams had managed.

It was as if Curtis could read his mind. "Maybe, but only because your girlfriend is an all-star," he teased.

"She's not my ..." Kase stopped himself. He wasn't going to get drawn into another debate. Curtis loved drama and enjoyed giving Kase unneeded advice. He decided to change the subject instead. "Can I hold your bow this time?"

Curtis chuckled. "What's wrong with your stick?"

Kase drew the twig from his sheath. He wasn't allowed to handle real weapons while shadowing Curtis, but it seemed like a joke for him to carry around something so useless. There must be a method to the madness. He hoped.

"I'm better than you with a bow," he replied. "If there's any trouble, I'll be able to handle it."

Curtis laughed again. "I know, Two Times," he said. "It might be the only thing you're good at."

Kase and Curtis had competed in a few archery contests, all of which Kase had won. It was the only game that he'd beaten Curtis at, which was why they played rounds of Warrior-Scholar-Wizard instead.

"But there hasn't been any trouble in the two years I've been stationed in this crumby town," Curtis said. "I doubt anything is going to happen in the time you're here to complete your practicum."

Kase looked back at the small crowd. Both he and Curtis were standing against a wall, on the edge of the main street of Flonkertown. There were a few shops scattered about, but it was nothing like the urban centre of Kimroad.

There were about twenty businesses on the strip, all on the same road. A few of them were food-based, but there were a couple that sold tools, and another that made furniture. There was no need to patrol the block, because they could already see everything. The only time they left their post was to check on the few shops that were scattered among the rural houses, but it was just an excuse to get some exercise.

The town mostly consisted of homes on large properties, unlike the clutter of the capital city. Kase had been excited about this post when it was assigned to him, because Flonkertown was where Lenia had grown up. On his first day, he realized why she wasn't in a rush to return to her hometown; it was pretty boring.

Curtis and Kase were both dressed in their Guardian uniforms, which consisted of a blend of green, gold, and grey fabric. They had rugged boots on their feet and open-faced, steel helmets on their heads. Their clothes weren't meant for battle: they were a symbol of status. If there was any trouble, they were easy to identify.

Their duty was to serve and protect everyone in their jurisdiction, but there was never any real action. Most of their time was spent people-watching and settling minor arguments. It wasn't the job Kase thought he would have as a warrior, but he was going to do his best just the same.

All warriors were expected to complete a practical work term in their third year at The Academy. Kase knew he should be glad that he'd managed to land a practicum with a group as prestigious as the Guardians at all. He'd be able to use it to get a better posting after graduation. His goal was to earn a post worthy of a great warrior.

"Mirror, mirror, show me moving images received today," Curtis commanded. He took a bite of Kase's—now his—apple and chewed it loudly.

A female voice emanated from the mirror, but Kase ignored it. Curtis had a lot of different girls sending him messages, but none of them seemed special. He bragged about being a social butterfly, but Kase had never met any of his friends in person. It was as if he enjoyed communicating through his sage mirror more than having real interactions.

Kase secured his twig and sneakily pulled his own sage mirror from his pocket. Guardians weren't supposed to use them for personal reasons while on duty, but it wasn't like his superior obeyed all the rules. He figured if he wasn't obvious about it, Curtis wouldn't report him and ruin his practicum grades. Kase didn't want to slow his trajectory to becoming a great warrior for anything.

He moved it close to his chin. "Mirror, mirror," he whispered. "Show me new moving images."

He slowly repositioned the sage mirror down to his side, keeping one eye on Curtis while a cloud formed on the mirror's face. His heart dropped at the empty words that appeared. No new images. He wondered if the moving image he'd sent Lenia was too lame to warrant a response. He started to question his dance moves.

"What's that?" Curtis asked.

Kase jumped, thinking he was caught, but Curtis was pointing in the other direction. He lazily followed Curtis' finger.

He expected to see another pretty girl that Curtis had picked out from the crowd, but he saw something much better. A small cloud of black smoke rose in the distance.

"Where there's smoke, there's fire," Kase said excitedly. "Let's go!" He slapped Curtis this time, knocking his superior off-balance, and started to make his way across the main street.

"Wait!" Curtis yelled. "Our orders are to stay here. We'll let the firefighters handle something like that."

Kase stopped and met Curtis' piercing blue eyes. "Let's just take a quick look. Besides, it's probably nothing, since there's 'never any trouble in this crumby town.'"

Curtis smiled back. He looked excited about his job for once.

Kase tried to pick up his pace, but it seemed like all of a sudden everyone in town was on the main strip. He carefully wove through the chaos, trying not to bump anyone in his hurry.

"Move!" Curtis yelled from behind him. Most of the crowd stopped to look at him. Curtis' strong, stocky arms were spread wide as he strode ahead. The crowd silently parted, and the two warriors hustled across the busy main street.

Once on a clear side road, they were able to run at full speed. Kase kept one eye on the sky to ensure they were on course. They ran through a rural area, where homes lined the street on either side. He thought about cutting through a few properties to get to their destination faster, but the roads were easier for running. There weren't any bushes, trees, or fences in their way if they stuck to the streets.

Kase looked back to make sure Curtis was still behind him. Even though he was a lot faster, he never lost sight of his warrior partner. After a few blocks of varied sprinting and a few more turns, he arrived at the scene.

A small group had gathered in the front yard of a two-storey house. Everyone there had a concerned look as they watched the heavy, black smoke billow into the atmosphere.

Even though the outside of the house wasn't on fire, Kase could make out some faint flickering through the downstairs windows. He couldn't help but smile as he thought about how much Lenia would love to see this.

"Running is the worst." Curtis put his hand on Kase's shoulder. Sweat dripped down his forehead. He was panting as he looked up to study the burning house. "Fires aren't much better," he added.

"There's someone in there!" exclaimed a young woman. She was the first to notice their Guardian uniforms. She jabbed her finger towards the house. "You have to go save her!"

Curtis shoved Kase out of the way. "You're right." Curtis' voice was pitched extra low. He put his hand on the woman's shoulder. "We'll put our lives on the line for whoever is in there, but we're here to protect everyone. Make sure you stay a safe distance away."

The woman looked at him and smiled, twirling her hair.

Kase tried not to roll his eyes. "Let's go," he said.

He jogged through the yard and climbed the two steps to the entrance. He put his hand on the door to check how warm it was. He couldn't feel any heat, but he could sense the fire burning in the room beyond.

"Move aside, Two Times." Curtis shoved Kase out of the way again.

Before Kase could reply, Curtis had his knee raised to his chest. With a powerful thrust, he kicked the door open. The crowd let out a soft cheer.

The door bounced on its hinges and more black smoke rushed out of the house. Kase was glad there hadn't been any fire directly on the other side. Curtis coughed and turned to avoid the escaping heat. "Ladies first," he said, continuing to clear his throat.

"You're such a gentleman," Kase replied sarcastically. He moved his right arm up and covered his mouth with the inner part of his elbow. He quickly dashed through the doorway and assessed the scene while Curtis reluctantly followed.

The front entrance was dark and cloudy; black smoke danced everywhere. A doorway led to the room on the left, and another to the

6

right. Straight ahead was a stairwell. Short flames at the foot of the stairs blocked off the second floor.

Kase heard a woman's voice from his left. "Anna-Bella!" she said, choking on the heavy air. "Anna-Bella, where are you?" She coughed harder.

Kase darted towards her, into a dining room. A long, wooden table spanned from the window at the front of the house to a doorway on the other side. Fire blazed in the room beyond.

A shadow moved back and forth amongst the mayhem. "Anna-Bella!" the woman said again, followed instantly by a deeper cough.

Kase rushed to her. She was an elderly woman, hunched over and clutching her chest as she coughed. He gently pulled her away from the flames. "I'm here to help. We have to get you to safety," he said. The severe heat pushed him back into the dining room.

They stumbled into Curtis, who appeared dazed by all the smoke in the air. "Curtis, I need you to take this woman outside right now!" Kase commanded. He tried to pass the old woman off to his partner.

"Curtis, we need to find Anna-Bella!" the woman said angrily. She coughed some more, and then looked up at the two warriors. She was about to say something else, but her eyes rolled into the back of her head, and she went tumbling to the ground.

"There's too much smoke," Curtis said. He bent down and picked up the woman. "Two Times, let's get out of here!" He stumbled towards the front entrance, keeping his head down. He didn't even look back to see if Kase was following.

That was perfect. Kase wanted to be alone.

He'd been practising his element control with Lenia, but he didn't get many chances to use his secret wizard powers on his own. If he were caught using magic as a warrior, he wouldn't just lose his job. The Triple Crown would condemn him, just like they had with the last person who showed two sets of abilities: the notorious criminal Mardious Hood.

Kase walked back into the heat. He extended his arms and closed his eyes. He had never tried controlling this much fire before, but he was excited to try. He didn't know what to expect, so he was unprepared for the wave of emotion that hit him. It felt like someone had punched him in the chest.

He took a step back to steady himself as he embraced the wild nature of the fire. He could feel it burning from the floor to the roof just past the dining room. He could sense its growing nature, stronger in some areas of the room than in others. He felt alive with the inferno, and couldn't wait to share the feeling with Lenia later.

He moved his hands from left to right, and the flames moved with them. It was like pulling back a curtain. He could create a gap, and have them sway from one side to the other. Unfortunately, he didn't know how to rip the fire curtain down or diminish it.

He smelled something pungent. He could make out hints of garlic, butter, and rotten eggs, but didn't recognize the combination. It was like a disgusting treat that fed the fire and helped it grow. He could feel the blaze getting stronger.

He tried letting go of himself to embrace his surroundings even more. If he increased his own power, perhaps he could counteract the strength of the fire. But then it hit him: he could sense an animal on the floor above him. He felt its rapid heartbeat. He experienced its fear and distress.

He turned from the fire and ran back to the entrance. Instead of going outside, he raced towards the stairwell. In mid-stride, he moved his hands together and apart, as if he were swimming through the ocean. The fire in front of him parted, and he ran up the stairs at full speed.

There was less smoke on the second floor of the house; the flames hadn't spread that far yet. Kase ran down the hallway and into a bedroom. He slid on the floor to look under the bed where the fear emanated from. He was met with two pairs of dark, piercing eyes and low growls.

"Easy, Anna-Bella," Kase said calmly. "I'm here to help." He reached his hand under the bed, but stopped when louder growls made him feel unwelcome.

He thought he was trying to gather a pair of scared pups, but he realized they were actually two heads attached to a single body. He had never seen a two-headed animal before, but he wasn't going to stop and analyze.

He rolled onto his side and drew his trusty twig. He had found a use for it after all. He pointed it towards the scared pup. But instead of allowing herself to be nudged from under the bed, Anna-Bella wrapped her teeth around it. She tried to wrestle it away from his grip, each head tugging in different directions.

Kase let go of his useless stick and sighed. He needed to connect with Anna-Bella in order to get out of this mess. He thought about the last time he was at the farm, secretly practising his animal control techniques.

Even though he hadn't let his aunt and uncle know what he was doing, Lenia had been more than happy to help him. There were a few times on their last visit where they were able to sneak off and practise their magic, among other things.

Even though he felt comfortable around the farm animals, Lenia had helped him find a deeper connection. He was able to herd the cattle as easily as his aunt and uncle did, and to calm the chickens so that they would stay well away from Lenia as they walked around. He was even able to attract a few wild squirrels to eat directly from his hand. He didn't quite understand how it worked, but he knew what it felt like. He tried to find that feeling so he could share it with his new two-headed friend.

He slowed his breathing and searched for the pup's heartbeat. He didn't want to overpower the young one and take complete control of its movement. Instead, he wanted to build trust with the animal. First, he needed to settle his new friend's emotions down, so it could make a decision on its own. It was Lenia's advice for helping control domestic animals on the farm, and Kase felt it would work the same way here, even if the situation was a little more intense. Smoke started to seep into the room.

He heard a whimper, and then felt two soft tongues lick his fingers. "Come on out, Anna-Bella. It's okay, I've got you." He slowly pulled his hand out from under the bed, and the small puppy followed it. "That's it," he said reassuringly. "Just a little more."

As soon as the puppy's heads were out from under the bed, she began showering him with kisses. She was a two-headed white bulldog. One of the heads had a black patch over her right eye, while the other had a brown patch over her left eye. Kase thought she looked kind of like a teacup pig.

He grabbed his trusty twig, tucked Anna-Bella under his arm, and jogged out of the bedroom. The flames were climbing higher, creeping through the cracks in the floorboards, but he was able to clear a path. He was a little surprised by his distribution of power: he was able to keep Anna-Bella calm with his connection to her and still handle the fire. He'd never tried using more than one wizard power at once. He felt proud of himself.

He ran down the stairs and was met by a few wizards near the front entrance. They were wearing red uniforms with their hoods up, symbolizing that they were firefighters.

"Get out! It's too dangerous in here," yelled one of them.

Kase didn't need to be lectured; he nodded and snuck past them quietly. As he stepped outside, he noticed that the crowd had grown substantially.

There were two horse-drawn carts equipped with large barrels of water in front of the house. A few of the firefighting wizards worked quickly to control the liquid, sending streams of water to slither through the air like flying snakes.

Curious onlookers crowded the carts, their sage mirrors flashing as they captured images of the scene. They weren't focused on the burning house anymore, but on the old woman lying on the grass in front of them.

Curtis knelt on one side of her, and a familiar healer knelt on the other. Kase rushed over to help.

"Two Times! There you are." Curtis looked up and smiled. "I thought I'd lost you!"

"Two Times?" Aura mouthed at Kase.

"I found Anna-Bella." Kase knelt down. The puppy tried to jump out of his grasp. He put the bulldog softly on the ground, and she hopped over to her owner's face. "How's she doing?"

"Her vitals are strong." Aura tapped the old woman's wrist as she held it gingerly. "She took in a lot of smoke, but she seems to be breathing fine now. I think she just passed out from the shock."

Anna-Bella licked the woman's face furiously until her owner started to squirm and giggle. Aura may not have been able to get the old woman out of her daze, but Anna-Bella seemed to know exactly what to do.

"Oh, Anna-Bella," the woman cooed as she regained consciousness. She cuddled her pet.

Aura introduced herself to the old woman and checked her again. "How do you feel?" she asked cautiously.

"Fantastic!" The old woman sat up, still clutching Anna-Bella. All three faces had big smiles. "Thanks to Curtis. He's my hero," she added loudly.

The crowd let out a cheer. More flashes flickered across sage mirrors.

"That's very kind of you to say," Curtis replied. He helped the old woman to her feet. Aura and Kase got up too and exchanged smirks.

"But Two Times and—" Curtis was cut off by more cheering and chants of his name.

"Curtis, over here!" someone shouted. She had a quill in her hand and a flipbook open to some quickly-scrawled notes. "How does it feel to be a hero?"

Someone else yelled before he could answer, "What was it like inside the house?"

"Were you scared at all?" Questions flew from every direction.

"It all happened so fast," Curtis replied, finally embracing the moment. He wrapped his arm around the old woman and walked closer to the crowd. "I'm just glad everyone is safe."

A loud crash came from inside the house, as if there were a thunderstorm trapped inside.

"That's not good," Aura mumbled.

"Should we go back in there?" Kase asked, ready for another battle with the fire.

"Curtis, can you pose so we can get a good image of you?" asked the reporter. They seemed unconcerned about the burning house.

Curtis and the old woman obliged, but Aura and Kase were still locked in on the firefight.

"No, we'll let the fire professionals handle the inside of the house," Aura said calmly. Her specialty was healing, and she knew nothing of Kase's burgeoning abilities. "I'm more concerned with why Curtis called you Two Times."

Kase couldn't help but chuckle. "He heard I'm a two-time champion of the Quest Series," he replied. "To be honest, I don't think he even knows my real name. He's used a nickname for me ever since my first shift."

"He's a little full of himself, isn't he?" Aura said. "Probably doesn't have time to learn people's names. He's not going to start calling me One Time, is he?"

12

"Probably." Kase and Aura both laughed.

Aura had only joined his Quest Series team, the Liberati, last year, but she was still a champion. In a proud moment she had grabbed the final trophy after their team had designed a goblin-inspired trebuchet to send her flying to retrieve it. Kase was impressed with her courage, but she'd been happy to make an impact for their team.

Kase gestured to Curtis, still telling his story to the crowd. "Sometimes I get variations, so he might call you One Time, O.T., or O-Time. He's surprisingly creative with it."

They heard another thunderous sound, and this time a couple firefighters came rushing out the front door with it. One was dragging the other away from the house.

"Oh no," Aura said. She rushed over to help, and Kase followed.

The two firefighters stopped on the opposite side of the front yard and collapsed beside one of their carts. A couple other wizards who were working with the water stopped what they were doing to help too.

"What happened?" asked Aura as she approached the group.

"Get out of here," said one of the wizards angrily. Three firefighters knelt beside their comrade, who writhed in pain on the ground.

"But I'm a healer," Aura said in defense. "I'm here to help."

"We can heal too," said the same wizard. "You can watch."

Aura and Kase both took a few steps back as the trio went to work.

"What do you think happened?" Kase studied the victim. The wizard's skin was discoloured on his neck and face. It looked like a crispy piece of bacon.

"I think the fire is getting the best of them," Aura whispered.

"But I thought they could control the fire?" Kase replied, shocked that the professionals were having difficulty with the blaze. He had been able to connect with it, after all.

13

"Oh, Two Times," Aura said with a sigh. "Fire is an unpredictable element, and even the best firefighters have trouble controlling it sometimes. Just because Lenia can control fire easily doesn't mean that every wizard can. She truly has a gift."

Kase knew that Aura was right: Lenia would have handled this fire with ease. But he was still a little confused because of his own experience. He felt like he was missing something, like there was another explanation.

He looked at the house, over at Curtis and the crowd, and then finally back to Aura. "I'm just going to step away for a moment," he said.

"I'll be here," Aura said, keeping an inquisitive eye on the firefighters.

Kase walked away from the wizards. He avoided his gloating comrade and the crowd's madness. He stood behind one of the firefighters' carts and pulled out his sage mirror. He moved it up to his mouth. "Mirror, mirror, show me new moving images," he whispered. The cloud seemed to hang on the mirror's face forever. Eventually, 'No new images' appeared.

He closed his eyes. He wished he could talk to Lenia. She was the only one who understood him; she would be thrilled to know that he was able to control the great fire when other wizards had struggled. He could still feel it burning away in the house, even though he was well beyond its reach. He felt oddly powerful in that moment.

"Kase!" yelled a familiar voice from the crowd. He looked over, but his eyes caught on a hooded figure standing in the distance instead. Dressed all in black, it looked almost like a shadow. He closed his eyes and shook his head, wondering if he was seeing things.

"Kase!" yelled Talen again. This time, he saw her as she pushed past two burly men in the crowd. She came running towards him, her arms open wide for a hug.

"Hey, Tal," he said, returning the embrace. "What are you doing here? I thought you worked only in Kimroad." Talen had also graduated last year, and gotten a real job out in the realm.

"Someone sent me a moving image of two warriors entering a burning building," she replied, her face expressionless as usual. "I knew it was you."

"Well, your story is over there," Kase said, pointing back towards the crowd. "Curtis is the hero of the day."

"I didn't come here for the story," she replied. "My editor already has a reporter to cover news in Flonkertown. I came because I haven't seen you in a while and wanted to know how you were doing."

Kase smiled. He needed a friend to talk to, not a reporter or a self-gratifying co-worker. "I don't know, Tal." He looked down and kicked the ground casually. "This Guardian business hasn't really turned out the way I thought."

"What do you mean?" she asked. He expected her to grab a quill and notebook, but she just stared at him instead. She seemed genuinely concerned.

"I guess I thought it would be more exciting," he replied honestly.

"Saving a woman from her burning house isn't exciting enough for you?" Talen tapped her chin, seeming puzzled by his response.

Kase couldn't help but laugh. "That's not what I meant," he replied. "Besides, the firefighters probably would've saved her anyway. I mean that my day-to-day as a warrior isn't that exciting. All Curtis and I seem to do is watch crowds and settle minor disputes. There's a lot of yelling, and some pushing sometimes, but that's about it. I haven't had to deal with any real danger."

Talen blinked a couple times. She tilted her head, as if to study his words.

"I kind of thought that once I was out of The Academy, I would be thrown into high-intensity situations," he continued. "I'd fight against giant beasts that threatened the land, or join battles against wild armies, or be sent on secret missions by the Triple Crown. I thought that this work experience would get me ready for all of that."

He didn't meet Talen's eyes, and instead fiddled with the sheath for his useless stick. "But it just isn't happening. I want to become a great warrior like my grandfather, but I don't feel like I'm doing anything great. I'm just walking the streets, stopping people from yelling at each other." He waved a hand at the commotion behind them. "Or maybe running into a burning house for a few minutes. I'm a nobody."

"I know what you mean," Talen said softly. She looked at the ground. "All I want as a journalist is to write brilliant stories that motivate people to see the world. I want to inspire the uninspired. I thought all my hard work at The Academy would pay off, and I'd be sent to remote locales all around the realm. But most of the stories I get assigned are just local, daily events. Yesterday, I had to write a piece about a man who has over fifty cats. It was ridiculous."

She sighed, and then looked back up at him. "But I know these minor assignments aren't the entire picture. They're just stepping stones to where I want to go. They won't define me as a journalist; they are practice for my chance to shine. When the story comes that takes me to the next level, I'll crush it because of all these little stories I put effort into."

Kase raised his eyebrow and took another look at Talen. He'd forgotten how wise she was. "Thanks, Tal," he said with a smile. "I needed to hear that. You're right: these small moments as a warrior don't define me. They're just stepping stones along the way."

He clapped her gently on the shoulder. "You really are inspirational, being able to give scholarly advice to a self-pitying warrior. I hope you get that chance to shine soon, and inspire everyone else in the realm."

"Thanks, Kase," Talen said. She turned away, but Kase could tell she was blushing. "I'm always here for you, but I wish I could take credit for that advice. It was actually Lenia who inspired me during the WHOOP last year."

The WHOOP, or the Winner's Hierarchy of Outstanding Performance, was the final tournament of the Quest Series. Only the eight best teams made it. Although the Liberati had started out the finals in first place, the competition was fierce. They had to face off against Talen's old scholar friends before defeating two teams made up of scholars, wizards, and warriors together.

Talen looked back at him, showing a rare smile. "In the second match, I thought I cost us our chance to win because I didn't get through that maze fast enough. But Lenia assured me that it was okay; it was just a small step towards something greater. She reminded me that I should enjoy the moment, rather than look back on it regretfully."

She clenched a small fist in triumph. "It all worked out in the end, because I was able to crush the design of the trebuchet in the final match, even though I'd tripped up earlier. I'm glad I took her advice instead of letting something minor get the best of me."

Kase reached down and felt his sage mirror through his pocket. He felt the urge to check it again.

"How's Lenia doing, anyway?" Talen asked. It was as if she knew Kase was daydreaming about something else.

"She's pretty busy," Kase replied. In only her first year after graduation, she was already working as an assistant for Professor Bright. It was nice that she was still at The Academy, but even before the work practicum Kase didn't get to see much of her. "We try and stay in touch by sending each other messages throughout the day."

Kase pulled the sage mirror out of his pocket and confidently moved it up to his lips. "Mirror, mirror, show me new moving images."

He held the sage mirror down so that Talen could see as well. When the cloud disappeared from the mirror's face, the words 'New message from Lenia Rie' appeared. A moving image followed.

Lenia was laughing hysterically. "You're such a dork!" she said between chuckles. "That's not how that dance goes! It's more like this!"

She put the sage mirror down and took a few steps away from it. Kase could tell that she was in Professor Bright's classroom. She started moving her hands and feet wildly, and then broke out into laughter again. Kase giggled too, even though Talen remained silent.

"Okay, it looks like we both need to work on it," she said. She picked up the sage mirror again. "Your rendition made my day, though. Thank you. Three days, three hours left. Threes!" Lenia smiled brightly, and then the message ended.

Kase moved the sage mirror back to his lips. "Save image in Lenia's message folder," he said.

"That's so funny," Talen said straight-faced. "You two are the best."

"Thanks, Tal, but ..." Kase stopped. Another notice came up abruptly on his sage mirror. It was a new message from their commanding officer.

"Kase," Davis said sternly. "I heard that you and Curtis broke away from your post. Return there immediately!" The image on the sage mirror disappeared, and Kase placed it back in his pocket.

"One step at a time," Talen said as she shook her head. She seemed to know how Kase felt about his orders.

"One step at a time," he repeated with a smile. "We should get together sometime. You, me, Lenia, Aura; the whole Liberati! We all need to catch up."

"Definitely," Talen said. "I'll check my schedule and send you a message. I'm not going to dance in it, though."

Kase laughed. He thought about Lenia's dance moves again, and then pictured her smiling face. He couldn't wait to meet with the entire Liberati, but he was even more excited to see Lenia sooner. Three days, three hours left.

CHAPTER 2

Too Strung Out On Compliments

L enia smiled and her eyes darted to the left. She'd told Kase that she felt silly when the students reacted to her trident, but he also knew she liked to showcase her special instrument. It was a bittersweet moment.

"Controlling fire is a battle," Lenia instructed. She expanded the flame around the head of her trident, and then let it diminish. The effect drew some more cheers from the class. "It's chaotic. It's aggressive. It will expose your greatest weaknesses, and then push you to your limits."

Lenia used her power to decrease the fire to the size of a candle flame, centred on the tip of the middle prong. "There is only one way to win the battle: to not fight back. You have to let it overpower you." She closed her eyes and slowly raised her arm. The small flame moved from the top of the trident to the palm of her hand. It didn't rest anywhere, but instead floated within her grasp.

"Realize that the fire is not your enemy, but your friend. You need to embrace it. Become one with it, and accept it for what it truly is." She clenched her fingers, enclosing the flame. She brought her fist close to her, tapped the middle of her chest three times, and then extended her arm, revealing her empty palm.

Although it appeared that the fire was extinguished, Kase knew what her plan was. He'd witnessed her practise countless times in preparation for this lecture. He couldn't wait to see how many cheers it received from the class.

"Only when it becomes a part of you will you become a part of it." Lenia snapped her fingers, and the three candles she had on her desk lit up at the same time.

Kase felt Professor Bright grab his arm and shake it a few times. She might have been the most excited spectator. He checked her grip, and then tried to politely make eye contact with her. She was so focused on Lenia's presentation that she didn't seem to know what she was doing. He decided not to disrupt her concentration.

"The importance of this exercise is to teach you how to feel connected to every aspect of elemental control, rather than just focusing on what's in front of you," Lenia continued. "Some applications require a lot of patience, strength, and control at multiple points. You'll need to know what it feels like to extend yourself beyond what you've already learned."

Lenia reached under her desk and pulled out her new and improved levitation device. With Talen and Kase's help, she had been able to construct a square, metal platform about two feet long and half a foot wide. It didn't look that impressive on the outside, but it was what was on the inside of this prototype that made it special.

Professor Bright let go of Kase's arm. She bent over, placed both palms over her mouth, and started to sway back and forth in her seat. She now looked like the most nervous spectator.

"What I have here is The Firefly," Lenia said proudly. A few murmurs bounced around the classroom, but she ignored them. "I'm going to demonstrate an application of today's exercise so that you know what you can work towards with this new skill."

Lenia went on to explain her design, using the giant sage mirror at the front to illustrate the inner workings when needed. There were two compartments inside the metal levitation board. The larger one held a mixture of butterfly tears, coconut vinegar, and lightning bolt powder. The smaller section above it was used to store magic magma.

Between the two compartments was a sliding door. Depending on the size of the gap, which was controlled by a simple lever, the magic magma would seep into the larger mixture. Lenia could focus her power on the reaction, and use the energy from the burning effect of the potion to control the levitation board.

"By influencing the quantity of potion in The Firefly, I can adjust how long it will perform for, how fast it can move, and how much it can lift." Lenia moved The Firefly below her feet, stood on it proudly, and rose into the air.

Professor Bright jumped out of her seat and clapped wildly. Kase glanced past her and noticed a couple other spectators whisper to each other. They smiled and also stood in applause. Lenia had told Kase that he'd have a chance to meet her family soon, which made him wonder if the excited pair beside Professor Bright was her father and brother.

Kase rose to his feet in support, and cheered Lenia with the rest of the group. Even though he had seen the demonstration before, he was proud that all her practice had paid off.

Lenia moved in front of her desk and stepped off The Firefly. She raised it to chest height, flipped the lever to close the mixing effect, and casually tucked the metal device under her arm. "I want you to take the rest of the class to experiment with the candles in front of you to work on your fire transfer skills," Lenia instructed.

She walked down the central aisle and glanced back and forth at her twenty-odd students at their table stations. Each of them had three candles, set up exactly as Lenia had at the front, only with a fire starter next to them instead of a one-of-a-kind black trident. Their challenge was to move the flame from one candle to the next.

"I will be walking around to help if you have any questions. If anyone can mimic the same fire control that I showed earlier …" Lenia snapped her fingers again, and all of the candles in the class ignited. "They will be rewarded with a chance to use The Firefly."

Excitement filled the room as the students quickly got to work. Lenia nodded in satisfaction and finally made eye contact with the extra spectators in the back. She nodded to Professor Bright, and then stared at Kase. His smile made her eyes dart to the left, and then she returned it with a beautiful smile of her own.

"Professor Rie!" shouted one of the students a couple rows from the back of the room. She eagerly waved her hand in the air. Kase had to look twice; she looked kind of like Talen.

Lenia casually walked towards the waving hand. "Yes, Tracie?"

"I don't have a fire starter. Is there one I can borrow?" Tracie asked.

Lenia smiled as she reached into her pocket. She pulled out a fire starter with a trident carved into it.

Kase tapped his own pocket, and felt his matching one.

"Here, you can borrow this for the rest of the class." Lenia looked up at Kase. "It's special, so be careful with it."

Tracie stuttered, but pulled herself together. "Thank you, Professor Rie!" she said gleefully.

"Professor Rie!" Professor Bright grabbed Lenia's attention away from the admiring Tracie. She placed her arm on the shoulder of the man beside her, who was smiling warmly. He had white hair that stuck straight out at the sides, but there was none on top of his head.

"Lenia, this is Stanley Zeller," Professor Bright said politely. "He was the elements professor here at The Academy before I started my tenure."

Lenia shook hands with the gentleman, rather than embracing him as if he were family. Kase had guessed wrong.

22

"Hello, Professor Rie," Mr. Zeller said. He shook Lenia's hand vigorously. "I've heard so much about you." His teeth looked like a forest of ugly, crooked trees. Kase didn't want to focus on them, so he stared at the giant mole on his nose instead.

"Wonderful lecture," Professor Bright said. "How did you make all the candles light up at the same time?"

Lenia smiled politely and stroked her braided brown hair. "I used the same flotation technique that you do in your element transfer demonstration, but with multiple tiny flames instead of one big one. I spread them out without anyone really knowing, and then expanded them all at once. I've been working on it with …" Lenia cleared her throat with a glance at Kase. "Sorry. I've been working on it for the last few weeks."

Kase winked back. He was happy to be the secret assistant to the professor.

"It's incredible!" Professor Bright said proudly.

"It is tremendously creative." Mr. Zeller smiled at Professor Bright. "This is exactly the kind of innovative magic we're looking for."

"I knew it," Professor Bright said. "Professor Rie is the best!" She clasped her hands together and covered her enormous smile. Mr. Zeller looked back at Lenia and kept smiling, as if expecting her to acknowledge something.

Lenia raised an eyebrow. "What is this about?"

"How silly of me." Mr. Zeller straightened his posture. "Professor Bright introduced me as a former professor, but I now work for the Triple Crown, along with Derek here." Mr. Zeller gestured to his much younger colleague, who gave Lenia a wink. "I oversee a research and development program that focuses on new and innovative creations. Do you have a sage mirror?"

Instead of answering, Lenia reached into her pocket and held up her sage mirror between them.

Mr. Zeller laughed. "I didn't mean that you had to pull one out. Just that the sage mirror is an example of what my program does for new innovations. I was able to coordinate funding for a team of researchers, which included some of the other professors here at The Academy. Together, we were able to create this unbelievable tool."

Lenia tucked the sage mirror back into her pocket, and then looked at Kase. All he could do was shrug in reply.

"In a similar fashion," Mr. Zeller continued, "I am recruiting a number of individuals to work on a new project. It has the potential to be as momentous as the sage mirror, if not greater. I was speaking about it with Professor Bright, and she told me all about a young professor who would be a great addition to the team. I can see from your sample demonstration that she is indeed correct."

Kase tried to judge Lenia's reaction. Mr. Zeller looked like he expected her to be happy, but she just slowly nodded her head. "Sounds interesting," she said.

"It's so exciting!" Professor Bright exclaimed. "It's such a great opportunity for you; you're going to do so much great work for the Triple Crown. I'm so happy for you!"

"Great!" said Mr. Zeller. He stuck out his hand and shook Lenia's again. "I'll get everything set, and you can start next week!"

Lenia panicked as she pulled her hand away from Mr. Zeller's grasp. "Wait." She took a deep breath. "I'm not sure if I'm ready for this."

"Oh?" said Mr. Zeller, his smile fading. He looked quickly to Derek, who hadn't taken his eyes off Lenia. "I am sorry to hear that, Professor Rie. In all my years of recruiting, I have never had anyone hesitate on an official offer from the Triple Crown."

"She's not hesitating." Professor Bright put a reassuring hand on Mr. Zeller's shoulder. "She still has a class to run, and it was rude of us to come into her classroom and catch her off-guard. I'll make sure she's ready for next week."

"Yes, of course," Mr. Zeller replied. He rubbed his chin and studied Lenia, which made Kase stare at the old man's mole again.

"No, I—" Lenia started, but Professor Bright quickly interrupted her.

"Why don't you go take care of your business with the Grand Master." Professor Bright turned Mr. Zeller towards the door. "I'll escort you to the administration castle before you have to head back to Kimroad."

"Yes, of course," Mr. Zeller said again. He politely waved goodbye as Professor Bright led him through the exit.

"It was nice to meet you, Lenia," Derek said. He stuck his arm out. "I look forward to starting our project together next week."

Lenia went to shake, but stopped. Instead of a hand, all he had was a stump. Derek laughed, and then stuck out his left hand in greeting. "I pull that joke on everyone," he said.

Lenia blushed, but turned to Kase instead of greeting Derek. "This is Kase," she said nervously.

Kase offered his left hand.

"It's nice to meet you," Derek said, taking it. He quickly turned his attention back to Lenia and smiled. "It was a pleasure."

Lenia watched him exit after Zeller, and then turned back to Kase. "What just happened?" she asked, eyes wide.

"I don't know—it happened so fast," he replied. "Congratulations?"

Lenia blinked a couple times. "Thank you?"

A bell chimed in the distance and they snapped back to reality.

"Class dismissed!" Lenia spun around and was met by a collection of groans.

"I was so close!" a student to Lenia's right grumbled.

"I was closer than you," another said.

"Professor Rie," Tracie said. "If we're able to ace this assignment next class, can we still try out The Firefly?"

"Absolutely, Tracie!" Lenia said.

The class cheered, and then packed up their supplies. Tracie returned the fire starter, and Lenia walked slowly to the front of the room. Kase could tell her mind was elsewhere. He grabbed his sac and rushed after her.

He had to fight through the crowd of students that piled into the main aisle, but he was able to catch up to her when she reached her desk.

"Your first lecture went really well," he said.

Lenia looked up at him and shrugged. "I guess," she said. "I'm sorry you had to take a day off to come watch. The way Brie—sorry, Professor Bright—was talking, I thought there were going to be more people here. But it was just you and the weirdoes from the Triple Crown."

Kase wished he could be in every class she taught. "I thought they were your dad and brother for a second," he said.

Lenia raised an eyebrow and smirked. "I look nothing like those two. You have to imagine this, but a male version." She waved her palm in a circular motion over her face to get the point across.

Kase laughed, but didn't want to imagine Lenia as a man. Instead, he put his sac on her desk and took out the gift he had prepared for her.

Lenia's eyes brightened in joy as she read the card. It had a drawing of a mermaid holding a trident. At the top was written 'Happy Birthday Lenia,' but Kase had crossed out the birthday part and written 'Congratulations' instead.

"Is this from Jude?" she asked. "Or another one of your helpers at Change the Realm?"

Kase spent some of his weekends volunteering at a help centre. Although he tried to spread his time evenly among the people there, he always ended up having fun with his young friend Jude the most.

"He made the card, but the gift is from me," Kase replied. "He didn't really understand the concept of giving gifts for something other than a birthday, so I had to modify it a little."

"He's getting better at drawing." Lenia brought the card closer to her eyes. "He obviously has a good professor."

Kase chuckled. "We're not celebrating me as a professor," he said. "We're celebrating *you*. Open your gift!"

Lenia's eyes darted to the left, and then she quickly unwrapped her present. Her smile faded as she cradled it in her hands. "What is it?"

"It's a scabbard for your trident!" Kase answered happily.

Lenia turned it in the air to study it, but she still looked confused. "Like, for my hip?"

"No, for your back," Kase said. He reached out for it. "May I?"

Lenia handed him the leather sheath and her trident. Kase let the straps dangle, and focused on the casing that the trident would slide into. Instead of encompassing the whole thing, like it would a sword, it wrapped around the stem of the trident, leaving the head and base open. He slid the trident through the support, and adjusted the height to suit Lenia. He secured it with the ties, and then held it up to gauge his craftsmanship.

"Perfect," he said with a nod.

"You sure?" Lenia smirked.

"Turn around, and we'll find out," Kase replied. He lifted the trident and held the contraption over her head. The straps criss-crossed at the front, so she had to extend her arms to slip into it. He lowered everything until it was secured around her chest and shoulders.

She turned around and then posed. "How do I look?"

The head of the trident extended just beyond her right shoulder, while the tail end could be easily touched by her dangling left hand. It was exactly how Kase had envisioned it, but he was still a little surprised by how cool it looked on her.

"You look amazing," he replied honestly. They stared at each other and smiled for a moment, until Lenia gently brushed her trident and disappeared. His gift was obviously functional if she was still able to teleport with it.

27

Kase glanced at the card again and smiled. A few seconds later, two arms gently wrapped themselves around his waist from behind. He looked down at Lenia's clasped hands.

"You're right, it's perfect," she said. She hugged him a little harder. "Thank you."

Professor Bright cleared her throat at the classroom entrance. Lenia let go of her embrace.

Kase turned around, a little disappointed at being interrupted.

"Lenia, I love the accessory!" Professor Bright said.

"Me too," Lenia said, elbowing Kase.

"Your performance was outstanding." Professor Bright walked down the aisle. "Mr. Zeller was so impressed, he can't wait to work with you. Are you excited to work with the Triple Crown?"

"I guess I don't really have a choice, do I?" Lenia replied, crossing her arms.

Professor Bright's smile faded at Lenia's unenthusiastic tone. "You always have a choice. But sometimes it takes someone who is much wiser than you, someone who cares about you very much, to push you to make the right one."

Lenia sighed. "I understand." Professor Bright was her mentor, and Kase had never seen Lenia be anything but appreciative of the older professor's advice. "But what about my duties as your assistant professor? I really enjoyed my lecture, and I feel like I'm getting better at element control. I don't want to just jump into something else on a whim."

Professor Bright put her hand over her chest and laughed. "Oh, you won't be abandoning your responsibilities here with me. Do you think I'd let you go so easily? No, it's just an on-the-side thing—almost like a secret club. Think of it like the Quest Series: it's something you do in order to challenge your skills, meet some new people, and learn new things. In fact, being involved with Mr. Zeller will help you become a better professor."

"So it's not a new job?" Kase asked. He was confused too.

"Yes and no," replied Professor Bright. "The Triple Crown is hiring Lenia as a consultant on this new project. She'll be able to supply them with innovative ideas, and in return she gets to learn what others in the industry are working on. She'll also make a little extra Aileron, and the Triple Crown will donate some funds to The Academy for our program."

"So it's good for The Academy." Lenia rolled her eyes.

"It's a win-win for everyone involved, and will enhance your career as a professor, like it did mine," Professor Bright said. "The Triple Crown has a special lab here at The Academy, so you'll work there a couple days a week, and be able to keep working with me here in my classroom."

"So you've done this before?" Kase asked. He was starting to get excited about Lenia's opportunity.

"Of course!" Professor Bright said. "How do you think I came up with my broken glass experiment? I've been involved in five projects, ranging from glasswork to fire control. Actually, Mr. Zeller came to me for this venture, but I told him that Lenia would be a better fit."

Professor Bright turned to her colleague. "I honestly think it will be a great experience for you, Lenia, and help you to grow. We all need to take advantage of new opportunities when we can. You're going to gain so much from this project!"

Lenia smiled. Professor Bright's enthusiasm and confidence had finally broken through. "Thank you, Brie."

"We're in this together," Professor Bright replied. "I'm glad I can help you, but you're going to have to share everything you learn with me. We're colleagues, and that means we have each other's backs."

Kase was really excited for Lenia, but he felt a little left out. "Can I be part of your club?"

Lenia and Professor Bright laughed. "Sorry, it's for professors only," Professor Bright teased.

"Maybe someday though," Lenia added. She grabbed his hand, which made him feel a lot better.

"Whether I'm a professor or not, I've still got your back, no matter what," Kase replied. He squeezed her hand back.

"Mine too?" Professor Bright added with a chuckle.

Kase laughed, and then agreed.

"Lucky for me, I need your support next Thursday." Lenia let go of his hand and looked at the ground. She took a deep breath before looking up again to meet his eyes. Her reluctance had Kase a little worried.

"My parents are having a small get-together," she said softly. "Will you accompany me?"

Kase smiled. It was *next* week that he would meet Lenia's dad and brother. He was honoured to meet her family.

"Of course he will," Professor Bright said, with a hand on each of their shoulders.

CHAPTER 3

It's A Game?

K ase tried to understand what Cali was talking about, but it didn't make any sense to him. "A cipher?" he asked.

"Think of it like a key," his older sister said excitedly. Her hair might have been a mess, and there were dark circles under her eyes, but she was energetic. "You need a physical key to get past a locked door: a cipher is like a key for words. You use it to decode a locked message."

"So you're able to read what's in dad's book?" Kase asked cautiously.

"Not the whole thing." Cali's smile disappeared. "There are five sections, each written using a completely different type of cipher. A couple are alphabetical, one is just lines and dots, there's some hieroglyphs that don't make any sense, and the last is just a bunch of ones and zeros. The first is the only puzzle I've figured out so far, but at least there's hope."

Kase had been worried that giving Cali the mysterious book he and Lenia had found would be too much for her to handle. Their dad had been a scholar, and when they were young, he left them with their aunt and uncle while he went on an expedition. Kase was only eight at the time, and didn't remember the details well, but their dad never returned. Cali had never accepted that he was dead, even when the Guardians came to their house to give them the news.

When Kase had found the book in the Badlands, there was a moment when he thought his dad could still be alive. He could only imagine how much stronger Cali's feelings were.

"Can you show me?" he asked.

Cali flipped to a page in the leather-bound book in front of her. It was different from the one Kase had found. It looked newer, and there were pages torn out.

She plopped it open in front of him and pointed to the left side. "This is copied directly from dad's notes," she said. He recognized her handwriting.

"Where's the original?" He wondered why Cali would make her own copy.

"It's old and smelly, and some of the pages are a little charred, so I didn't want to ruin it," she admitted. "I made a book for each section, to try and clear my mind to decode it. Don't worry; his is in a safe place."

Kase was only worried about how much time Cali had spent on this project. It must have taken a long time for her to copy, and then translate. He understood now why she looked so tired.

"Ymjit qt fjhxouron ..." Kase started.

"Crazy, right?" Cali interrupted.

"It sounds like gibberish." He had already given up trying to read it, and waited for Cali's explanation.

She didn't disappoint. "It's a shift cipher," she said. "Each letter is replaced by a letter further along in the alphabet. The trick is that you have to find the pattern to reveal the original script. Usually, the same shift is used in the entire document, so it's easy to figure out using trial and error or by recognizing what some of the common, repeating threads are. But in this case, you have to look at each word."

Cali pointed to the sentence Kase had started reading. Her finger was shaking a little. She didn't look nervous, so Kase assumed it was from fatigue. He had noticed earlier that there were a lot of dirty coffee mugs around her office.

"In this case, you have to look at each word in the sentence to figure it out," she said. "The number of letters in the word represents the shift. The first word has five letters, so for each letter you move up the alphabet five places."

Cali stood and grabbed one of the mugs, looked carefully at the bottom, and then moved it to her lips. "Try it out," she said. She tilted her head back and tapped the bottom of the cup to try and force a few more drops down her throat.

Kase used his fingers to count back up the alphabet. "Thedo," he mumbled.

"Good," Cali replied. She sat back down behind her desk and awaited the next word.

"Or," he continued. Cali nodded.

Kase took a little extra time to figure out the last word. "Wayoflife," he finally said. "Thedo or wayoflife."

"Perfect!" Cali said. "The spacing is messed up, which is the final challenge in this particular cipher, but when you say it out loud you can hear it a little better."

"The doorway of life," Kase said, understanding what Cali meant. He shook his head and stared at the pages again. He remembered what Talen had translated from the walls of the hidden castle of the Eidola they had found during last year's Quest Series. "I thought it was a myth?"

"That's why we have to decipher the entire book." Cali rubbed her face and leant back in her chair.

"Right now?" he asked. He'd just dropped by Cali's office to see how she was doing, and didn't have plans to stay much longer. He flipped through her notebook and the multiple pages of coded notes. It was going to take a long time for him to count out the words with his fingers.

"No, I've translated this section already," she replied. "I never would have guessed what the pattern was if I hadn't worked on a project for High Scholar Sheese about … well, never mind."

She leant on her desk. Sharaine was the only one that Cali shared an office with, but she was away for a few days. The door was shut, the window was closed, and there was no way their voices would carry through the thick stone of the castle walls. Even though no one else could possibly hear, she kept her voice low. "If I tell you what's in this book, you have to promise you won't say anything to anyone else."

"Of course," Kase said. He leant in closer so he could hear better.

"Not even Lenia," Cali said sternly.

Kase hesitated. He didn't want to keep it a secret from Lenia. She'd been with him when he found the book, and had encouraged him to give it to Cali. However, the look on his sister's face was serious, and he wanted to hear what she had to say. "I promise."

"The doorway of life was used by an ancient group of wizards who called themselves The Chosen," Cali explained. "When an outsider almost stole their power away, they realized that the doorway was a curse rather than a gift. They knew that it would tempt those who used it, and possibly corrupt them, so they took it upon themselves to make sure that no one else could. They tried to destroy it, but they only succeeded in breaking it apart."

Cali cleared her throat and shimmied her chair forwards. Her voice lowered even further. "Four pieces were scattered throughout the realm, hidden and protected by The Chosen's appointed guardians: the Eidola of the desert, the giants of Jenim Island, the mermaids of the deep blue sea, and the dragons of Skyland."

"So the castle that we found during the Quest Series." Kase paused. "It was the real hiding place for one of the pieces?"

Cali nodded. "These notes not only outline where the secret hiding place for the Eidola was, but also what happened to the piece after it was found. There's a map that leads to where it's now hidden, and it's …" she put her right hand over her mouth and whispered. "It's here in the castle of the Triple Crown."

"Where?" Kase whispered back.

"According to dad's notes, there's a secret room on the top floor of the castle." Cali continued whispering. "It's not as glamorous as you might think though; it's behind a broom closet." Cali flipped to another page of her notebook. "This section outlines where it is and how to enter."

Kase froze. He had been on the top floor of the castle with Lenia when they were searching for her lost trident last year. Her ring had led them to a lone broom closet, but they weren't able to make it any further before being caught.

"I think the real question is why," Cali added.

"Why what?" Kase asked.

"Why is it here?" Cali said. "Who knows about it? Is the Triple Crown protecting it now?" She ran her fingers through her greasy hair. "What about the Money Jane copycat? Why did he have dad's book? Is he working with the Triple Crown? Are they trying to put it back together, and use the power that was feared by The Chosen hundreds of years ago? Does this book unlock a government conspiracy?" Cali rubbed her face again.

"And why was dad involved?" Kase mumbled. He leant back in his chair and sighed. Cali was right; this book was creating more questions than answers. He wondered whether their dad had abandoned them in order to protect the secret doorway or to chase after its power.

"I'll have to translate this journal, and understand what's in it, before I'm able to answer those questions," Cali stated.

"We," Kase corrected her. He reached out and touched her hand. "*We* have to translate this journal."

Cali laughed and swatted his hand away. "No offence, brother, but I don't think you'll be able to help with the ciphers."

Kase pulled his hand back. He felt useless. "I just—"

"But when the time comes for action, you'll be the first person I go to," Cali said. Her smile didn't make him feel better. "You're the only one I trust with this."

He still felt a little worried about Cali's fatigue. He wanted to help lift some of the weight off her shoulders. "If you need help with decoding the message, can't we just invite Talen?" he asked.

"Absolutely not," Cali said. "We won't share this with anybody. You promised."

Kase felt a little guilty for the suggestion, even though Talen was one of the smartest scholars he knew. He nodded in understanding.

"Besides, I can't be seen talking to Talen," Cali added.

"Why not?" Kase thought Cali was being especially flippant, considering her and Talen's friendship.

"She's a journalist now," Cali explained. "Politicians and journalists are like … Guardians and criminals. If you were friends with a criminal, and people saw you talking with them, they would question you as a Guardian. They might think you were a criminal too."

Kase rolled his eyes. "That's a little extreme," he said. "It's Talen."

"This isn't the Quest Series anymore," Cali said. "This is the real world. If people saw me talking to her, assumptions would be made. They might even think I'm leaking confidential information about the Triple Crown."

"Like a super powerful, mystical doorway." Kase gave her a sideways grin.

"This is serious, Kase," Cali replied. "We have to be careful. If the wrong people find out, we'll be in danger. I would hate to drag anyone else into this without first knowing the consequences."

Kase nodded, but he didn't agree. He knew that when they stuck together he, Cali, Talen, and Lenia could do anything. He tried to think of a way to convince Cali of this, but a knock on the door stopped him from answering.

Cali snapped the book shut and shoved it in her drawer. She leant forwards and plunked both elbows on her desk. She took a deep breath, cleared her throat, and smiled brilliantly. "Come in!"

"Two Scoops!" Curtis shouted as he entered.

"Two Scoops?" Cali sat back in confusion.

"I had two helpings of berries with my breakfast this morning," Kase explained. "It's not that clever of a nickname," he added.

"It doesn't have to be clever, Two Scoops." Curtis jabbed Kase in the shoulder with his fist, giving him a charley horse. "We did it!"

Kase tried not to rub his arm; he knew it would encourage Curtis to hit that spot again. "Did what?" he asked.

"Finally earned a transfer—to a new post in Kimroad," Curtis said, throwing his hands in the air. "It's the break I've been waiting for!"

"Congratulations!" Cali said.

"Thanks, Cali." Curtis gave her a polite nod.

Kase scratched his head in confusion. "Does that mean I have to get assigned a new practicum partner?"

"No way," Curtis said. "You're coming with me. After all, you're my lucky charm! If you hadn't convinced me to check out that fire, I never would have gotten this opportunity."

"Fire?" Cali asked. "What fire?" She gave Kase a worried look.

"Two Scoops didn't tell you?" Curtis asked.

"I'm good at keeping secrets," Kase said, causing Cali to smirk.

"It's a secret no more," Curtis said, oblivious to what Kase really meant. "We're official heroes!"

Curtis went on to share the entire story with Cali. He embellished his role a little, and overstated his bravery, but Kase didn't mind. Curtis was a confident storyteller.

"It's a good thing that fire was no match for you." Cali gave Kase a wink. She knew he was comfortable around fire thanks to Lenia's passion for the elements. She didn't know he had power of his own, though.

Kase had to admit, it felt good to get a promotion. He was excited for Curtis, but also for his own journey to becoming a great warrior: he was finally moving in the right direction. "So what happens now?" he asked. "Do we go to our new post right away?"

"We start next week," Curtis said. "Today, we celebrate! Want to join us, Cali?"

"I have some extra work to do still, but thanks for the offer," Cali replied. She gave Kase a nod.

"Next time," Curtis said with a smile. "Let's go, Two Scoops." He raised his arms in celebration, and hurried out the door.

"Hey," Cali said, stopping Kase from leaving. "If you're stationed here in the city, come visit more often. I'll give you updates on our ..." she hesitated, but a crash from outside the doorway interrupted her thought.

Kase and Cali leant to peer out the open door. A handful of papers floated in the air. Curtis already had his head down in shame. "I'm so sorry," he said softly.

Kase stepped out of the room and was met by the creepy stare of High Wizard Zuke. "Kase Garrick," Zuke said in surprise. His dark eyebrows raised. "It's nice to see you again. It seems like you're getting to know your way around the castle a little better."

Kase looked down to avoid the gaze of the High Wizard and noticed Derek on his hands and knees, trying to collect the mess of papers. He piled the pieces with his left hand, but his right stump didn't do much more than jab at the floor.

"I wanted to congratulate you on all your success at The Academy," Zuke said. "I've been watching you, and was glad to see you do so well during the Quest Series. Keep up the good work."

Although Zuke was smiling, Kase thought it was forced. The High Wizard had never been this pleasant to him; it felt like he was trying a little too hard to get on his good side.

Curtis jabbed him in the ribcage.

"Cali, I was meaning to talk to you," Zuke said, brushing past Kase and into Cali's office. He closed the door behind him, leaving Kase, Curtis, and Derek in the mess of papers.

"Let me help you," Kase said, kneeling down too.

"That's very kind of you," Derek replied. He stuck out his stump to introduce himself. "I'm Derek, by the way."

Kase was a little off-put, having met him only a couple days prior. Was Derek that forgetful? He hesitated and just stared at the offered stump.

Derek laughed. "That's just a joke I usually do," he said, pulling back his right arm and offering his left hand instead.

Kase reached out his own. "We've already met—"

"Oops, I'll take those," Derek said, disregarding the handshake altogether. He reached past Kase and grabbed the papers that Curtis was staring at. "Let's just make a pile here in the centre, and then I'll grab them all."

Curtis shrugged and started pushing the papers together rather than looking at each one. Kase turned his attention back to the papers too, until he saw what looked like a drawing of Lenia's levitation device, The Firefly.

There was a large orb drawn on top of a block in the diagram. The words 'magic magma,' 'butterfly tears,' and 'lightning bolt powder' were scribbled on the side. A table of numbers was listed below. It looked similar to the plans that Talen had made when she helped to design the prototype.

Kase went to pluck the page from the pile, but Curtis pushed a few more papers on top of it. "Hurry up," he whispered.

Before Kase knew it, they were done. Curtis tapped the edge of the papers to straighten the pile, and then handed them to Derek. The stack nestled nicely in the armpit of Derek's shorter arm.

"Thank you for your help, gentlemen," Derek said. Kase wondered if Derek had forgotten his name already.

"I apologize again for my clumsiness," Curtis replied. "Have a good day." He tapped Kase on the shoulder, and they walked away from the scene.

When they were out of earshot, Curtis nudged Kase. "I didn't know you were on a first name basis with High Wizard Zuke. That's amazing! Do you also know High Scholar Sheese and High Warrior Mac? What other secrets are you keeping from me, Two Scoops?"

Kase raised his eyebrows and forced a smile. Instead of responding to Curtis, he looked back at Derek, who still waited patiently outside Cali's office.

He had plenty of secrets, but he had the feeling that Derek and Zuke might have more. He wondered what else could have been hidden in those notes.

CHAPTER 4

All That Glitters Is Not Gold

Lenia didn't want to teleport directly in front of the house in case anyone saw. As she had explained to Kase, she hadn't told her family about her special gift—they just wouldn't appreciate it. He didn't understand why not.

They walked the last block of the now-familiar roads of Flonkertown and were met by a happy young couple. "I didn't think you'd show up," the male said with a cynical smirk. "You usually don't come to any of mom and dad's parties."

"If it was optional, I wouldn't have," Lenia retorted. "Kase, I'd like you to meet my brother, Leland."

Kase shook Leland's hand politely. His hands were soft, his robes were rich, and his hair was perfectly combed. Lenia was wrong: her brother wasn't a male version of her.

"This is my fiancée, Gwen," Leland said, gesturing to the girl he was with.

"Your fiancée?" Lenia's mouth gaped open in shock.

"Hi, Lenia." Gwen reached out and hugged her fiancé's sister. Kase was surprised that Lenia returned the embrace, since she wasn't a big fan of hugs. "It's nice to finally meet you."

"It's nice to meet you too," Lenia said with a smile. "How did you? When did you? Why didn't you … I mean, congratulations! I'm going to have a sister." She let go of Gwen, but instead of hugging Leland, she shoved him playfully.

Leland laughed. "It all kind of happened pretty fast. We haven't even told anyone yet. Well, except for mom and dad."

Lenia turned to stare at the front door of their parent's house. "So that's why they insisted I be here," she said softly.

Kase checked the two-storey home, and found it welcoming. Steps led up to a wide porch filled with potted plants. The large windows were open to let in the gentle breeze, but the warm chatter and light music of a pleasant get-together escaped instead. He wondered what kind of reception the greatest wizard he'd ever met would get when she entered.

"Is that the trident?" Leland asked excitedly. He reached out to touch the top of it.

Lenia took a step back when his elbow ungracefully clipped her forehead. "Ow." She rubbed above her left eye. "What else would it be?"

"I'm sorry," Leland said, holding his hands up in defence. "Here, let me heal you."

Leland went to touch Lenia's forehead, but she swatted his hands away. "It's not that bad."

Leland stepped away. "Sorry. You can hit me back if you want. Just don't stab me with your weapon."

Lenia laughed. "It doesn't work like that."

"How does it work?" Leland shared a look with Gwen, who also seemed intrigued.

"I'll show you later." Lenia shoved her brother again and nodded towards the entrance. "Let's go inside."

"Cool." Leland grabbed Gwen's hand. They walked up the stone path towards the house.

Lenia and Kase stayed further back. They stopped at the foot of the porch to wait as Leland and Gwen opened the door.

"There they are," someone yelled. Cheers erupted from those inside. Leland put his arm around Gwen and smiled, strolling into the house.

Lenia sighed and grabbed Kase's hand.

"I can't wait to see how loud everyone cheers when you enter," he said.

"Yeah, right," she replied. "My brother is the golden child. They probably won't even acknowledge me."

"Golden child?" Kase asked. He wondered what was better than a golden child, because Lenia was obviously more talented than her brother.

"He's the perfect son." Lenia shrugged. "He's always been well-behaved, a great student at The Academy, and now he's a healer like both of my parents. With his engagement, he deserves all the attention."

"What?" Kase didn't think that those accomplishments were all that impressive. "I thought your parents would have a Lenia shrine. Aren't your Quest Series medals on display at least?"

Lenia laughed. "My parents aren't as dorky as your aunt and uncle," she teased.

Kase was proud that his family displayed his medals. It made him feel appreciated. "Does that mean I'm a golden child?" he asked.

"No, your aunt told me that Cali is their favourite." Lenia poked Kase in the ribs, but he wasn't sure if she was kidding. "It's okay though; sometimes it's better to just lay low, and not have all the pressure that comes with the golden child status."

Kase didn't understand. It sure seemed like being the golden child was better. He played along anyway. "Should we go in then, fellow silver child?"

Lenia laughed. "Absolutely, Silver Times."

"That's inaccurate," Kase chuckled. He liked every nickname she gave him, but it didn't suit his latest ones. "If anything, it's Two Silver Times."

"Much better," Lenia said sarcastically. "Make sure to tell Curtis, so he can update his list of names for you."

Lenia and Kase walked up the steps and entered her parents' house. She was right: no one really noticed them. In the living room to the left of the entrance, everyone's attention was on an older man, who had his arm around Leland and a glass in the air.

"And then he healed the horse!" the man joked, causing everyone to laugh.

"This way," Lenia said, pulling Kase to the right. They walked past the stairs in the hallway and into the kitchen at the back of the house. An older woman had her head down, fiddling with some food on a silver platter.

"Couldn't you have worn something other than your hooded uniform?" She said without even looking up.

Lenia sighed and shook her head.

"Can you at least hang that thing up in the back room? It's so dark and depressing."

Kase felt Lenia squeeze his hand a couple times. "It's nice to see you too, mother," she replied in a Talen-like monotone. She looked up at Kase, nodded towards the doorway, and turned to exit the kitchen.

"Wait," said her mom, turning around. She sighed and shook her head. "I'm sorry. With everyone here, and your brother's big news … it's just a little overwhelming." She smiled warmly. "It's good to see you. Who's your friend?"

Lenia smiled and introduced Kase, who extended his hand.

Lenia's mom leant back and took an extra-long look at him. "I'm Grace." She lifted her hands away. "My hands are all dirty, so you'll have to excuse me. Do you two work together?"

"Umm …" Kase mumbled. He had expected Grace to know who he was.

Lenia rolled her eyes. "We were in the Quest Series together, mother," she said. Maybe Grace was supposed to know, but she forgot.

"I'm training at The Academy to become a warrior," Kase added.

"Mmm-hmm," Grace said, squinting at Kase. "Well then, I could use your strength. Would you mind taking this tray of goodies to the other room for me? It would really help me out."

"Absolutely," Kase replied with a smile.

"Dragoon," Lenia said with a cough. He looked back at her and met her grin.

"Excellent," Grace said, missing out on the teasing. "Place it on the table near the window. That way our guests can pick at it while they visit."

Kase promptly took the plate and returned to the hallway. When he entered the main room, he was finally noticed by the hoard of guests.

"Oh, look at the treats!" a woman to his left said as she took a sample.

"I didn't know this party was catered," another said. "Are there any appetizers, or just goodies?"

"I'm not sure, I just—" Kase jumped when a hand touched his shoulder.

"These are so delicious!" exclaimed another stranger.

Kase glanced towards the window and saw a table with jugs and glasses. There was an empty spot where he could place the tray. He took a few steps forwards, but was met by more hungry guests.

By the time he made it to the table, there was one treat left on the tray. Instead of leaving it, he decided to head back. He thought that Grace might have extras for the rest of her party. The last goodie disappeared while he was making his decision.

He was halfway to the kitchen when he heard Lenia's frustration echo into the hallway. "I'm not having this conversation with you again, mother!"

"All I'm saying is there are some nice boys that your brother works with," Grace said. "You don't have to be afraid of going on a date, just …" she stopped when she saw Kase walk through the doorway.

Lenia turned. When she saw Kase her eyes went soft and her cheeks flushed. She took a few steps towards him, but then looked at the ground. "I need some air," she said as she brushed past him to leave the room.

Kase turned to follow, but as soon as Lenia was alone in the hallway, she touched her trident and disappeared.

"Did they go that fast?" Grace asked, seeing his empty tray.

Kase looked between her and the hallway, hoping Lenia would come back.

"You're an excellent helper," Grace added. "Can I fill up the tray again for you?"

Kase smiled politely. "Of course, Mrs. Rie."

"You're sweet, but please, don't be so formal," Grace replied. "Call me Lenia's mom," she added with a laugh.

Her laughter was welcome, and Kase enjoyed being a helping hand. It reminded him of time spent with his aunt and uncle potion making.

Grace and Kase chatted while they set up the second tray. Grace named the treats that she had prepared, which included macaroons, chocolate chip cookies, and—Lenia's favourite—snickerdoodles. They talked a little about the Quest Series, and his new practicum placement in Kimroad. They even enjoyed a few of the goodies as they conversed.

When they were finished, Kase took the tray back out to the main room. This time he wasn't bombarded by hungry guests, and made it to the table without anyone sneaking treats. He placed the tray down and looked around the room for Lenia.

There were about twenty people crammed into the main room. Most of the guests were older, but there were a few his age. He didn't find who he was looking for, but he did recognize a familiar face.

He strolled over to her and tapped her on the shoulder. "Hey, One Time. What are you doing here?"

Aura turned with a smile and gave him a big hug. "Kase! You made it." Aura pulled back, but kept her hands on his arms. "Lenia and I grew up together, so the Ries are like a second family to me. Where is she?" She looked around the room.

"I'm not really sure," he admitted.

"I want to know how her first class went." Aura hopped on her toes. "She was so nervous, but I'm sure she did well. I mean … it's Lenia."

"It was amazing!" Kase said. "Her experiment went well, the students were so excited about The Firefly that—"

"You were there?" Aura's face fell. "Why wasn't I invited?"

Kase laughed. "It wasn't a big crowd. It was just Professor Bright, a couple wizards from the Triple Crown named Derek and Stanley Zeller—"

"Derek Glisterin?" Aura shook Kase excitedly. "Was it Derek Glisterin?"

"I didn't catch his last name." Kase tried to step back, but Aura was holding on too tight.

"Describe him to me," she pressed. "Blond hair? Dreamy eyes?" She looked away and sighed.

Kase tried to remember Derek's distinguishing features. "He was missing a hand."

"That's him!" Aura shook Kase a little more enthusiastically, but he held his ground so that he didn't bounce around. "I heard he lost it mixing ingredients during a potions class. He's so cool …" Aura trailed off again, and then shook her head slowly. "Lenia and I used to have huge crushes on him."

Kase felt his chest drop. But Lenia had barely even acknowledged Derek after her presentation. Maybe it was another one-handed Derek that Aura was talking about.

"There's my daughter!" A man with a peppered moustache pointed towards the doorway. Lenia sheepishly walked across the room. She grabbed Kase's arm as she went past, and they both made their way to the welcoming gentleman.

"Dad, I want you to meet someone." Lenia pushed Kase forwards a little, and dipped her head behind his shoulder.

"Hi, Mr. Rie. I'm Kase," he said politely. Lenia's dad squinted at him, sizing him up with his green eyes.

He relaxed and patted Kase on the shoulder. He stood on his tiptoes to look over him, trying to get the attention of his daughter. "I have someone I want you to meet too," he said. He moved his eyes to the left, like Lenia often did, and turned to the man beside him.

"Hi, I'm Michael." The new man reached out to shake Lenia's hand. "Eric has told me how proud he is of you."

Lenia moved beside Kase and looked up at her father before shaking Michael's hand.

"We actually have an opening at the healing centre that I run, and we would be happy to bring you aboard." Michael smiled proudly.

"You're offering me a job?" Lenia said cautiously.

"Of course!" Michael replied. "We would love to have a Rie on our staff! From what your father has said about you, you're going to be a better healer than he is." The old men laughed, but Lenia curled back towards Kase.

"That's very generous of you," Lenia said levelly, "but I already have a job."

"You mean the one where you play with fire at The Academy?" Eric said. "That's a great hobby, but working at a healing centre is a *career*. It's an opportunity to do something worthwhile with your education, and really help people in the realm. Isn't helping people more important than fire tricks?"

Kase didn't understand. He was proud of Lenia's abilities, and how elated her students were with her teaching, but Eric's eyes only showed pity.

"Those fire tricks got me a consulting job at the Triple Crown with Stanley Zeller," Lenia said in defence.

"Stanley Zeller?" Michael laughed so hard he had to hold his belly in place. "You mean Professor Moleface? Remember that class, Eric? That guy was such a nut!"

"I still remember the day he set his own hair on fire." Eric laughed. "Classic Moleface."

Lenia's small smile was stiff and forced. "Thank you for the offer," she said to Michael. "I need to think about it." She turned and walked away.

Eric and Michael were still laughing as Kase and Lenia fought through the crowded room. Just before they reached the exit, a couple women blocked the way completely.

"Lenia, have you met Gwen yet? She's such a dear. When are you going to get engaged?" one of them asked.

"Someday, Aunt Gloria," Lenia said simply, dodging the question. She pulled Kase through the last barricade, and they exited the house together.

When they got outside, Lenia leant on the porch railing and stared out at the front yard. Kase stood in silence beside her. He knew she was stressed, but didn't know what to say to comfort her.

"Your family is really nice," he finally said. He put his hand gently on her shoulder, hoping she wouldn't teleport away without him.

"They're selfish and full of …" Lenia stopped herself and took a deep breath. She looked up at him with watery eyes. "They're trying to impose their will on me, as if they know what's best, but they don't even consider how I feel. How am I supposed to figure out who I am, or what I'm supposed to do, with a dozen different people pulling me in every direction?"

Kase rubbed her back softly. He could feel her frustration and vulnerability. He didn't have an answer for her, but wanted to make those feelings go away just the same. His only solution was to do something that she might hate.

Kase snuck his left arm around her waist and pulled her close. "I'm sorry, Lenia. It must be tough to feel that way, and face that all the time. Tell me more." He held her tighter.

Her hands dangled around her sides at first, but then she returned the hug with as much force as he was applying.

He wished he could hold her there forever. He wanted to put the burden on his shoulders, so that she wouldn't have to carry the whole load. He wanted to listen to her further, but another fugitive from the party interrupted them.

"Is this a good time to witness a trident demonstration?" Leland asked.

Lenia rubbed her face on Kase's shirt, and then spun them both around to look at her brother instead of disengaging from the hug. "Touch the top of it gently, and I'll show you how it works."

Leland smiled brightly and rushed over. He reached out, careful not to hit Lenia in the face this time. He gripped the trident just below the prongs. "Like this?" he asked.

"Exactly," Lenia said. Kase felt her left arm release from the hug. A moment later, they all stood on a floating island of rock just below cloud level.

It was one of a series of floating rocks that led from the mainland below to the giant island in the sky known as Skyland. Ladders and stairways had been built to connect the islands, making the vertical hike a little easier. Despite that, the gruelling trek had been dubbed the Skyland Grind. Even though Kase had hiked it before, teleporting to the top was much easier.

Clouds scudded past just above them and their island. The breeze was a little cool at this altitude, even as the sun was shining bright.

"What just happened?" Leland let go of the trident and took a few steps back. "Where are we?"

"We teleported," Lenia said. She finally let go of Kase, and they all walked to the edge of the tiny island. Kase couldn't help but look up and think about the satyrs and dragons that lived in Skyland.

"You can teleport?" Leland shook his head as he stared at his sister. "I hate you so much right now. You're like, the greatest wizard in the history of—"

"Want to see something else that's cool?" Lenia interrupted.

Leland nodded rapidly.

"During the Quest Series," Lenia said, "we had to climb up all of these tiny islands in order to complete one of the events. If you look over the edge, you can see them all."

Leland did as instructed. The land thousands of feet below them looked like a patchwork quilt, with greenery, lakes, and grasslands intermixed elegantly. No islands from the Grind blocked their view. "That's crazy. I wish I had done the Quest Series." He leant a little closer to the edge.

Lenia slowly lifted her leg, softly placed the bottom of her foot against his backside, and shoved him off the cliff.

Kase heard Leland scream as he plummeted to the mainland below, but it was soon drowned out by Lenia's laughter. "That was really mean," he said.

"It's fun!" Lenia chuckled. "Your turn." She grabbed Kase by the waist and tried to hurl him over the edge.

He didn't budge. Instead, he wrapped his arms around her as she laughed and struggled to move him. It was good to see her smile. The way the sun reflected in her beautiful green eyes and bounced off her soft cheeks was perfect. He felt the urge to put his lips on hers and finally get the kiss that had eluded him for months now. He leant in a little closer, but then hesitated.

Lenia looked up at him. "What?"

He thought about what she'd said of her family pulling her in different directions without acknowledging how she felt. He didn't want to do the same: to force her into something because of his urges and emotions. He felt his own vulnerability take control.

"You have a lash under your eye," he said. He rubbed his thumb softly on her cheek, and then showed her the hair that he'd removed.

Lenia looked at it, and then met his gaze again. "Make a wish," she whispered.

Kase closed his eyes and took a deep breath, blowing it away. He knew the wish he made wouldn't come true.

He still had one arm wrapped around Lenia's waist, so he gripped the back of her scabbard and flung her off the edge.

He heard her cackle as she fell through the air. He opened his eyes and smiled. He peered over the edge, expecting to see her flailing around. She wasn't there. He closed his eyes again as he realized that he wasn't the master of mischief he thought he was. He was still the student.

He felt a foot on his backside. There was nothing he could do.

The wind rushed around him as he was forced off the edge. He stretched his arms out like a bird and glided free. He had no worries in the world, and took in the beauty of the terrain rushing towards him.

The cool wind was comforting, although it stung his eyes a little. He closed them so he could enjoy his peaceful journey. He knew Lenia would teleport to him, but he was a little worried about what her brother was thinking. Was Leland confident that Lenia would reach him and teleport him to safety? Did he think she'd killed him? That she wanted to send him to his demise?

Before Kase could think of an answer, the wind around him stopped, and he opened his eyes to the island in the sky. He and Lenia stood tall, but her brother was quivering beside them on his hands and knees. He gripped the grass with everything he had, breathing heavily.

"Is he okay?" Kase whispered to Lenia.

"He's fine, he's just a little … wet." Lenia chuckled as Leland looked up at her.

"I didn't pee myself," Leland said angrily. "Don't tell people that."

"When we were kids—" Lenia started.

"Don't!" Leland yelled.

"He peed himself?" Kase asked, getting in on the teasing.

Leland tried to stand up, but his legs were still shaky, so he collapsed to the ground. He had such a defeated look on his face that Kase felt bad for him.

"I'll tell you later," Lenia whispered.

"I still can't believe you can teleport," Leland admitted. "It's just … next level."

Lenia offered to help Leland up. He grabbed her hand, but still struggled to get to his feet. Kase reached out too, and together they were able to get Leland standing. He held onto Lenia's trident to steady himself, and Kase knew he wasn't about to let go.

"Let's head back," Lenia suggested. Before Leland could nod, they had all returned to his parents' house. This time, Lenia didn't worry about being seen, and teleported them back to the porch. When they arrived, the wide eyes of Gwen were the only things that met them.

"Where did you come from?" Gwen asked. She blinked a couple times.

Leland let go of the trident and quickly clutched Gwen. He hugged her tight. "We teleported," he said. "I need some water." He rushed into the house.

Gwen blinked at Lenia again, and then smiled. "I was hoping for a chance to get to know you better. Leland says you're an elements professor at The Academy. That's so cool! Professor Bright was one of my favourites. What's it like working with her?"

"He told you I'm a professor?" Lenia asked.

"Well ..." Gwen put her hand on her hip. "He did say how happy he was that you didn't become a healer, because that's his thing, and you're a much better healer than he is." She laughed, which caused Lenia to smile. "Don't tell him I said anything, but he's pretty proud of you."

Lenia sighed. "Let's go back to the party, and I'll tell you all about it." She put her hand on Gwen's shoulder, and headed for the door. She looked back at Kase and gestured for him to follow.

Gwen and Lenia found a corner where nobody seemed to bother them. Gwen talked about her experience at The Academy, and how she'd met Leland through work. She shared some details of their first date, and how happy she was when he proposed to her. She admitted that she was nervous to meet his family, but found them welcoming and accepting.

Leland joined the group and shared more stories of his time with Gwen. Kase was hoping that he'd have some stories of his sister, but his focus remained on his fiancée instead. The two of them made a lot of inside jokes, answered some trivia about their relationship, and talked about their plans for the future.

Aura found them, and the conversation moved back to Lenia's work at The Academy. Aura still wanted to know more about The Firefly demonstration, which also impressed Gwen and Leland. Lenia promised to show them her invention another time, since she hadn't brought it with her.

As the party continued, Lenia and Kase bounced around the room, and he got to know the rest of the group. Although other members of Lenia's family sounded interested in her work, the conversations ultimately ended up with their healer stories. Kase found it extremely interesting, even though he couldn't directly relate. He wanted to tell them about his own wizard experiences, but didn't want to expose himself as a warrior practising magic.

After a few hours, it was time for them to leave. They said their goodbyes, Lenia hugged her future sister, and then she and Kase walked away down the street.

But before they teleported, Lenia stopped. "Thank you for coming today. I know time with my family can be a little … unpredictable."

"I just wish I could've fit in a little better with your family of healers," he admitted. Lenia had wowed his aunt and uncle, and he wanted to reciprocate with her family. He felt like he had failed.

Lenia laughed. "You're perfect just the way you are." She touched his cheek, but it didn't make him feel better.

"Can you teach me how to heal?" Kase moved his eyes to the left. "Just so I can be a little more perfect?"

"Fine," she grumbled. "It's not as difficult or prestigious as my family makes it out to be, though." She reached into her pockets, but came up empty-handed. "Do you have a knife or anything?"

Kase wasn't armed. Since he couldn't carry a weapon while on duty, he was in the habit of not carrying one at all lately. He reached into his pocket and grabbed his fire starter. "Will this work?"

Lenia studied the edge, and then wrapped her fingers around it. "Stick out your arm," she said. "I'm going to scratch you and heal you first, and then we'll switch. Only do this with another wizard around— even the best healers can't heal themselves."

Kase rolled up his sleeve to his elbow, exposing his left forearm. Lenia took the edge of the fire starter and placed the tip of it on his skin, just below the design he had gotten on their last visit with the mermaids. She pressed hard and whipped her arm back, producing a deep scratch. A little blood popped through the surface, but he didn't flinch.

Lenia frowned. "Doesn't it hurt?" she asked.

"A little," Kase said with a shrug.

Lenia shook her head slowly, and then concentrated. She held her palm against the minor wound. "Remember how this pain feels, because you're going to have to search for it when healing someone else."

Kase could feel Lenia's magic go to work. A soft glow surrounded her palm, and the cut quickly healed. "It's like a whirlwind," she explained. "There's a lot of emotional strain flying wildly about, so the trick is to focus on the source of the pain. If you can concentrate on the injury, rather than the wild emotions of the struggling victim, your power will absorb the discomfort."

Kase nodded confidently. Like all things Lenia taught him, there was a major difference between understanding his power and feeling it. He was ready for the new challenge.

Lenia used the fire starter to scratch herself. She shook her arm a little bit, and then smiled. "You made it look so painless."

Kase placed his palm on her wound and closed his eyes. He tried searching for her pain, but he couldn't feel anything different. He had half-expected to succeed right away, and felt like a failure. "I can't do it."

"Yes you can, Two Silver Times," Lenia replied.

Kase smiled, but kept his eyes closed. He felt her free hand touch his gently, and relaxed. All of a sudden, he felt a shooting pain slice through his heart. He scrunched his nose as he tried to absorb it.

"That's the way," Lenia whispered. "Find it."

Kase felt something move inside of him. It flowed away from his heart and up to his shoulder. From there, he expected it to fall towards his right hand touching Lenia's arm, but instead it flowed towards his left. He felt the pain focus on his left forearm, in nearly the same spot that Lenia had marked earlier. The pain grew, and then was wiped out completely. He opened his eyes in shock.

Lenia smiled and lifted her left arm. "Not even a scar. You're a natural!"

Kase felt proud, but he still didn't really understand what happened. "I must have a good teacher. Thank you, Professor Next Level."

Lenia laughed. "How long have you been sitting on that one?"

"What do you mean?" Kase laughed too. "When your brother said it, I knew that it was good. Way better than 'golden child.'"

"I'll show you what's next level." Lenia touched her trident, and they disappeared together.

CHAPTER 5

A Rookie And A Vet

Curtis tapped his palm against Kase's closed fist. "Scholar beats warrior," he said. He had won three games to two again. He grabbed Kase's apple and leant against the wall.

Kase stared back at the street, listening to the crunch of Curtis' appetite being satisfied. He thought things would change with their relocation, but their post in Kimroad wasn't much different than Flonkertown. The losing still felt bad, and the grind was still the same.

He closed his eyes and hoped for some action.

Curtis choked, causing Kase to glance over. He was holding his sage mirror while a moving image flashed over its face. He spat chunks of apple to the ground and bent over in laughter. He bellowed louder once air filled his lungs again. "Two Three, you've got to see this," he said, moving the sage mirror back to his lips. "Replay image," Curtis said between breaths. He held his hand out so Kase could see.

A man appeared in the image wielding a wooden sword. Beside him was a toddler, who struggled to swing his matching weapon. It looked like the man was trying to teach the toddler some moves, but wasn't having much luck.

The man's attention turned towards the sage mirror capturing the moving image. He stopped engaging with the toddler, but the young student hadn't been told the fight was over. With a wild but swift swing, he made contact with the distracted adult, hitting him squarely in the crotch.

The man keeled over as Curtis laughed again. "Such an idiot," he said. He tucked the sage mirror away and returned to his apple. "That kid is awesome!"

Kase didn't laugh, but he understood Curtis' amusement. "Kids are the best," he agreed. He turned his attention back to the street, and tried to figure out how far Change the Realm was from here. He wondered if any of his young friends were interested in warrior training.

While Kase daydreamed, Curtis took a few more bites of his snack and then offered the rest to his trusted steed. "That's a good boy, Bojangles," Curtis said, stroking his horse's mane gently. Although he was a new horse to Curtis, Bojangles was old, overweight, and slow. His brown hair looked brittle and dull, instead of shiny and smooth.

After Bojangles was done with his treat, Curtis mounted up. "Break's over, Two Three." He lifted the reins and made a clicking sound with his tongue. Bojangles slowly picked up his hooves, and eventually entered a steady trot.

Although there was space on the horse's large hindquarters, Curtis made Kase walk. Kase was still technically a warrior-in-training, so he didn't qualify for his own horse. He thought he would get a little something extra for Curtis' promotion, but he didn't even get a replacement twig for his sheath.

Since Curtis was newly appointed to his post, his orders were to walk the streets, get to know the locals, and familiarize himself with the area. He wasn't required to engage with anyone or get involved in any disputes. He didn't even have to report any questionable activity. He only had to become a part of his new neighbourhood.

They made their way down the cobblestone lane, which was littered with small businesses and shops. Kimroad was so large that even streets like this were full of people running about. Even though they weren't in the busiest area, it was exponentially more packed than being in peaceful little Flonkertown.

To his left, Kase noticed a shop called Flower Power. On his right was a small fruit grocery with a sign that had nothing but an apple on it. Behind him, he heard a shopkeeper pleading with those around him. His attention turned to the warriors.

"Stop, Guardians," he pleaded. "We need your help!"

Curtis pulled on Bojangles' reins. "I'm sorry, sir, but we—"

"Up there," the shopkeeper said, pointing to a tree beside him.

Kase shaded his eyes and looked up. On one of the branches, a hairless kitten shivered against the trunk. Its skin was a deep green that matched the leaves of the tree, but it had brown patches mixed in, like a leopard. Its eyes were wide and its legs were stiff.

"I'm sorry, sir," Curtis repeated, "but that seems more like a job for the firefighters."

As wizards, firefighters and healers were usually called upon for animal-related incidents, so it wasn't unusual for Curtis to defer. Kase tried to see if there were any branches for him to climb to reach the scared animal.

"Please," the shopkeeper begged. "I know the regular Guardians in this area wouldn't be able to help us, but I'm sure you new recruits are more willing."

Curtis smiled and dismounted from his horse. He was always pleased with the opportunity to shine. "Let's take a closer look," he said, patting Kase on the back.

"Wonderful!" the shopkeeper said.

Curtis led Kase to the tree and looked up again. The kitten was only twelve feet above the ground, but there were no branches within their reach. Even the ones that were there were too skinny to support either of their weights.

"Give me a boost, Two Three," Curtis said. He leant on the tree and waited for Kase to follow.

Kase judged the height to the kitten. He wasn't confident that a boost would get Curtis close enough, but he obeyed his commanding officer.

He stood beside the tree and clasped his hands together. Curtis put one foot in his grasp, and then pushed on his shoulders. Kase lifted Curtis up and rested his hands on his lap, securing Curtis' boot and using his legs to support the extra weight. He leant against the tree to make it a little easier on himself.

"I'm going to stand," Curtis said. He steadied his free foot on Kase's left shoulder and stood tall, holding the trunk to balance.

Kase leant harder against the tree and held Curtis' feet. They both wiggled a little, but once he steadied himself, Kase felt like he could hold Curtis for hours.

"Oh no." The shopkeeper pointed up. "She moved to a higher branch."

"C'mon, kitty," Curtis said softly.

Kase didn't want to look up and lose his balance; he knew he wouldn't be able to see anything, anyway. Instead, he closed his eyes and tried to connect with the kitten, like he had with the puppy during their fire rescue. He didn't know if it would work, but he wanted to try.

He slowed his breathing and searched for a connection with the little animal. He felt the cool breeze flow through his hair. He felt his heartbeat slow down. But he didn't feel the kitten; nothing was happening. Then, in an instant, the pure terror of the kitten filled his entire body.

He wanted to say something to calm himself down, but he couldn't. He wanted to reach out to the kitten, but he didn't want to do anything to make him look like a wizard. Instead, he concentrated on his breathing. He slowed it down so that his heartbeat would follow. In a few seconds, both he and the kitten were completely relaxed.

Instead of trying to coax the kitten into trusting Curtis and waiting for it to move on its own, Kase tried to control the animal so that it could be rescued faster. He thought about how a cat might balance in a tree, and visualized its four legs moving with poise. He focused on the precision the feline would use with each step, and he could feel his power working.

He imagined the kitten creeping slowly to move its paws to a lower branch. He visualized how it would turn its body around to climb backwards down the tree. He thought about how welcoming Curtis' big, bulky hands would be as they safely carried the kitten from the height of the tree.

"He's got her!" the shopkeeper exclaimed.

"Two Three, I'm coming down," Curtis said.

Kase opened his eyes, but didn't break his focus. He helped by grabbing Curtis' right foot and guiding it down to his supported waist hold.

Curtis held the kitten in one hand, but kept his other steady on the tree trunk as he made his way to the ground. Once he was flat-footed, Curtis presented the kitten to the shopkeeper.

The shopkeeper was thrilled. "You're such a great addition to our community," he said. "I'm Wally, the owner of The Juice Moose." He pointed to the storefront beside the tree. "Come to my shop, and let me make you a smoothie for your hard work today."

"We're not supposed to—" Kase started.

"We'd love to!" Curtis interrupted.

Wally hugged his hairless kitten and led them inside his shop. He stepped behind the counter and placed the speckled animal onto a tiny, furry bed. The kitten instantly curled up to clean itself while Wally enthusiastically went to work.

The entire shop was filled with baskets of fruits and vegetables. There were even jars of liquid lining the shelves on the walls, which looked like premade juices for sale. A menu board above the counter listed the types of smoothies and their main ingredients.

As Wally grabbed random samples from his inventory, he told Kase and Curtis the story of his little friend, whom he named Battlecat.

Although Battlecat was from the jungle, she had snuck a ride with a banana shipment. Wally had taken the poor orphan in, and provided food and shelter while he arranged to return her to her natural habitat. But after a few weeks, he felt that their bond was strong enough for them to remain friends under the same roof.

"She's not going to get much bigger than a regular cat," Wally explained. "Her camouflaged skin and slender tail make her a good hunter in the wild. Her instincts are starting to develop, seeing as she's climbing trees—hunting for birds, you see—but she isn't a threat to people. She's a great pet!"

Kase thought about how much Lenia might appreciate a bird-hunting pet. Wally slammed two cups in front of the warriors. "Enjoy," he said happily.

The smoothies were surprisingly cool and delicious. Kase tasted mango, peaches, and bananas, all perfectly blended together. He wondered how Wally mixed all of the fruit, juices, and ice together. He made a mental note to add another drink to his friend's old Slup-a-lurp competition.

Curtis and Kase gulped their drinks back, thanked Wally a few times, and then headed back to the grind. They walked up and down the streets of Kimroad, memorizing the street names, studying the businesses, and speaking with the people in the area.

They didn't find anything exciting on their walkabout. Although they engaged with a few more people, most of them were travellers that needed help with directions. Kase wondered why he had spent so many hours at The Academy working on battle strategy, weapon techniques, and his physical strength when it would have been more beneficial to study maps and geography.

After a few hours of staring at rows of buildings that looked the same, Curtis decided they needed some refreshments. They headed back to The Juice Moose for another delicious smoothie. Kase was determined to watch Wally make the drink this time, to figure out his methods. There must have been some magic involved.

Kase froze when he saw a familiar face engaged with Wally outside the store. He quickly recovered and slipped behind Bojangles, hiding his head from view.

Questions raced through his mind. Why was J.R. in Kimroad instead of the Badlands? Were the other members of the Brotherhood around? Was the gang hunting Kase down?

Kase thought about his and Lenia's last encounter with J.R., Porkchop, and Money Jane. Their enemies couldn't have been pleased with their escape, but Kase had thought since they left the Badlands, they were safe. He didn't know what would happen now if J.R. noticed him.

Kase tugged on Curtis' leg to get him to stop. "Don't look, but there's a criminal at The Juice Moose."

Curtis pulled on the reins, and Bojangles plodded to a halt. He peered over his trusty steed. "Where?" he asked.

Kase peeked around Bojangles, careful not to move too suddenly. J.R. shook hands with Wally, and then walked down the street. He wasn't dressed in his tattered Badlands garb: instead, he wore a navy, glittering robe.

"The guy in blue," Kase stated. "He's part of the Brotherhood."

Curtis sat straight and put his hand on his helmet. "A gang member? From the Badlands?" he turned to Kase. "He sure doesn't look like he's part of the Brotherhood."

Kase took a step away from Bojangles and stared down the street. J.R. was walking away briskly, like he was on a mission. His hair was neatly combed, and his fancy robe glimmered in the afternoon sun. Kase knew he was up to no good. He wanted to follow him.

"Let's go talk to Wally," Curtis said. "I'm thirsty."

Curtis made a clicking sound, and Bojangles sauntered towards The Juice Moose. Kase kept his eyes on J.R., but tried to discretely look around to see if he recognized anyone else. He didn't.

"Gentlemen," Wally said with open arms. "Welcome back! Two more smoothies?"

"Do you have any other flavours?" Curtis asked. "I have a craving for strawberries."

"I know the perfect drink," Wally said with a wink.

Kase had thought Curtis would get to the point quickly. Instead, he slowly dismounted, pulled on his belt, and then ran his hands through Bojangles' mane.

Kase couldn't wait any longer. As Wally stepped towards the counter, Kase blurted out his question. "Who was that man you were talking to?"

"Who?" Wally looked in J.R.'s direction. "You mean John Ross?"

J.R. must be short for John Ross. Kase nodded, but he kept one eye on the street. It wasn't difficult to lose the sparkles in his peripheral vision.

"John Ross works for Brothers' Inc.," Wally explained. "They're a property management company. He collects all the rent from the businesses around here. I was just giving him my payment for the month."

"Hmm." Curtis tapped his chin. He finally seemed interested. "How many businesses does Brothers' Inc. own?" he asked.

"Oh, they must own half of Kimroad," Wally said. He turned his attention back to making drinks for his newest customers.

Kase froze. The words came out of his mouth before he had time to process them. "The Brotherhood owns half of Kimroad?"

"Brothers' Inc., Two Three," Curtis said with a laugh. He patted Kase on the back. "Pay attention," he added. He raised his voice to address Wally. "My partner thinks John Ross is from the Badlands."

Wally looked at Kase, then waved his hand and chuckled. "No way. John Ross has been collecting from me for the last few years, and Brothers' Inc. has been around for decades. Besides, he smells too good to be from the Badlands."

"You see, Two Three," Curtis said, wrapping his arm around Kase's shoulders.

Kase didn't have time for a lecture, but he could tell Curtis was already relishing the moment.

"You have to be able to read the situation," Curtis said. "It's critical that you pay attention to every detail. Although your gut might tell you one thing, you have to gather all the facts before making any accusations."

Curtis turned Kase back towards the street and pointed at a hooded shopper across the way. "See that person over there?" he asked. "Their clothes are a little worn out, and their hood is up, so that must mean they're a criminal, right?"

Kase tried not to roll his eyes. "Probably," he said sarcastically. J.R. was getting away, and he wanted Curtis to finish so he could get back to what was important.

"C'mon," Curtis said, patting Kase on the shoulder again. "They're just a regular patron in our wonderful community that … wait a minute."

Curtis gripped Kase's shoulder and stared across the street. The shopkeeper was helping another customer with some jewellery, but left the display case open. While the shopper modelled the necklaces in front of a mirror at the back of the shop, the hooded patron nudged the glass door open, grabbed a ruby-handled dagger, and slid it into their pocket. They then ducked their head down and hustled out of the store.

"Your gut was wrong," Kase quipped, but Curtis was already on the move.

"Hey, there," he shouted. When he didn't get a response he added, "You, in the hood!"

The culprit stopped and turned their head. Kase couldn't see the criminal's face, but he felt like he and Curtis were recognized as Guardians. After a moment of hesitation, the robber took off sprinting.

"Oh, it's on," Curtis said in a huff. He mounted Bojangles quickly, which spooked the old gelding. The horse neighed and took a few wobbly steps, but Curtis was able to calm him down. "Let's go!" Curtis jammed his heels into the side of his not-so-trusty steed. The horse neighed again, and then raced down the street.

"Where are you—" Wally started.

"We'll be back!" Kase said, chasing after his superior.

Bojangles didn't run that fast, so Kase was able to keep up. The street wasn't that crowded either, so they could see their target clearly.

The hooded thief ducked into an alley half a block away. It was a narrow path, too narrow for a warrior on horseback.

"Two Three, go follow the perp," Curtis said, pointing down the alleyway. "I'll go around the block and cut him off."

"Dragoon!" Kase said, picking up speed. When he made it to the alley's entrance, he slowed to survey the scene. The thief stumbled down the open backstreet, and looked pretty tired already. Instead of heading after him, Kase hesitated and looked back down the main road.

Curtis was rounding the corner, but further down Kase could see J.R.'s glimmering blue robes. For a moment, he thought about disobeying Curtis' orders and following his nemesis instead. Curtis was wrong; it was more than a gut feeling. He needed to find the connection between J.R., the Brotherhood, and Brothers' Inc.

Curtis disappeared from his view; Kase had to make a move. He reviewed his options again, took a deep breath, and headed down the alley. The thief was a problem now; he could pursue J.R. another time.

The criminal had made it to the end of the alleyway, where they leant against the wall. When the perp looked back, Kase was a little surprised to see the face of a scared young boy; he couldn't have been more than a few years older than the kids that he helped out at Change the Realm.

The young boy darted left, away from the alley to where Curtis would head him off.

"Wait!" Kase yelled, but it was useless. He tried to run faster, to catch the criminal before he was trapped.

When he rounded the corner Curtis was there, sitting on his horse and blocking the street. He held his bow high and steady. An arrow was drawn, its point aimed at the criminal.

The young boy turned around and locked eyes with Kase. He was caught between the two Guardians, but was closer to Kase and the alleyway. There were buildings on either side of the street, but no traffic. He had nowhere to go.

"Don't move," Curtis demanded in his deepest voice.

The boy's eyes watered as panic gripped him. He reached into his pocket and took a step towards Kase.

"I said don't move!" Curtis yelled again. He released the arrow, sending the soaring assassin towards its prey.

"No!" Kase yelled, but it was too late. Curtis' aim was off: instead of a warning shot, the arrow was headed straight for the boy's heart. Nothing could stop it. Even Kase couldn't react quickly enough.

Time slowed. The arrowhead pierced the boy's back. His body reacted almost instantly: his eyes grew wide and his hands spread as he fell to the ground. His head bounced off the street's cobbles, causing him to let go of the item he'd pulled from his pocket. It was a wooden figurine of a Guardian.

Kase rushed over to help. He knelt beside the boy and turned him over. His eyes were closed. A little blood oozed from his mouth and a small gash on his forehead.

Curtis trotted over and slowly dismounted from Bojangles. "Gotcha," he said proudly.

Kase turned to Curtis, but his vision was blurry. He clenched his teeth together. "You got him square," he said softly. "He's just a kid."

Curtis moved his hand to his face. "Oh, no," he said. "No, no, no …" he kept repeating. He knelt down and pulled the hood back from his victim's face. The boy's sweaty black hair was stuck to his forehead.

"This isn't happening," Curtis said. He stood and took a few steps back. "I'm in so much trouble. What am I going to do?" He put his hands over his eyes and started pacing.

"We have to get him to a healing centre," Kase said. He brushed the wet hair away and tapped the boy's cheek to get him to wake up. He pulled the boy closer so that he could get to the arrow. He pulled on it a little, but it wouldn't budge.

"Are you crazy?" Curtis said with a scowl. "We need to get rid of the body and forget this ever happened. I'm going to lose my job for this! I wasn't supposed to engage with anyone yet, and on top of that I used my bow. The scrutiny I'll be under will be—"

"We can still save him!" Kase said, cutting Curtis off.

Curtis' face softened. "You're right." He sighed. "I'll use my sage mirror to message for help. Then we'll work on our story."

Curtis turned and walked away, but Kase turned his attention back to the wounded. He couldn't believe that Curtis had shot so quickly, and was now thinking of covering up his mistake. Their duty was to the people, not to themselves.

He tapped the boy's cheek again, but there was still no response. He leant over and pulled the boy closer. He tried to fight away tears, but he could feel the cool drops slide down his face. He felt guilty for hesitating in the alleyway. He should have been able to do more.

He closed his eyes. "I'm sorry," he whispered.

He felt his heart cave a little bit. It was like something had pierced his soul. He could feel the pain flow through his core, around his stomach, up through his lungs, and into his head. He wanted to scream, but he kept his mouth shut. He wanted to sob, but he pinched his eyes tighter. He wanted to get up and fight, so he clenched his fists taut.

He felt the arrow loose in his hand.

Kase leant back and opened his eyes. He pulled the arrow from underneath the boy. The blood on the tip had dried.

The boy's eyes fluttered open. The cut on his forehead had disappeared. The instant he locked eyes with Kase, he rolled onto his side and pushed Kase's arms away.

The boy scrambled to his feet, eyes darting around in confusion. He stared at Kase, who still knelt on the ground, then glanced at Curtis. He quickly pulled his hood back over his head. He reached into his pocket, tossed the stolen dagger to the ground, and took off running. He dodged past Bojangles and didn't turn back.

Kase was left sitting dumbfounded in the street, still holding the arrow. Was the pain he felt real? Had he healed the boy by accident?

"Your hands glowed," Curtis said. He held his sage mirror limply by his side.

"What do you mean?" Kase tried to keep his voice steady. Had he been caught using his magical abilities? His mind raced, trying to figure out what happened. He needed to think of a clever excuse.

"They glowed the way a wizard's do when they ..." Curtis put his hands on Kase's shoulders. "Are you a wizard?"

Kase tried to stand, but Curtis was leaning on him too hard. Their eyes met, so Kase felt obligated to answer. "No, I—"

"You are though!" Curtis smiled and shook Kase excitedly. "That is so cool! I wish I could heal people like you. What other tricks do you know?"

"You wish you could be a wizard and a warrior?" Kase was confused. He'd kept his power a secret because nobody would understand. Having two sets of abilities would make people assume that he was evil. But instead of being threatened, Curtis celebrated like it was a special gift.

"Of course I do!" Curtis pulled Kase to his feet. "If I had special powers that set me apart from all the other warriors, it would make me be a better Guardian."

"Won't that cause more harm than good?" Kase asked. "Won't the Triple Crown lock you up for that sort of thing? They might think you're the next Mardious Hood or something."

"Look, Two Three." Curtis wrapped his arm around Kase's shoulders. "This is the real world. It's not like The Academy. The school is set up so people can focus on their specialty, but life doesn't follow the same rules. Yes, maybe tradition keeps things in order, but in the real world, things change. We have to adapt in order to rise through the ranks."

Kase still wasn't willing to share his full secret with Curtis, but he liked the enthusiasm. "I thought Guardians were supposed to do their job every day and just grind it out. That after years of service, new opportunities will arise for those that have put in the time and earned the right to move ahead."

Curtis laughed. "No one is guaranteed to rise through the ranks. Everyone is competing for the same roles, and they'll pull you down if you're falling behind. You don't start slow and get faster. You need to start fast!"

He clapped Kase on the back hard enough to knock him forwards a step. "I know it took a while for me to get from Flonkertown to Kimroad, but if I had some extra wizard skills like you, I'd be even higher up the chain by now. If you learn anything from me during your practicum, I hope it's this: be everything you can be, use every advantage you have, because no one is going to just give you a better title. Your healing power, and whatever else you might be able to do, won't make you a threat to the Triple Crown. It'll make you the greatest warrior in the realm."

Kase looked at the ground. His dream was to become a great warrior, but he never thought that his wizard ability would be the way to reach that goal. It was just something that he enjoyed, something that built a connection between him and his favourite wizard. Yes, he found opportunities to sneak it into his daily life, but he didn't think it would amount to greatness.

It sounded too good to be true. "How will I know when to show it?" he asked.

"You don't have to be flashy with it," Curtis said. "You just need to do little things, like what happened today. You saved that boy's life, true, but you also saved mine. My career would've been over if we'd have taken him to a healer. I owe you everything, and am in your debt forever." Curtis extended his hand.

Kase felt like he could trust Curtis, but that didn't mean he was in a rush to show off all his talents. He was still worried that people who didn't know him would isolate him for being different. On the other hand, he was happy to have someone else on his side.

Instead of taking Curtis' hand, he stuck out three fingers. "Wizard beats scholar," he joked.

CHAPTER 6

Just Having A Friend Couldn't Be No Crime

Talen offered a Jam-Jam to Kase, but he refused. He wanted to wait for everyone to join them before he started eating. He fought the urge to check his sage mirror again, but it was getting difficult.

"Sorry I'm late," Aura said.

Kase turned around and smiled, but Talen jumped up and gave Aura a hug. "You're just in time," she said. "Our drinks are still cold and our dinner is still fresh."

Kase sat under a tree on a picnic blanket that Talen had brought. In front of him was some food that she'd prepared, including a charcuterie board filled with meat, cheese, and a few vegetables. There was also a separate plate of baked goods. Kase had brought some smoothies from The Juice Moose, but he only knew what was in one of them. He had asked Wally for the top four flavours.

"This looks lovely!" Aura said. "Where's Lenia?"

Kase shrugged. "She's probably just running behind."

"As usual." Aura joined Kase on the blanket and grabbed a drink right away. "Slurp-a-lurp!"

"Shouldn't we wait for her?" Kase asked, but Aura had already taken a sip.

Aura froze. She eyed both Kase and Talen, then shrugged and continued drinking. She didn't seem too concerned about Lenia's absence. "Do you know when she's coming?" she asked.

Kase looked at Talen's expressionless face. "I guess we could start without her." He also shrugged, and Talen followed suit.

"Good. I've had such a long day, and this smoothie is already making it better." Aura took another few sips, then leant back and sighed. She looked up at the sky and basked in the late afternoon sunshine.

Kase picked up his cup and held it out to Talen. She sat down, grabbed her own drink, and they tapped them together in an informal toast. Kase could taste strawberries and blueberries in his. He decided to grab a Jam-Jam to pair with it.

"This is such a nice park, Talen," Aura said. She took another sip of her drink. "How did you find it? Did you write a story on it or something?"

Talen moved her hand to her mouth, trying to finish the cheese she was chewing on quickly. "When I was younger, I used to escape here to read. I'd sit under this tree with a full sac of books until it got too dark out to see."

Kase stared up at the big oak beside their blanket. It was the tallest, widest, and oldest tree in the park, but there were other large oaks around. There was even a little pond not too far away where some other people sat on the grass and relaxed. The square field was in the middle of a few streets of houses, away from the business of Kimroad.

"So that's how you got so smart," Aura said. She reached for some salted meat, and picked up some cheese too.

Kase laughed at Aura's joke, but Talen didn't seem to care for it. "I didn't study here. I mostly read my favourite adventure series. It was just a lot quieter here than at my parents' house. They live a couple blocks that way." Talen pointed over her shoulder casually, and then grabbed a slice of cucumber.

Aura and Kase both stopped eating and leant in.

"Are you going to show us where you grew up?" Aura asked.

"Are we going to meet your parents?" Kase asked. Talen didn't really share her past, so he was incredibly intrigued.

"Absolutely not," Talen said. She grabbed another cucumber. "My parents work a lot, so they're probably not home anyway," she added.

Kase looked down in disappointment.

"What do they do?" Aura selected some more meat and cheese.

"They're both real estate agents," Talen said. "In fact, they're the best in Kimroad. They've helped countless families find the right homes at affordable prices. They've successfully set up businesses in ideal locations. They've helped many farmers expand their land rights and titles. They are highly intelligent and have worked very, very hard in order to be successful." She sounded like she was reciting from a textbook by rote.

"Have they ever worked with a company called Brothers' Inc.?" Kase interjected. If her parents were the best real estate agents in Kimroad, they must have dealt with a property management company that owned half the city. He swiped some cucumber to match Talen.

"I didn't pay attention to who my parents partnered with, or the details of their services. They literally worked all the time, and rushed through dinners just to get back to it. It always seemed like their job was more important than ..." Talen looked down at her hands. "Me," she mumbled.

"That's horrible," Aura said. She reached over, but instead of grabbing more food she rested her hand on Talen's.

Talen looked up and forced a smile. "It's okay," she admitted. "It was probably for the best; it gave me a chance to sneak out of the house. It made me smarter."

Aura smiled, and went back to eating. Kase was still eager to tell Talen about J.R. "Do you remember our trip to the Badlands last year?" he asked.

"How could I forget?" Talen retorted.

"I saw J.R. the other day in Kimroad," he said. "Apparently he works for a company called Brothers' Inc." He eyed the dessert plate.

Talen dropped her cucumber slice and quickly reached into her sac. She pulled out a notebook and quill, flipped to the middle of the book, and scribbled something down. She looked back up at Kase and leant closer to him. "Tell me every detail," she said.

Kase went over the events, including how he had been careful to not be seen by their enemy. He described how different J.R. looked, the comments made by Wally, and the possible connection between Brothers' Inc. and the Brotherhood.

"I think your suspicions are warranted," Talen said, making some final notes. "I'll look into it and see what I can find."

Talen was about to put her notebook away when Aura pointed at the cover. "Why do you have 'Night Projects' written on it?"

"This is where I keep all of my Money Jane notes," Talen said. She flipped through the notebook, showing that most of the pages were covered in her handwriting. "I still haven't been able to figure it all out yet, but every bit counts."

"Still having trouble relating Money Jane to Mardious Hood?" Kase asked.

They had first travelled to the Badlands to do some research on the notorious criminal Money Jane. When they met J.R. and his father Porkchop, it was suggested that Mardious Hood and Money Jane were the same person, even though Talen's previous studies stated otherwise. Kase knew Talen was frustrated with the puzzle, but he admired her tenacity.

"I can find lots of information on Mardious Hood, but nothing about Money Jane," Talen answered. "It's like history went out of its way to erase everything about one evil icon, but at the same time created all this fearful propaganda about the other. It's difficult to even figure out what's real and what's fake."

"Fake history?" Aura asked. "What do you mean?"

Talen flipped to one of the first pages in her notebook, and showed them. She had drawn a horizontal line across the centre. Random numbers were circled and scattered about, with lines connecting them to the main one. Kase didn't understand it at all.

"I created a timeline, and marked the pages where I have notes corresponding to each event." Talen traced her finger around the numbers, and stopped when she hit the end of the page. "The right side marks the death of Mardious Hood, his involvement with the Brotherhood, and how he was defeated by Roman Garrick. There is a lot of information on his doom, so all these numbers are cluttered."

Talen then moved her finger to the left side of the page. There was another cluster that she circled with her finger. "On this side, I have information about when Mardious Hood worked for the Triple Crown. He actually led a research team with Zuke, before Zuke became the High Wizard. Together, they uncovered a lot of new magic in regards to animal control, specifically which ones can be controlled and which ones can't. Most of his publications were on dragons and their environment in Skyland. In some circles, he was regarded as a trailblazer because of his discovery of the rogue nature of the fire-breathing beasts. He also was a beloved pianist."

Kase didn't care if Mardious was a musician or not, but he was interested in the magic. He wondered what being a trailblazer meant.

"The clusters of circles show that there are many articles and books on the subject, which supports the facts about Mardious Hood at these times. Despite that, there are a couple gaps in my research."

Talen pointed to a space on the left of the page. "This area shows the information I found about Mardious Hood before his time with the Triple Crown." There were only a few numbers on that side of the page, and most of them were crossed out.

"Why do some have an X through them?" Aura asked.

"Those are the fake stories," Talen said.

"How do you know they're fake?" Kase asked. There were a lot of Xs on the page, even in the clusters.

"This one is a prime example," Talen said. She pointed to the number 13, which was on the left—from before his downfall. She flipped to that page in her notebook and read her notes. "Mardious Hood had a wizard mother and a wolf father. Human by day, but beast by night, Mardious roamed the woods of the Amber Forest until he was discovered by …" Talen stopped reading and started to laugh. "I'm sorry; this one is so ridiculous it always gets me."

Kase was happy to see Talen smile. "So he's not a werewolf?" He tried not to laugh too.

"Fake history," Aura said with a nod.

"All of the past stories are ridiculous," Talen admitted. "He was born in a volcano. He was possessed by a demon. His family were all jesters. The stories are all scary, but they provide no real, consistent background information."

"Jesters aren't scary," Aura said. "They're always so joyful and funny."

Talen's brief smile disappeared. "Jesters are the scariest," she said. "They paint their faces so that they're always smiling, even when they don't mean it. They wear ridiculous clothes and laugh like maniacs. They're deranged." She pulled her notebook in close to her chest and shivered.

"Don't worry, Tal," Kase said. "If there are any jesters around, I'll protect you from them."

Aura laughed, but Talen shuddered again. She put her notebook back down and grabbed some cheese. "Thank you, Kase," she said. She nibbled on her snack, but still seemed rattled.

Kase tried to change the subject to make Talen feel better. "There was one number that had a star beside it. What does that mean?"

Talen took a deep breath. "That page relates to our encounter with Porkchop last year. He said that Mardious Hood was the real Money Jane, which proves a connection to the Badlands. I don't have any information to support his claim, but I believe him. I even suspect that Mardious Hood is from there originally."

"But if he's from the Badlands, how did he make it into the Triple Crown?" Kase asked. The Badlands were segregated from the rest of the realm. It seemed strange for someone to climb their way into working for the entity that kept them in poverty.

"You uncovered one of the two major questions that I don't have answers to," Talen said. "But when I figure it out, I'll let you know."

"What's the other question?" Aura asked. She took a final slurp of her drink, and then tapped the bottom to get the last few drops.

"How did he leave the Triple Crown?" Talen said. She opened her notebook to her timeline again, and pointed to a gap on the right side of the page. "I know a lot about what Mardious did while he worked there, and his terror-filled war against them after, but nothing about what happened in between. What made Mardious leave? Who helped him? Why was he such a respected leader at one point in time, and such a villain on the other? What made him snap?"

"That's more than one question," Aura pointed out. "It does sound complicated, though."

"If there's anyone that can figure it out, Talen can," Kase said.

Talen closed her notebook and put it back in her sac. "I feel like I'm missing one major piece; like once I find it, it will all make sense. I wish I had more time to spend on this project," she admitted. "I like solving puzzles. It's much more enjoyable than the stories I have to write at my boring job."

Kase thought about Cali's puzzle dilemma. He knew Talen would be able to help. The Triple Crown seemed to have a lot of secrets—since Talen was researching its past, maybe she could help Cali with its present.

"Have you ever heard of ciphers?" he asked.

"Of course!" Talen perked up. "Those are my favourite kinds of puzzles. There are a lot of them in the stories I used to read. Why do you ask?"

Kase hesitated, and took a sip of his drink. He was sworn to secrecy by Cali, but wanted to tell Talen the truth. "I—"

He was saved by the sound of Lenia's voice. "Sorry, guys, but I can't make it tonight." Lenia's moving image flashed across Aura's sage mirror. "I'm stuck at The Academy. Please don't hate me!" The message ended, so Aura put the mirror back in her pocket.

Kase looked down and sighed. It felt like he hadn't seen her in years. "So much for our Liberati reunion," he mumbled.

"I'm sure she'll make it next time." Talen put a hand over Kase's.

He checked the food that was left. "If she can't make it here, why don't we take our picnic to her? There's still plenty for her to enjoy." He lifted the full smoothie beside him. It was still cold.

"That sounds like a great idea," Aura said, grabbing the last slice of cucumber. "But I'm going to head home. I still have some things to do tonight, so I don't want to be out too late."

"I think you should definitely take the rest of our food to her." Talen gave him a definitive nod. "But if you don't mind, I'm going to head home too. I need to start researching Brothers' Inc. for us."

They all made a promise to get together next week. It felt good to be team Liberati again, even if all of their teammates couldn't be there.

Talen headed home from the park, but Aura and Kase made their way to the gateway portals. The nearest gateway had ten portal doors side-by-side. Aura stopped at the first triangular door, while Kase went to the second. He wasn't interested in where she was going, focusing instead on his own quest to meet Lenia before the smoothie melted.

He slipped a couple Aileron coins into the keystone in front of his door and calibrated the destination for The Academy. He waited patiently in front of the twenty-foot portal while the bright light between the panels pulsated. After the seventh flash of light, the stone panels split apart and slowly slid towards the edges of the triangular arch, as if disintegrating into the border. He could see the glimmer of his destination through the gateway.

On the other side of the portal, students enjoyed the remaining evening sunlight in the outdoor common area. There were some warriors doing sprints next to the warrior castle, and some scholars reading in the shade of the scholar castle. As he glanced around, Kase saw a dandelion patch next to the administration castle. He knew Lenia would love a bouquet of her favourite flower, but he didn't have time to stop.

He hustled to the wizard castle and the familiar route to Lenia and Professor Bright's classroom. The halls were fairly quiet, since classes were over for the day. He was glad he didn't have to fight through any crowds to reach his destination.

When he got there, Lenia had her entire head buried in one of the lower cabinets at the front of the class.

"Did you find it?" she asked in a tight, high-pitched tone. She turned her attention to the doorway. When they locked eyes, her panic seemed to disappear. "Hey, you!" She stood up and opened her arms.

Kase rushed to the front of the classroom, put his sac and the smoothie on the table, and embraced Lenia. He picked her up and twirled her, which always made her giggle. He turned a bit too far, and the bottom of her trident smacked the open door of the cabinet. They both stopped and laughed a little more.

He set her down, but didn't let her go just yet. "I brought you some food," he said, staring into her green eyes.

"You're a lifesaver," she said. Her eyes moved to the side and her lips curled up a little. "Are you going to let me enjoy it?"

Kase mimicked her expression. "No," he replied, dropping his arms.

He pulled out the charcuterie board while she took a sip of her drink. "I can taste peaches!" she said. She must have been hungry, because she started shoving food into her mouth. Kase quickly caught her up on his conversation with Talen and Aura, his gift from The Juice Moose, and his encounter with J.R.

"There's something else I've been meaning to tell you," he said.

Lenia slowed her chewing, recognizing his seriousness. "Is it a secret?" she whispered.

Kase looked around the room to make sure they were alone. He wanted to tell her all his secrets. "I healed someone," he whispered back. "In public."

Lenia stared intently while he described his showdown with the young criminal: how Curtis had been wrong for firing, but how he had rectified the situation by accidentally saving the boy's life. He told her the pain he'd felt through his whole body, his embarrassment at being caught, and how different he felt after hearing Curtis' support for his abilities.

"He told me that it's nice to have gifts, but unless you're going to do something with them, what's the point?" He put his hand on Lenia's and took a deep breath. "I want to become more than just a warrior who can do a few magic tricks. I want to become a wizard. Will you teach me how to be a real one?"

Lenia gripped Kase's fingers. She looked deep into his eyes and smiled. "You're already a wizard," she said. "You have the ability to connect with everything around you, whether it's animals, elements, or the injured. You've already learned the hardest part, but I think I know what you need next."

She opened a cabinet along the wall and tapped her chin. The inside shelves were lined with books. Her fingers scanned the titles, and then wrapped themselves around a bright green one. She proudly handed the book to Kase. "I want you to read this," she said.

The title of the book was *Wizardry 101*. The cover showed a unicorn jumping over a rainbow. Kase wondered if that was something that Luna and Turanus, the unicorns that he knew, enjoyed. He flipped the book over a couple times. It was pretty thick.

"Like, the whole thing?" he asked.

"I want you to read all of these." She pointed back to the cabinet. "You'll need to understand all the applications for a wizard's power, like healing, potion making, illusions, and so on. I want you to study hard."

Kase scratched his head. He thought Lenia would be his private tutor like before, and they could increase the time they spent together. But instead it felt like she was acting like a professional, treating him like any random student who'd asked for help. "I kind of thought you would be able to show me what to do."

Lenia's smile disappeared. "I don't have time to walk you through everything. I know you can learn some things on your own, because of how you studied your grandfather's notes before becoming a warrior. For wizardry, you have to first figure out what you're passionate about, as well as what your boundaries are." She tapped the book. "Then I'll show you how to break through those boundaries."

Kase felt his heart beat faster. He was excited to learn as much as he could, and happy to have Lenia's support. The road to becoming a real wizard wasn't as direct as he'd first thought, but he was up to the challenge. It felt right.

"Thank you, Professor Next Level." Kase smirked. "I won't let you down."

Lenia laughed and shoved Kase playfully. He tossed the book on the table and was about to push her back when a knock sounded on the open door.

Derek stood in the doorway, holding a dark-coloured vial. He rattled it a little bit, which made Lenia squeal in delight. Kase had never heard that sound from her before.

"You found it!" she said. She ran over to the doorway and grabbed it from him. "Let me just get my levitation board and we can go," she said. She clutched the vial close to her chest and skipped back to the front of the room.

Kase wondered why Lenia was acting so weird. "You have to go?" he asked.

"I have to work on my project with Derek," she explained. "We're working on …" she hesitated and looked back to the doorway. Derek was slowly making his way towards the front. "I can't really say, but it's super cool!"

Kase felt a lump in his throat. He remembered the plans for The Firefly that he had seen in Derek's papers; they must have been working together from the beginning. He was disappointed that Lenia had a secret project with Derek, but then again, he was keeping secrets from her, too.

"Kase Garrick," Derek said. He had reached the front table and extended his left hand. "It's nice to see you again."

"You remember me?" Kase asked. His bad feeling was only getting worse. First Derek couldn't be bothered to know his name, and now he was acting oddly friendly.

"Of course," he replied. "High Wizard Zuke had so many good things to say about you."

"What?" Kase looked over at Lenia, who already had The Firefly under one arm, ready to go. The confused look on her face probably matched his own.

84

Derek laughed. "Well yeah, you know the High Wizard, don't you?" he chuckled again. "You're a funny one." He turned to Lenia and put his good arm around her. "Ready to go, beautiful?"

Kase glared at Derek as they left the room, his blood coursing through his veins. He held himself as still as a statue to prevent himself from acting on the impulses racing through his mind.

Derek whispered something to Lenia, his lips getting closer and closer to her ear. She giggled, and then turned away from him bashfully. He looked back to Kase and nodded his chin.

Kase clenched his fists. He wanted to remove Derek's good arm from around Lenia's shoulders. He wanted to tell Lenia to teleport Derek to an isolated part of the realm, so he could never interrupt them again.

Without saying good-bye, Lenia and Derek left.

Kase stared at the doorway, his breathing getting heavier and heavier. Did Derek always talk with Lenia like that? Did she enjoy it? Was Derek a big priority in her life? Kase wanted to be the one that was close to her.

He shoved the textbook in his sac, leaving the charcuterie board on the table, and sprinted to the door as fast as possible. He looked left and right, but didn't see them anywhere. He checked again, but still nothing. They were gone.

He walked back into the classroom and slowly cleaned up the charcuterie board. He focused on his breathing, and his heart started to relax. He drank the last of Lenia's peachy Juice Moose drink, and ate the scraps of meat and cheese. He tossed the dirty dishes in his sac, and then walked over to the library cabinet to scan some more books.

He studied the titles and flipped through a couple of them. He picked out three more and threw them in his sac. He hustled out of the room and left the wizard castle quickly.

He was on a new mission: to become a better wizard. He needed to study hard in order to get to the level that he so desperately desired to reach. He was determined to learn as much as he could, and to figure out his boundaries as soon as possible.

He needed a chance to break through them with Lenia.

CHAPTER 7

Swinging Sword Lecture

Cali's hair was the most chaotic Kase had seen it. The back stood straight up, while other parts were pulled back. It looked like it hadn't been washed in weeks.

"I've tried everything." Cali leant on her desk and rubbed her face. Her eyes were darker than normal. "I'm getting nowhere. I've looked at every cipher example the Triple Crown has on record, but none of them match. I don't know what I'm going to do. I've failed."

Kase put a hand over his heart. He didn't want his sister to feel like a failure. "It's okay, Cali. There's no rush. Maybe we can leave it for a while, and come back later?"

"I can't stop," Cali said. "I won't stop. I have to know why dad made this mysterious book. It must be able to lead us to him somehow." She took a deep breath, and then shook her head. "I miss him."

"Can I take a crack at it?" Kase suggested. He knew he wouldn't be able to solve it if Cali hadn't, but he wanted to relieve her of her struggle.

She peered at him between her fingers. "I know your tricks, brother. You'll just give it to Talen."

"What would be wrong with that?" Kase asked. He was getting tired of Cali's selfish unwillingness to trust her friends. "Maybe a fresh pair of eyes will help you figure something out. Maybe she's read books with ciphers, and knows a few tricks. Maybe she grew up loving puzzles, and would step up to the challenge."

Cali tilted her head. "Those are oddly specific examples," she mumbled. She leant forwards. "Did you tell her already?"

"No." Kase matched her glare. "I didn't break my promise to you." He looked down and twiddled his thumbs. "I wanted to, though."

"How many times do I have to—" Cali started.

"Just meet with her," Kase said, cutting her off. He raised his voice. "What's the harm in talking to her? If I could arrange a place where no one would find you two together, would you consider it?"

Cali crossed her arms and leant back in her chair. Her eyes were angry. "No way," she said. "It's just too dangerous."

"I thought you liked a little danger," Kase said. He expected Cali to at least crack a smile, but instead she closed her eyes. He thought for a second that maybe she had fallen asleep at her desk.

A knock on her office door caused her to rouse herself. She jammed her secret notebook back into her desk and cleared her throat. "Come in," she said. She glared at Kase, but smiled brightly as Curtis entered the room.

"Great news, Two Skills!" Curtis said. "The Grand Master is at the castle today, so I was able to get you into a meeting right away."

Kase wasn't in the mood to be as excited as Curtis. He couldn't believe that Cali wouldn't even consider seeking another solution to her problem. They were in a staring contest, and neither of them was going to break.

"Did I interrupt something?" Curtis asked. He looked back and forth between them to gauge the situation. The silence was deafening. "I've only seen you this quiet when I bug you about your girlfriend." Curtis slapped Kase on the back. "Was your sister teasing you too?"

Cali smirked, breaking her glare. The twinkle in her eye was a sign of mischief. "Do you mean Lenia?" She uncrossed her arms and leant forwards again.

Kase looked down. He felt his cheeks get rosy, but he didn't want to play their game. He wished he had the trident so that he could teleport out of Cali's office.

"I'm pretty sure she's the only girl he knows," Curtis said. "I keep telling him to make a move, but he hasn't yet. I don't really know why."

"Are you too nervous, brother?" Cali's voice rose an octave, a technique she'd used since they were kids to mock him.

Kase gave her a dirty look.

"Maybe you should talk to her," Cali said, her lips puckered out. Another move Kase hated whenever she made fun of him. "What's the harm? If I could arrange for a place where no one would find you two together, would you consider it?"

Kase grinned. Cali was trying to be condescending by turning his words against him, but she was too clever for her own good. He could use it to bait her into a solution. "It's too dangerous," he retorted.

Curtis laughed, and hit Kase on the shoulder. "Relationships aren't that scary, Two Skills. I'm sure your sister has some good advice. You should listen to her." He looked at Cali and smiled.

Kase thought for a second that Curtis was trying to flirt with Cali, but she wasn't paying any attention to him. Her eyes were locked on Kase. Her face softened. "I'll make you a deal," she said.

Kase did his best to look innocent, so she wouldn't realize she was walking into his trap. He knew that being bashful would make her come to a resolution on her own. "I'm listening," he said.

"If you promise to finally talk to Lenia about how you feel, then I'll talk to that person we were chatting about earlier." Cali tapped her desk drawer to make sure it was shut.

Kase smiled. He had gotten what he wanted, but he suddenly felt nervous. Was it worth the cost? He puffed up his chest to push past his hesitation. "Deal. I'll pick a time and place, and we'll all get together."

"Deal," Cali confirmed.

Kase looked up at Curtis and stood. "Let's go." He tapped Curtis' shoulder and walked towards the door.

"Do I get anything out of this?" Curtis asked.

"You can have the rest of my cinnamon bun, if it makes you feel better," Cali said. She reached across her desk and grabbed her snack. There were a couple of bites missing, but it still looked delicious.

"Deal," Curtis said.

They said their good-byes and stepped into the hallway. Kase waited for orders.

Curtis had already inhaled his tasty treat, and was licking his fingers clean. "This way." He pointed down the hall.

They were on their way to meet with Commander Davis and the Grand Master. As part of the practicum program through The Academy, Kase was obligated to regularly meet with his superiors so that they could evaluate his performance. It was the third meeting of many throughout his term, so he wondered why Curtis seemed excited about it. To Kase, it was just a formality.

Curtis led Kase down some stairs, past the main floor of the castle of the Triple Crown, and into the second basement. Kase heard that the castle had just as many levels underground as it did above, but he hadn't gotten a chance to explore it all yet. He'd always been more concerned with what was on the upper levels.

Curtis opened a large door, and they walked into an auditorium-style room. The ceiling was high, but there were no tapestries or other ornaments on the walls. A large, circular platform made of red bricks stood in the middle of the room. It was about thirty feet wide, but it wasn't tall enough to block Kase's view of the table at the back of the room, where Commander Davis, Grand Master Carter, and High Wizard Zuke sat.

Davis and Carter were preoccupied with the paperwork in front of them, but Zuke was alert to Kase's presence. He stroked his beard as the warriors made their way to the table.

Kase wondered why Zuke was there. He couldn't think of a reason why the High Wizard would sit in on a warrior's evaluation, unless his wizard power was known. Had Curtis revealed the details of their latest pursuit? He felt vulnerable, but tried to hide it as he took a seat opposite his superiors. Curtis sat down beside him.

"Here it is," Grand Master Carter said. He placed a piece of paper in front of Zuke.

After an awkward moment, Zuke finally looked away from Kase and studied the paper. He picked it up, moving it back and forth in front of his face, and then put it down. "Go on," he said with a roll of his gloved hand.

"Curtis has told us a lot about your time in the field," Commander Davis said. His forehead was crinkled, his voice was low, and his face was stern. He also took a look at the sheet in front of him.

Kase prepared for the worst. Curtis had probably been obligated to tell them of his healing power. He would have to accept whatever punishment was to be handed out, whether it was expulsion from The Academy, exclusion from the Guardians, or being arrested by the Triple Crown. He wanted to close his eyes and accept his fate, but he remained frozen.

"You also have exemplary grades in your classes at The Academy," Davis continued. "Grand Master Carter has provided us with the details. You are a model warrior student, as well as a Quest Series champion. We'd like to applaud you for all your hard work, because it has grabbed our attention."

Kase glanced at the Grand Master, who had his head down and was staring at the table. His shoulders were slumped forwards, but his eyes darted from left to right nervously. Kase wondered why he was being so quiet; usually, he led the evaluations.

"Because of your impressive service and training," Davis continued, "we'd like to offer you the chance to compete for a role on a special task force, codenamed Triple Thunder. This team, led by High Wizard Zuke, will be made up of three other wizards and two warriors. The specifics of the task force will remain confidential until you prove yourself worthy of being one of the two warriors chosen."

The Commander leant forwards. "It is rare for us to offer this to a warrior who has not yet graduated, and is thus a great honour. Do you accept?"

Kase scanned the panel again. High Wizard Zuke wore his creepy smile, Grand Master Carter still hadn't looked up, and Commander Davis held a quill steady over the paper in front of him.

He wanted to say yes, but he was dubious. He was reminded of Stanley Zeller's offer to Lenia, and how Professor Bright had supported Lenia's development. Why wasn't the Grand Master just as excited? Although it seemed quite glamorous, an opportunity to get ahead in his pursuit of becoming a great warrior, he suddenly felt uncertain.

"How will I prove myself?" he asked.

"Your credentials are well documented, but we need to see you in action," Zuke said. "If you accept our offer, then your first trial will start right now."

Kase looked at Curtis, who gave him a reassuring smile. It seemed like the kind of situation that would accelerate his career, but the mystery of it bothered him.

There was no more time to think, though: it was time for action. "I'm in," he said.

"Yes," Curtis said with a dramatic fist-pump.

Kase glanced back at the panel, and saw Commander Davis give Grand Master Carter a pat on the back. This time, the Grand Master looked up. He appeared worried.

Davis brought his sage mirror up to his lips, and talked into its face. Kase didn't hear the words, but a few seconds later, the door to the room opened.

Kase turned around in his chair. A large warrior in heavy armour stepped into the room, a morning star in hand. The club-like weapon had a wooden shaft, at least three feet in length, and a fixed metal head. Spikes protruded from the head in all directions, with a single, larger spike extending from the centre.

"You will face High Guardian Mason in combat," Davis instructed. "The circular stone platform is your arena. The warrior that is either knocked off the platform or willingly yields will lose the match. Do you understand, Mr. Garrick?"

Kase nodded and stood. "Where do I get my morning star and armour?"

"You have a weapon," Zuke said.

Commander Davis looked at the High Wizard. "I was going to—"

Zuke held out his palm. "This is the test. You still have the option to deny our request," he said to Kase.

Kase took the twig out of his sheath and stared at it. His weapon was no match for a bone-crushing instrument of death, but he would have to make do. He didn't think he was in any danger, and he would try his best either way. It was just like a sparring session at The Academy. At least his training would be useful for a change.

He watched the High Guardian step onto the circular platform. The heavy armour curved around the warrior's belly. Kase figured that his opponent outweighed him by at least a hundred pounds.

Kase walked to the edge of the platform and stopped. He removed his helmet, stepped out of his boots and took off his Guardian uniform. He needed to be fast and agile, and he knew the extra apparel would slow him down. It wouldn't protect him against a heavy weapon with deep spikes, anyway.

"Interesting," said Zuke, but the rest of the panel remained quiet.

Kase slipped his twig out of its sheath and snapped it in two. He wrapped his fingers around each piece, so that the protrusion of wood stood about four inches above his grip. He intended to use the twigs like twin daggers, instead of a sword.

"Let's go, Two Sticks!" Curtis yelled. He had turned his chair around so that he could witness the battle.

Kase tried not to smile and focused on his opponent as he stepped up to the ring. High Guardian Mason's armour covered all the major body parts, but Kase knew there were weaknesses to be found at the joints. He'd be able to jam his sticks into the armpits, elbows, or behind the knees. There was a guard around Mason's neck, so he didn't think he'd be able to inflict any damage there. Only the eyes were an option on his head, but not something Kase was willing to consider for a match.

"Begin!" Commandar Davis shouted.

Mason took a step towards Kase and gripped his morning star tighter. The weapon was used for brute bludgeoning force, not for finesse, so Kase wanted to avoid it at all costs. He watched Mason's movements carefully, assuming Mason would aim for his arms and legs to avoid any real damage.

His assumption was wrong. Mason began with a swing of the morning star at head level. Kase had to duck to get out of the way of the spiked point. Was there a chance he could get seriously injured during this test? His heart pounded.

Mason switched his grip for an overhead strike. Kase knew he'd have to be more agile than his opponent; he'd have to move in creative and unexpected ways to gain the upper hand, as he'd been taught in Professor Valas' combat classes. He slid out of the way as the head of the morning star hit the ground, and took a step forwards to counter the attack.

But Mason was already ahead of him. As Kase raised his arm to jam a stick into his opponent's armpit, Mason's fist was already on its way to its target. Kase took a heavy, metallic blow to the face.

Kase stumbled and shook his head, feeling dazed. Black spots clouded his vision. But he didn't have time to recover, because a darker spot was coming for his head again. He leant forwards and rolled to the side, away from Mason and towards the open part of the circle. He felt the rush of air from the morning star as it missed his back.

"Good work, Two Sticks!" Curtis cheered. "Keep it up!"

Kase jumped to his feet and was able to catch a few deep breaths. He rubbed away the blood that trickled from his lips. Mason was still coming towards him, but not as fast as before. Kase decided that he would tire out the High Guardian before trying his next counter-attack.

Mason started swinging again, but Kase was able to avoid every strike. He dodged left, ducked a few more times, and dodged right. He relied on his flexibility, in addition to moving his feet, so that he could remain in the combat ring. He was quick, his eyes were alert, and his breathing slowed. It was quite a contrast to the strong, flailing, panting High Guardian.

Mason held the morning star high, and came down with another overhead strike: powerful, but slow. It was Kase's time to attack.

Before Mason could land another punch, Kase jammed both sticks into the inner elbow socket of Mason's armour. For a split second, Mason's grip on his weapon loosened, which was all Kase needed to yank it free.

Mason tried to grab Kase's shoulder, but Kase swatted the metal glove out of the way with an open palm. He spun to Mason's non-dominant side, gaining momentum. With a lunge, he swung the weapon with all his might at the back of Mason's leg. One of the spikes on the side of the head drove into the back of the warrior's knee.

Mason screamed out in pain and crumbled to the ground. He immediately raised his hands and shouted, "Yield! I yield!" He grabbed at his wounded knee, but his flexibility was limited because of the armour.

Kase knelt down and reached for the warrior's leg. He hesitated before touching him, worried for a second that his power would unleash itself. "I'm sorry," he said.

Mason removed his helmet and tossed it to the side. His greying hair was sweaty, his eyes were closed, and his teeth were clenched together hard. He took a couple sharp breaths and then laughed. "You got me good." He opened his eyes to study Kase. "You did a lot better than I thought you would."

Kase turned to face the panel. High Wizard Zuke was leaning across the table, talking to Commander Davis. Grand Master Carter was staring at Kase with a look of fear, slowly shaking his head. When Zuke leant back, the Grand Master hid his expression by looking down at the table again.

"Congratulations, Mr. Garrick," Commander Davis said. "You have passed the first trial with flying colours. You may collect your things and be off." He set Kase's paperwork aside and picked up his quill. "I'll remind you that you are not to tell anyone of this task force. We will contact you with further instructions."

Kase wasn't worried about keeping secrets: he had become quite good at that lately. He glanced at Mason's pain-ridden face, and then back to the panel. "Aren't you going to heal him right away?" Why wouldn't the most powerful wizard in the realm come to the aid of a fallen warrior?

"We have a perfectly acceptable healing centre upstairs," Commander Davis said. He was busy making notes, and didn't seem to care. "You are dismissed, Mr. Garrick."

High Wizard Zuke got out of his chair, but instead of walking towards the ring and the injured Mason, he exited through a door at the back of the room. Curtis also got out of his seat and hurried to collect Kase's uniform.

"Let's go," Curtis said, moving his chin towards the main entrance.

Kase took one last look at Mason, who had his fist over his heart. "Dragoon," Mason said.

Kase reciprocated the gesture and left the arena. He didn't think he'd have been able to gain the respect of an experienced warrior by stabbing him in the back of the knee with a morning star. It made him feel better, anyway. He knew Mason would be okay, and with the healers' help, would fight another day.

In the empty hallway, Kase put his uniform back on. Curtis was still reliving the battle. "He was swinging so hard, but you were just too quick for him," he said. He danced around a little, but he didn't look very agile at all.

"I'm lucky I didn't get hit," Kase replied. "He could have killed me."

"I knew he wouldn't though, Two Sticks." Curtis was still wrapped up in his own movements. "It's such a rush! What a beginning to your illustrious career."

Kase wasn't as optimistic about his career if he kept getting in the ring with people who were out to kill him. "Do you really think it's worth it?" he asked.

"Of course!" Curtis put his arm on Kase's shoulders. "Look, Two Sticks, I'm proud of you. You're a lot more gifted than I am, and I know you're headed for greatness. All I ask is that when you're climbing the ladder, you'll remember to take me with you."

Kase understood why Curtis was pushing him to be part of the task force. He was a little disappointed that the invite came from his own self-interest, but it felt good to have the confidence of his partner nonetheless. He didn't want to let Curtis down.

"If I make it out alive, you'll be the first person I partner with when I get promoted," he said.

Curtis pumped his fist again. "Now I know how it feels to be part of your Quest Series team—and why you won it twice. I bet the next trial is going to be even more exciting."

Although it seemed like Kase was finally on the path to fulfill his dreams, he was a little worried about what came next. It wasn't like the Quest Series at all. He wouldn't know what these trials were beforehand, but they would be difficult, and likely even more dangerous than the first. With them, he wasn't aiming to be a part of the Triple Thunder task force, or even to become a better warrior; he just wanted to survive.

CHAPTER 8

It's Like This And Like That And Like This

Talen gripped her stone, took a step forwards, and followed through with her toss. The rock skipped four times before sinking to the bottom of the lake.

"You did it!" Kase said. He was impressed that Talen's initial throw was a success. He remembered trying to teach Cali, who had stayed out until past sunset before she'd finally gotten a rock to skip.

"Is four good?" Talen asked in a monotone. "Yours skipped eight times."

"Four is outstanding, considering you've never done this before," Kase said. "With a little more practice, I'm sure you'll be a professional."

He looked around the lakefront and picked up another smooth, flat rock. He took a step back and set his feet. "I like to do more of a side-arm toss, spinning the rock a little bit, and then cheering it on. It usually helps if I name it first."

He looked back. Talen already had her notebook open. He thought it odd to take notes on something as casual as skipping stones, but it was Talen.

Kase looked at his rock and rubbed it. "Let's do this, Turtle Power." He took a step forwards and chucked his pet rock into the lake.

Turtle Power hit the water and bounced high. "Uh, oh," Kase said. "Too high of a bounce isn't good." When the rock hit the water again, it dribbled twice before sinking.

"Is three good?" Talen's look was unwavering, but Kase knew she was making fun of him.

"Think you can do better?" he challenged.

Talen looked at the lake, scribbled something in her notebook, and then carefully placed it back into her sac. She searched the lakefront and picked a beautifully flat stone. She rubbed it between her palms. "Let's do this, Shark Tooth," she said.

"I love that name," Kase said.

Talen bent her knees to get a little lower, pulled her arm back, and whipped the rock towards the surface. Shark Tooth didn't bounce high at all, but kept skipping along the top of the water. It made so many ripples, Kase lost track.

"How about seventeen?" Talen asked. This time, she couldn't contain her smile.

Kase stared at the water. He couldn't remember what his record was, but he knew it wasn't that high.

"That was amazing," Cali said from behind them.

Talen and Kase both turned. Cali was leaning against Lenia, trying to orient herself.

"Yeah, it was an incredible throw," Kase agreed.

Cali and Lenia shared a confused look, and then Cali stood up straight. "I meant the teleporting," she said. "How does it work?" she asked Lenia.

"I just touch my trident and visualize where I want to be," Lenia said. "If I can see it, I can save a few steps by imagining that spot. For anything farther away, though, I can only teleport to places I've actually been, because I know how it feels to be there."

Lenia touched Cali's shoulder and teleported them twenty feet down the lakefront. She used Cali's arm to wave at Talen and Kase, and then returned to them a moment later. Cali swayed a little bit, and then sat on the ground. She looked dizzy.

"We have a blanket over here." Kase walked over to the spot that he and Talen had set up. It was under the shade of a tree, but still had a good view of the lake.

"It's good to see you two," Talen said. She walked up to Lenia and gave her a hug. Cali grabbed Talen's leg and hugged it from the ground.

"You getting in on this?" Lenia asked.

Kase rushed over and wrapped his arms around everyone. "It's good to have the original group of Liberati back together. The O.G. Liberati!"

"That name's a bit of a stretch," Talen pointed out. "But I love it!"

The O.G. Liberati gathered on the blanket. Cali looked over the water and sighed. "I know it's near the farm, but I haven't been to this lake in forever," she said. "I forgot how pretty it is."

"It's a good spot away from it all," Kase said. "Somewhere secluded where we can all relax and not worry about being interrupted."

Cali smirked at Kase. "You're really not wasting time, are you?"

Kase scratched his head and looked at Lenia. She was basking in the sun, oblivious to her surroundings—at least, until she noticed everyone looking at her. "What?" she said.

"Brother?" Cali prompted. She smiled a little more.

Kase took a deep breath. "I invited everyone here for a reason," he said. "It's more than just a friendly get-together. There are some things that I've kept secret, and I feel like I need to get them out in the open with the people I care about most."

Lenia and Talen leant closer, but Cali just kept smiling. Lenia's hand brushed his, and he turned to meet her gaze. Her lips were tight in concern, but she gave him a reassuring nod. He looked directly at his sister. "I can do more than just use Lenia's trident. I'm an actual wizard."

Cali's smile disappeared. "What?"

Kase knew it wasn't the secret she was expecting. Talen's eyes were wide, her mouth forming a silent, "Oh."

"I'll show you." He pulled the fire starter from his pocket and flicked it to produce a flame. He made a turning motion with his hand, and the flame moved from the fire starter to his palm. He let the fire expand and contract, and then manipulated it into different shapes. He started with a heart, then shot an arrow through it. He turned it into a shark, and then swam it close to Talen before letting it disappear.

"That's so cool," Talen said. "What else can you do?"

Kase told the group about how he healed the boy in Kimroad and Curtis' reaction to it. He talked about how empowering it felt to be encouraged to harness his wizard power by his warrior partner, and how it could make him a better Guardian. He told them how he had been studying Lenia's books, and had taken his magic to the next level.

He also told them about his meeting with the Commander, Grand Master, and High Wizard, even though he'd promised not to mention the task force. He was still unsure of what it all meant, but it made him feel better to share the news with his friends.

"I don't know when my next trial will be, but it's going to be intense," Kase said. "It's a lot more serious than anything I've done at The Academy, or during my practicum."

Cali blinked a couple times. "And I thought I had a lot going on," she admitted.

"Have you ever heard of secret task forces before?" Talen asked Cali.

"No I haven't," Cali said. "Everything I've done at the Triple Crown has been well-documented. I'm not surprised there are things going on that I don't know about, but I'm a little shocked that you're a part of it, brother."

The group went silent, until Lenia jumped in to unveil a secret of her own. "I'm also part of a special team," she said. "Did you know that some of the professors at The Academy have been sponsored by the Triple Crown for research?"

Cali rubbed her face. "I don't know if I can handle any more of this," she said with a laugh. "Yes, I know that the Triple Crown funds projects that include professors. There are finances that get allocated to innovation, but my department doesn't deal with any of the specifics."

"Well, my group doesn't have a cool name like Triple Thunder, but it's still pretty secretive," Lenia said. "I also had to pledge that I wouldn't tell anyone, but I know I can trust the O.G. Liberati."

Kase gripped Lenia's hand. He was happy she was using his new nickname for the group.

"I work within a team of five wizards. We're led by an old elements professor from The Academy named Stanley Zeller. His research now revolves around minerals, metals, sands—anything that has something to do with the earth. He's really knowledgeable, but a little detached from reality at times."

Kase thought about Mr. Rie's comments about 'Moleface'. He thought Mr. Zeller was just eccentric.

"The rest of the team are recent grads that work for the Triple Crown. Lucy is a water element specialist, while Rick focuses on wind. Derek is the final member, but he's more involved in potions instead of elements. I've learnt the most from him so far, but he's really … complicated." Lenia looked down at her hands and brushed Kase's away.

He instinctively pulled it in close to his chest. He felt a shortness of breath.

"He's been really interested in the potion I use for the levitation board. We've been working on adding ingredients to accelerate the burning process, but it hasn't worked out as he'd hoped. He keeps pressuring me to come up with alternative solutions, but it's been stressing me out."

Kase wanted to put Derek in his place. Lenia had already invented something amazing—she shouldn't feel pressured to make it better if it wasn't on her own terms.

Lenia reached into her pocket and pulled out a full glass vial with a cork in it. "This is the closest we've gotten so far. This potion contains butterfly tears, coconut vinegar, lightning bolt powder, death adder scales, and pinecone dust."

Lenia reached into her pocket again, and pulled out a small stone. "This is a hardened piece of magic magma," she explained. "We've found that in solid form, there's a delay before the burning effect of the lava occurs."

She pulled the cork off the top of the flask and dropped the stone into the solution. She replaced the cork, touched her trident, and disappeared.

"Where'd she go?" Cali said, looking around.

"She's about forty-three feet behind you," Talen said.

Lenia set the flask on the ground, touched her trident again, and then reappeared on the blanket. "Just wait a few seconds," she said.

The O.G. Liberati all turned to watch. Moments later, the solution exploded, causing the ground beneath it to shoot into the air in tiny pieces. When the dust settled, it left a hole the size of their blanket; Kase couldn't tell how deep it was.

"That is really cool," Cali said. "What are they planning to do with a potion like that?"

"Ultimately, they want to use it for mining," Lenia replied. "A version of the potion that's smaller and more powerful could be used to break up hard rock in tight places. It would also work a lot faster than people with pickaxes. When the earth is soft enough, they would be able to transport it all away by using a larger levitation platform." She tapped the trident. "So I guess there are two separate things in development right now."

"That really is fascinating," Talen said. "I wish I had a job like that."

Lenia laughed. "It's not that glamorous, and really more of a hassle than anything. At first I thought I would be excited to meet new people in the field and work on something ground-breaking, but I've found that I enjoy teaching at The Academy more. The special research will help me become a better professor, so it's something that I'm obligated to do, but I'd much rather just work with the students all day."

"I'm sure your students appreciate you too, Professor Next Level," Kase said.

"I'm not as good as Brie, but I'll get there," Lenia replied, using Professor Bright's first name. "Oh, wait! I totally forgot. I'll be right back." Lenia touched her trident and disappeared.

The rest of the O.G. Liberati sat in silence as they waited for Lenia to return. Kase looked out at the lake and felt at peace for the first time in weeks.

"When are you going to tell Lenia your other secret?" Cali asked. Now she was the one not wasting any time.

"Soon," he said, deflecting Cali's fervour. He was more annoyed at her than he was nervous about Lenia.

"What secret?" Talen asked.

"Kase is going to—"

"Don't."

"Ask Lenia to be his girlfriend," Cali said in a playful tone.

"How old are you?" Kase said.

A puzzled look crossed Talen's face. "I thought you two were already dating."

"Why would you think that?" Cali asked.

Before Talen could answer, Lenia reappeared with a tray of four bowls. Steam rose from the surface, and Kase could already smell its delicious aroma.

"Soup-a-loop!" he exclaimed. "Is this Professor Bright's famous recipe?"

"Not quite," Lenia said, passing the bowls around. "I'm now a part of Brie's soup exchange. It's my turn to make some this week, so I've been practising. This is the third batch I've tried, but I think I've got it now. It's a beet soup with celery, potatoes, onions, cabbage, and garlic."

Kase dipped his spoon into the bowl and blew it off before he brought it to his mouth. He wasn't surprised that it was the best soup he'd ever had. "It's better than Professor Bright's," he said.

"Are you implying that it's the best in the realm?" Lenia said.

"We're in the circle of truth right now," Kase pointed out. "I have to be honest."

"Do you want to be honest about anything else?" Cali chimed in.

Kase took another sip of his soup. He was tired of being teased by Cali. He wanted to tell Lenia his biggest secret on his own terms.

"While you were gone, Lenia," Cali said. "We were talking about relationships."

"Oh, really?" Lenia replied. "You have a new boyfriend?"

Cali laughed. "I wasn't talking about me."

Kase stirred his soup, methodically scooping up a spoonful and then dumping it out. He took a deep breath. He was ready.

"I have a new girlfriend," Talen said.

The rest of the O.G. Liberati stared at Talen. She casually lifted another spoonful to her mouth and gave Kase a small smile. "This really is good," she agreed.

Lenia smiled. "What's your girl's name?"

"How did you meet?" Cali added.

"Her name is Harlow," Talen said. "She's funny, considerate, and a few years older than me. I work with her at the news centre. She has my dream job." She took another sip of her soup.

"Your dream job?" Kase also kept eating. He forgot about his own nervousness and focused on Talen's revelation.

"She gets to go on elaborate trips all over the realm, writing short stories for avid travellers," Talen said. "She finds the best spots to eat, the special historical sites, and the must-see entertainment. Even the stories she doesn't write down are interesting. I would do things a little differently, but she's in a great position."

"Like, you'd write the stories differently?" Cali asked.

"My goal is to inspire the uninspired," Talen answered. "I wouldn't just tell people where to go or what to see; I want to share the importance of it all. There's so much to learn from history, but we're also making history every day. I'd want to remind people what they're really capable of. I want to be part of something great."

Kase looked at Cali, who returned a smile. She reached into her sac and pulled out the original copy of their dad's notebook: the one that Lenia and Kase had found in the Badlands. "Talen, I have a special historical project I need your help with."

She tapped the cover. "I need your help to make sense of it, but you have to promise not to write or tell anyone about it. I want you to be a part of it, because it's too big for me to handle on my own."

Talen put her soup down, recognizing the seriousness of the situation. "You have my word," she said, placing her hand over her heart.

Cali took a deep breath and handed the book over. Talen carefully accepted it and turned to the first page. "Dominic Garrick?" she asked, touching the signature at the bottom.

Cali explained what the book was about, what she had deciphered so far, and how dangerous it might be since their government was involved. She was able to teach Lenia a little bit about ciphers as she uncovered how she had decoded the first section. She was still stuck on the others.

"I've looked through countless resources, but the coding doesn't match," Cali said. "I just don't know what else to do."

Talen turned a page in the notebook and moved her head closer to examine it. She tapped the paper and nodded. "This one's a pigpen cipher."

Cali looked at Kase, and then back at Talen. "You figured one out already?"

"Did you ever read *The Legend of Blue Cider*?" Talen asked. She reached into her sac and grabbed a notebook and quill.

"No, why?" Cali asked.

Kase looked at Lenia, and they exchanged shrugs. They both slurped their soup a little softer so they could listen.

"It was my favourite series when I was younger," Talen said. "Blue was a treasure hunter who explored magical, far-away lands. Sometimes, in order to get past a certain obstacle or discover some hidden cove, she had to solve a puzzle. One of those puzzles was a pigpen cipher."

Talen drew some lines on the page in her notebook. The first two were four-line grids, one with dots and the other without. The second two were X's, also with dots on one and not the other. "Instead of using a regular alphabet," she explained, "the pigpen cipher uses symbols, created from the shape of the grid, that correspond with letters."

She filled in the spaces around the lines with letters, completing the alphabet in the last X. She then wrote the letter "A", and the shape that the "A" square made from the grid.

Cali looked at Talen's notes, and then at the simple symbols in their dad's notebook. "That's brilliant, Talen. I don't know why I didn't think of it."

"The pigpen cipher is a pretty simplistic, monoalphabetic substitution scheme. I don't think it's normally used for coding, because it's mostly seen in literature." Talen ran her finger along the first set of symbols on the page. "Unless you've seen this type of cipher before, I don't know how you'd be able to guess. Let's see if I'm right."

Talen picked up her quill and started scribbling in her book. After writing two words, she showed the results to the rest of the O.G. Liberati.

"Jenim Island," Kase read aloud.

"Giants," Lenia said, referencing the primary inhabitants of Jenim Island.

Cali moved closer to Talen so she could see both the original notebook and Talen's shorthand. "Let's finish the rest of it."

Kase was proud that Talen was able to help Cali. He knew their combined minds would be able to crack the code. He also knew that he and Lenia were not going to be able to chip in much for this project. The time had come to make his move.

"I need to stretch my legs," he said to Lenia. "Do you want to go for a walk with me?"

"I want to know what happened on Jenim Island," she said, watching Cali and Talen carefully. "Maybe it will give us a chance to go visit Cooper and Lyla."

One of the challenges in the Quest Series last year had been to teach the giants how to use larger versions of a sage mirror. In return, they had learned about the culture of the island and made some new friends.

"We'll need some time on this," Cali said. She smiled at Kase. "You two can take a break together."

Kase waited for a little more teasing from his sister, but she was focused on Talen's handiwork. Lenia stood up, stretched her arms, and grabbed his hand.

They walked along the lakefront and stared at the water. The early evening sun reflected off the surface, turning the blue lake orange. A cool breeze floated through Kase's hair, but it didn't keep him at ease.

He let go of Lenia's hand and rubbed his sweaty palm against his pant leg. "I have something for you," he said.

They stopped walking, and Lenia looked up at him. He was more focused on the tree that stood a few feet away from the beach.

Kase pointed towards it, where a bushy-tailed squirrel climbed down the trunk. It scurried through the weeds and across the hardened mud, but stopped near the edge of the water. It looked over at them and then went still.

"It's beautiful." Lenia clasped her hands in front of her. "Well done, my young pupil."

The squirrel stood on its hind legs, folded one arm in front of itself, and bowed before fading into nothingness. "I've been working hard on my illusions," Kase admitted. "How did you know it was fake?"

"Squirrels move as if they've just eaten a handful of sugar," Lenia said. "Yours walked as if it were a cat, so that was my first tip-off. But animals are tough to create as illusions, because wizards can connect with them. I couldn't feel the squirrel, so I knew it wasn't real. If it was something that wizards couldn't connect with, like a dragon, mermaid, or centaur, then it would have been more believable."

Kase had hoped it would impress her. "I guess I still have lots to learn." He slumped over in defeat.

"You're already so good though." Lenia wrapped her arms around his waist and hugged him tight. "Just creating an illusion that looks like the thing you're trying to produce is a major breakthrough. I bet most wizards at The Academy couldn't make a squirrel look that good." She smiled with a flutter of her eyes.

He felt a little better.

"Once you get the motions down, you can focus on the little details too," she added.

"What do you mean?" he asked.

"The surroundings are just as important as the illusion itself," Lenia said. "If we go back to your squirrel, how does it interact with the environment? Does the grass sway when it crawls through? Are there tracks in the sand that it leaves behind? What does it sound like? All of these things serve to heighten the illusion and make it more realistic."

Kase was glad he had Professor Next Level with him. She knew so much more than what was in the books he'd read, and she'd already proven that she went past limits. He was ready to break down more barriers with her.

He reached around her waist and held her tight. His heart started to beat a little faster. This was the moment he had been waiting for.

He stared into her green eyes, took a deep breath, and leant forwards. He brushed her nose as he nudged his mouth towards hers.

He felt her grip his shirt and push back against his chest. Her head moved well away from his. "What are you doing?" she asked.

Kase felt his heart drop. He struggled for words. He didn't even think he was breathing. "Oh, I was just …" he trailed off, trying to think of the perfect thing to say.

"Were you going to kiss me, Kase Garrick?" Lenia smirked playfully.

He tried to step back, but she still clutched his shirt. He let go of her waistline. "Yes, I was." He didn't feel nervous anymore, just embarrassed. He had been honest all day, and he wasn't going to stop now—not with his favourite person. "I've wanted to kiss you for a long time. I was hoping that you'd want to kiss me too, but I understand if your feelings are different than mine. I don't want to pull you into something just because I'm wanting more."

He tried to step back again, but Lenia didn't let go. Her expression softened, and her beautiful, genuine smile returned. "I want to kiss you too," she admitted.

Kase tilted his head. He hadn't expected that answer, even though it was the one he wanted most. He wrapped his arms around her again.

Lenia moved her head back. "But this isn't the right moment," she said. "My breath smells like garlic from dinner. There's a dead fish floating on the shoreline. Talen and Cali are over there staring at us."

Kase turned his head. The dead fish was gross, but Talen and Cali's stares were worse. They had obviously stopped working on the Jenim Island puzzle. Cali had her notebook closed, and Talen leant over hers with her chin in her hands.

He turned back to Lenia and shook his head. "I don't care about all that stuff."

Lenia sighed. "I do," she said. "I want our first kiss to be perfect. I want to feel it with everything I have, because I want to remember the moment forever."

Kase still felt that moment was now. It was a special day already, and he'd remember their first kiss no matter when it happened.

But even though he disagreed, he respected that she wanted it to be special. "How will I know when the right moment is?"

"We'll both know." Lenia smiled. "And trust me, when it does happen, it will blow your mind." She leant in and gave him a peck on the cheek. It wasn't the kiss he wanted, but he would take it.

They disengaged and turned back to the rest of their group. "Now, let's go learn more about the doorway of life on Jenim Island."

They held hands as they walked down the lakefront. Kase didn't notice the shining sun, the gentle breeze, or Cali's and Talen's smiles. All he could think about was how exciting it would be when he and Lenia had their moment.

When they reached the blanket, Cali and Talen were silent. They were each pretending to be busy taking notes, but Kase could tell they were writing down the same thing.

"Anything useful?" he asked. He sat back down with Lenia, and they cuddled together on the blanket.

"Almost," Cali said. She looked up at them, and then quickly back down. Her smile was wide, but she didn't say anything else.

Talen looked at Cali strangely and stopped writing. "There's a lot of useful information here," she said.

Cali pulled her dad's notebook closer. "You can tell them while I keep working," she said.

Talen nodded, and then turned to her audience. "The notes describe a portal door, just like the one we found in the desert," she explained. "Instead of being identified by a flat stone in the middle of nowhere, it's hidden at the base of a giant maple tree."

"That's a lot easier to spot than a short stone in the desert," Kase said.

Talen scratched her head. "The tree isn't in a clearing," she said. "It's in the middle of a forest. It's like trying to find a needle in a haystack. The odds of stumbling upon it are …"

"There's a map," Cali said, not waiting for Talen to calculate it out. She didn't look up from her notes.

"Right," Talen said. "There are details on how to get there, but that's not the hard part. The true danger lies in the creatures located on Jenim Island, and in the forest in particular."

"Like giants?" Lenia asked. "But they're so friendly."

"No, not the giants," Talen said. "I mean the larger-than-normal insects and animals that also make Jenim Island their home. The beetles there are the size of Kase's legs, and the wasps have stingers as long as your arm. Imagine seeing a rat the size of a tiger, or a tiger the size of a—"

"We've handled tigers before," Kase said. He remembered how he and Lenia had conquered that Eidola sandcastle challenge during the Quest Series. He wasn't worried about rats.

113

"I agree," Lenia said with a wink. "They're not really dangerous."

"What about giant birds?" Talen said.

Lenia froze, her eyes widening. She curled her legs into her body and wrapped her arms around them, as if she had just woken up from a nightmare.

"Okay, there are a lot of dangerous animals," Kase admitted. He rubbed Lenia's back as she worked through her biggest fear. "What else?"

"The portal door is located in the base of the tree," Talen said. "But in order to get to it, someone would have to scale to the top branches, find the access hole marked by the ancient order of The Chosen—if it's still visible—and then traverse down the inside of the tree to the bottom."

"Sounds intense," Kase said.

"And … done." Cali put down her quill and took a deep breath. She looked around the circle and smiled at everyone in the group. "Thank you all for helping me with this. I don't know what it means yet, but it feels like we're making progress." She nodded to Kase. "It was a good idea to get the O.G. Liberati back together."

"Agreed," Lenia said. She put her arms around Kase. "We should do this again."

Kase held Lenia tight. He was glad that his friends were all with him again. Even though things hadn't gone as well as he'd hoped, it did feel like they had moved to a higher level.

He couldn't wait to see what happened next time they all came together.

CHAPTER 9

Feel It Coming In The Air

Two weeks later, Kase stood at attention with nine other warriors awaiting further instructions. All were Guardians and dressed in their uniforms. Kase only recognized one of them, because she was one of his classmates at The Academy.

They overlooked a valley that was covered in mist. In the evening's dying light, only the tops of the highest firs poked out from the thick fog. Kase heard a few wolves howl, which made it seem all the more eerie. He wondered if he'd be able to use his animal control skills on them—he'd never tried on a dangerous animal before.

High Guardian Mason checked his sage mirror. He turned towards the group and raised his hands. "We're ready to begin your first group trial," he said. "In front of you lies the Valley of Shadow. It's a murky forest with a reputation of capturing lost souls and never letting them go."

The warrior beside Kase chuckled.

Mason glared at the young Guardian. "Is something funny, Paris?"

Paris put his fist over his mouth and cleared his throat. "Sorry, sir," he said. "It just seems like you're trying to scare us. It's a little overdramatic, that's all."

Mason grinned. "You should be scared. There are animals here that prey on the weak. They're waiting for you to get lost, tired, or injured so that they can feed on you. This forest is one of death, and is thus feared by many."

Mason turned his attention back to the group and raised his sage mirror. "But that's not what we're here for today," he said. "We're not testing your fearlessness, because you've already proven your courage by signing up for this task force. Today, we're testing your focus."

Paris stopped smiling and stood tall once again.

"The fog of the Valley of Shadow is so thick it's difficult to see what lies ahead. Right now, we're able to overlook the valley as a whole, but when you're in the heart of it, it's different. You must concentrate on moving one step at a time in order to see the obstacles ahead. Trees, pits, fallen debris, and animals are just a few examples. It's a test of mental fortitude, because the smallest distraction will cause you trouble."

Kase scanned the valley again. It seemed to stretch for miles and was already intimidating from up here. He wasn't looking forward to being in the thick of it.

"It's hard to keep one's sense of direction," Mason said. "Luckily, you're all equipped with a compass that will help you to navigate." Mason pointed to his sage mirror. The face had marks to show the four cardinal directions, with an arrow pointing towards north. "Because the valley runs east to west, you will head due north to the other side. The valley is about five miles wide, so it will take some time to traverse the terrain. It would be easy to walk through, but this is a race."

Mason's smile returned as he looked at each warrior in turn. "Only six of you will be moving on to the next round of trials, so you will want to travel as quickly as you can. If you jog too slowly, your competition may surpass you. Sprint too fast, and you might not see what's ahead in time to react. Your mission is to get to the other side of the valley, pick up the package that Derek has waiting for you, and return it to me here. Does everyone understand?"

Kase frowned. The only Derek that he knew of was the one-handed wizard who worked with Lenia. He shook his head. It must be another Derek. "Dragoon!" he said in unison with the squad.

Mason sat down in a chair that he had brought along. He wasn't limping at all, so he must have fully recovered after his combat with Kase. He stretched his legs out and put his arms behind his head as he looked out across the valley. He sat for a few moments before addressing the warriors again. "What are you waiting for? Go."

Paris sprinted down the hill, and the rest of the warriors followed. Kase tried to keep his feet moving so he wouldn't trip, but it didn't take long to reach the fog from their starting point. As soon as he hit the thick cloud, he knew he was running too fast.

He could barely see the warrior in front of him: he recognized A.J.'s hair flopping on her shoulders as she ran. A.J. sprang forwards, lifting her legs high. A dark black log appeared out of nowhere. Kase jumped over it too.

A few howls distracted Kase, but he kept his gaze straight ahead. He wanted to make the same moves as A.J. They both darted left around a tree, and then leapt over another log. Kase was starting to breathe a little harder. He wondered how long A.J. would keep sprinting for. His answer came a few seconds later.

A.J. darted to the right to avoid the tree trunk in front of her, but didn't see the low-hanging branch in the way. Her head snapped back when it hit the protruding limb. She fell to the ground and landed square on her back.

Kase darted left and brushed the trunk. He dug his feet into the ground and stopped after a few quick steps. He turned back towards his fallen competitor. She rolled from side to side, her hands covering her face. Her helmet was beside her.

"Hey, A.J." Kase knelt down beside her. "Are you okay?"

A.J. rubbed her forehead with one hand. "Am I bleeding?"

Kase studied her more closely; it was difficult to see in the dark and the fog. But there weren't any cuts, lumps, or bruises. The helmet must have absorbed most of the blow. "Doesn't look like it."

A.J. dropped her other hand and then sat up. "I guess I need a new strategy," she admitted.

Kase stood and tried to look at the forest around them. All he saw was white. "Mason wasn't kidding around," he said. "It's impossible to navigate this forest at full speed."

"I guess it really is a marathon, and not a sprint," agreed A.J. "You should probably get going if you want to keep up with the rest of them."

A wolf howled in the distance, and a raven crowed as if in response.

"You sure you're okay?" he asked. He wasn't worried about the trial anymore; he was confident he could make up ground on the rest of the pack. He didn't want to leave A.J. alone if she was seriously injured.

"I'm fine," she said. "I just need a minute, and I'll be back on track. You better get going; I want a good race. I hate to break it to you, but I'm going to beat you."

Kase laughed. He'd forgotten how competitive A.J. was. "See you at the finish line."

He pulled out his sage mirror as he walked away. "Mirror, mirror, show me the compass," he said. A cloud appeared on the mirror's face before the directions were shown. He adjusted his position and started to jog.

He wasn't running as fast as before, and yet it was still difficult to manoeuvre within the mist. Trees would pop out of nowhere. He had to watch his step so that he didn't trip over dead branches. There were even some birds that swooped down on him at times. It would have been a nightmare for Lenia.

He stopped running and checked his sage mirror again. He was veering slightly too far east, so he adjusted his position back to due north. He took a few breaths, and started jogging again. He had been going for about half an hour, but he wasn't tired at all, and thought about picking up the pace. No sooner had he put on some speed than he tripped over a rock and nearly went down.

He wondered how the other warriors were doing. They must have been going at the same speed, but he wasn't certain. There had to be a faster way through the forest. He remembered what Curtis had said about using all his abilities to give himself an edge. He could use some of his wizard skills here to gain an advantage.

He couldn't close his eyes and keep running, so he focused on his breathing instead. He felt his chest expand, and then contract. In and out, in and out. His heart was steady.

At first, he tried to sense what was around him. He could hear birds flying overhead, but he couldn't feel them. There was more howling in the distance, but the wolves were too far away. The sound of his feet trudging through the mulch seemed to get louder. He tried to run lighter and swifter, and sidestepped another tree.

A slight breeze tickled his neck. It felt cool against the beads of sweat that slid down his back. It was more than just refreshing, because it gave him an idea.

In the Wizardry 101 textbook that Lenia had given him, there was an overview of element control. It described the fire, water, and sand forms that he had already worked with in his private tutoring sessions, but there were others listed. One of them was air.

Air control was similar to the other elements, but Kase hadn't tried it yet. His understanding was that the force of air couldn't be changed, just the direction that it blew in.

He jumped over a moss-covered stump.

When he had read about it, he was reminded of Lenia's manipulation of the sand tornado during their first Quest Series. She had created a hole within the swirling winds for them to pass through. Even though those winds had blown with much more force, he knew he'd be able to do something similar with the mist. He didn't know exactly how, but he was excited to try.

He focused on his breathing again. His success with the other elements had come from feeling them with everything he had. Therefore, he needed to feel like one with the breeze. He needed it to touch not only the back of his neck, but his entire soul.

A rush of chaos flowed through his body. He felt free and trapped at the same time. A heavy pressure bore down on him, but at the same time it felt weightless—like being underwater. He was swimming through the air.

He launched himself over a fallen log.

He unclenched his fists and made a cup with his hands instead. The pumping of his arms while he ran was like doing a shortened backstroke. He was able to feel the air flow in his grasp. He imagined pushing the air up and out of his way. His path started to become a little less foggy.

He wasn't creating an open corridor through the forest, but the little pockets of air that he manipulated made it clearer. Instead of only seeing a few feet in front of him, he was able to see ten to twenty feet ahead. He picked up his pace and ran harder.

Excitement coursed through his veins. The burst of chaotic energy made him run faster than ever. He could see the obstacles with enough advance to dodge them. He noticed birds perched on branches instead of having to wonder where their hoots or calls were coming from. He was even able to check his compass while he ran instead of having to stop.

He was a little disappointed when he reached the end of the valley, but then he remembered that he'd be able to run back.

Out of the fog, the moonlight was bright enough to see a young man sitting in a chair similar to Mason's on the slope above the valley. He didn't have to get too close to recognize one-handed Derek.

"Kase Garrick!" Derek stood up and gave a welcoming smile. "I knew you'd be the first to arrive." He looked over Kase's shoulder. "Not by much though."

Kase turned, wondering how many others trailed him. But only A.J. ran up the hill.

"This is great! I can give both of you an explanation at the same time," Derek said. He stood and gestured to a row of ten oddly-shaped logs. He waited for A.J. to stand tall beside Kase before he continued.

"Each warrior is required to carry one of these timbers back through the Valley of Shadow to the starting line. They all weigh the same, but they differ in thickness, length, and balance. Kase, since you were the first to arrive, you will get the best choice."

Kase looked at A.J., who was already studying the logs intently. He didn't really have a preference, but he accepted his award of first pick.

He walked down the line and tried to judge which log was the most even. All of them were over six feet long and at least a foot in diameter. A couple of the logs had huge stumps on the end, so he didn't want those. Another was shaped like a V, and looked like it would be extremely awkward to carry. He stopped at the fifth log and pointed to it.

"You have impeccable taste," Derek said. He reached for a jar and brush. He pulled the lid off the top and covered the tip of his brush with the liquid inside. It looked as glittery as the night sky above them.

Derek painted Kase's name on the bottom of the log, along with the number one. "I'm marking your timber with a unique potion. This way, you can't ditch it in the forest and find another one. You also won't be able to steal anyone else's and claim it as your own."

Kase picked up the log and nested it against his shoulder. He wasn't able to grip it with one hand, so he hugged it instead. He took a few steps back down the hill, but the rough bark rubbed his neck. He leant the base of the log on the ground so he could reposition it. He didn't know how he was going to run with this additional encumbrance.

"I'll take this one," A.J. said.

Derek took his brush and wrote the number two on her log before hesitating. "What's your name again?"

"A.J.," she said.

"That's an easy one to remember," Derek said politely. Despite that, Kase had a hunch he'd forget again.

Kase lifted the log and rested it on his neck. He let the weight of the top fall past his head and onto his shoulders so that it lay horizontally along his back. He felt really wide, and knew that he'd have to be careful running around trees, but at least he was comfortable enough to run.

He walked down the hill, hoping that A.J. would pass him and enter the forest again. He didn't want her to see him using magic.

She hadn't run past him, so he decided to stop in front of the mist. He waited a few minutes and then turned to see if she was struggling. She stood directly behind him, also stopped and with her log across her shoulders.

"What are you waiting for?" she asked. "Let's get going."

Kase felt nervous. "You're waiting for me to start? Did you follow me through the forest on our way here?"

"Of course I did," A.J. said candidly. "And it worked; it was much easier to see you and your reactions than it was when I was watching for trees earlier."

Her log shifted in what Kase assumed was a shrug. "When I hit my head, I may have been acting tough, but I came to a realization. You're the best warrior here, Kase. You're guaranteed to make it through. If I do what you do, I can be the second warrior chosen for this task force."

Kase was confused. "I like what you're saying, but nothing's guaranteed."

"Give me a break." A.J. laughed. "You're a two-time winner of the Quest Series. I know you have a strategy for this trial, and it'll probably be better than any of the others'. Not only that, but I heard from one of the other candidates that you were the only one interviewed by High Wizard Zuke."

Kase didn't believe her. "Why would High Wizard Zuke single me out?"

"Because you're obviously guaranteed a spot on the task force. Haven't you been listening?" She laughed again. "Everyone else got interviewed by their commanding officer, the Grand Master, and Derek. I'm actually surprised I made it this far if Derek can't even remember my name."

Kase didn't agree, but he didn't want to waste any more time. "So you want to form an alliance? Isn't that against the rules or something?"

"There are no rules," A.J. said. "So I think we can do whatever we want."

Kase shook his head. He didn't want A.J. to follow him, but there was probably a way to lose her in the Valley of Shadow. He turned back to the mist, reached into his pocket, and pulled out his sage mirror. He was already facing due south.

"There might be a better way for us to carry these logs together too," A.J. said.

Kase put his sage mirror away. "How?"

"Have you ever gone hunting before?" she asked.

"Not really," he said. His aunt and uncle were farmers, so they had all the food they needed and were against killing animals for sport. He had joined them when they tracked the odd predator that wandered onto their property, but that was only to chase it away.

"One time I was hunting a wild boar with my brother," A.J. said. "We were successful, but we still had to carry our trophy through some rough terrain before we could load it onto our cart. It was about two hundred pounds and super awkward."

A.J. dropped the log off her back. It hit the ground with a thud. "We ended up tying the boar to a long branch, and we each took an end." She stood at the base of her log and pulled it up to her shoulder. "I was thinking if we carried our logs together, one on each shoulder, it would help us move our load a little faster."

Kase checked his dangling hands. It would be difficult to keep checking to see if A.J. was following him. If she were behind him the whole time, he'd at least know where she was. It would also be tough for her to see too far ahead if she was staring at his back.

"Let's try it out." He dumped the weight off his back, grabbed one end, and dragged it to A.J.'s free side. He helped position the log onto her shoulder, and then walked to the front. He squatted down and heaved both logs into a similar position. A.J. was right; it did feel less awkward.

"Ready?" he shouted.

"Let's do this," A.J. replied.

Kase couldn't help but smile. Her response reminded him of his Liberati teammates during the Quest Series. It felt good to be on a team again, instead of feeling alone. He checked his sage mirror, and then re-entered the Valley of Shadow.

He started off slowly to get a feel for how A.J. would react to his movements. He moved left around a tree, and she followed flawlessly. He decided that they could go a little faster.

He slowed his breathing to become one with the soft airflow once again. Instead of using his hands to cup the pockets of mist away, he used his elbows. It wasn't as effective, but he didn't want to use his power as openly with A.J. directly behind him. He was still able to see more clearly, and that was enough.

Just like his first run, focusing on manipulating the air kept his mind from wandering aimlessly with the thick mist. He was able to dodge obstacles well in advance, and stayed the course while A.J. followed behind. There were a few instances where he jumped over a rock or a fallen tree, but A.J. didn't see it in time. He tried to communicate as best he could, but there were still a few stumbles.

They took breaks when they needed to check the sage mirror for directions, catch their breath, or rest from carrying the awkward logs. They were both sweating heavily, but it didn't matter. The excitement from the challenging run gave both of them extra energy.

After running for what seemed like much longer than the first half, Kase heard a voice ahead of them. "Is someone there?" It sounded like Paris.

"Where are you?" Kase yelled. He slowed down a little bit.

"Over here," Paris said. It didn't really help, but Kase could tell he was somewhere straight ahead.

"Keep talking until we find you," Kase shouted.

"Kase, stop," A.J. said.

The duo took a break. Kase heard a thud and felt the logs pivot: A.J. had dropped her ends to the ground. Kase did the same, and then turned to her.

"Talk about what?" Paris yelled. "I can't even move. My ankle is mangled, and my sage mirror is broken."

"We can't go find him," A.J. said in a low voice. "We can't let the others know of our alliance. We should finish the race first, and then we can come back."

"Are you there? I … I don't even know if you're real. I feel like I'm going crazy, surrounded by nothing but all this mist." There was fear in Paris' voice.

Kase took a deep breath. "I'm not leaving him out here any longer," he whispered back. "You can go if you want, but I'm going to help out a fallen brother."

A.J. nodded. She bent down, checked which log was hers, and then hoisted it onto her shoulders. "You don't owe him anything, you know. It's all part of the game."

"A game with no rules," Kase said. Although he disagreed with A.J.'s actions, he understood them. He wanted to help out his injured comrade, but that was because, to him, it was more important than the race, the task force, or their alliance. It was the right thing to do.

A.J. smiled at him. She checked her sage mirror, angled herself away from Paris' cries for help, and took off into the mist.

"Please … if you're really there. I'm right over here," Paris shouted.

"Tell me more," Kase yelled back. "I'm almost there. You're going to be alright."

Kase picked up his log and secured it over his shoulders. He started walking in his original direction, but didn't use his magic to make the path any clearer. He just followed Paris' voice.

"I'm going to try and stand," Paris shouted. "I couldn't put any pressure on my right foot earlier—I thought it was broken—but now I can't even feel it. I'm going to try again."

Kase kept walking. He knew he was getting closer. He thought he saw an outline of a warrior beside him, but it was just another tree.

Paris screamed. There was a pause, then a raspy, "Nope—still broken."

Kase picked up his pace and finally saw Paris sitting on a stump. He clutched his ankle, his teeth clenched together as he breathed hard.

"I'm here," Kase said. He dropped his log, knelt down, and went to touch Paris' ankle. Paris had removed his boot, but it looked like his foot was bent the wrong way. Kase hesitated.

Paris put his hand on Kase's shoulder. "Good, you are real." He threw his head back with a laugh. His eyes were wide. Kase wondered if Paris had already lost his mind.

He wanted to heal Paris, but he knew he couldn't. Even as delusional as Paris seemed, his magic would be too noticeable. "Let's get you out of here and to a healer."

Paris nodded. Kase pulled out his sage mirror and checked their direction. He looked at his log. If he left it here, he wouldn't be able to find it again. He picked up the edge of it in his left hand, and steadied

Paris with his right. Paris stood on one foot, and leant heavily on Kase to get his balance.

The two warriors shuffled forwards. Kase dragged his log, and Paris hopped beside him. They were going incredibly slowly, but they were making progress.

"How did it happen?" Kase asked. "That looks pretty bad for a fall."

"I honestly don't even know," Paris admitted. "I remember sprinting and jumping over a log, but I got bumped in midair. My foot landed between two rocks. I think someone must have kneed me in the back of the head after that. When I came to, my foot was throbbing. I tried to pull out my sage mirror to get help from Mason, but it had broken in my pocket."

They stopped walking, and Paris pulled out a shard of his sage mirror to show Kase. "I wish I knew who bumped me, because I would shove this right into their throat."

"You would kill them?" Kase asked. "That's pretty hard-core."

"This game is ruthless." Paris returned the mirror shard to his pocket. "It's about life and death. I'm lucky you found me. Otherwise, I would have met my doom."

Kase thought Paris was being overdramatic, but he was still glad to help. "You're welcome?"

Paris laughed. "I wish I could repay you somehow. You deserve to make the task force, now that I'm clearly out. Just promise me that you'll keep your head up: don't trust anyone. The others will do whatever it takes to bring you down."

They had cleared the mist. They both looked up the hill, where a torch marked the finish line. Mason was patting A.J. on the back, beaming proudly.

A.J. locked eyes with Kase, and then pointed to him and Paris. She rushed down the hill and helped Paris on his other side. "Are you two okay?" she asked. Paris wrapped his arm around her shoulder.

"I'll survive," Paris said with a weak smile. "Are you the only one that finished?"

"Yes," A.J. replied. "Mason said he's never seen someone make it back this fast. He told me it must be a record."

All three warriors hobbled up the hill. Mason started clapping when they reached him. "Such resilience," he said. "You really have proven yourself today, A.J. Well done."

They helped Paris into Mason's chair. Mason knelt and helped Paris to stretch out his leg. He examined the injury.

"Thank you, sir," A.J. replied. "Kase made it here too, though."

Mason looked up at the two warriors. "Humble as pie," he said. "But there can only be one true winner."

Kase dragged his log beside A.J's and sat down on the grass. He was exhausted. It felt good to have helped Paris back to safety, and he was glad that A.J. had made it ahead of the other warriors. Despite that, he couldn't help but wonder if she had manipulated him into helping her.

He looked back across the Valley of Shadow. He felt torn. On the one hand, his competitive side was a little disappointed that he'd lost to A.J. On the other, if this was only the first competition, what would the cost of winning a spot on the task force be?

He didn't want to manipulate anyone, or win because another warrior got hurt. He wanted to be awarded a higher position because of his skills and hard work. How much was this game worth? It was starting to feel like he had only a little to gain, and a lot to lose.

CHAPTER 10

Got The Right One

The Triple Thunder task force was down to six. Paris had been unable to complete the first event, and three others were disqualified because they didn't make it through the Valley of Shadow fast enough.

Kase was anxious to get through the second challenge, and he hadn't been able to sleep the last few nights because of it. It was affecting his work with Curtis, and the load of the daily grind felt heavier. Bojangles seemed to trot around slower than usual. Curtis' teasing was less funny. Travellers asking for directions were more annoying. He felt on edge, and thought a drink from his favourite café in Kimroad, Co Co., would help. It didn't.

The remaining competitors stood in front of a large set of double doors on the first level of the castle of the Triple Crown. Mason had to open a locked gate first, and then there were two more locks on the large oak doors behind it to bypass. Kase was curious to know what was so important to be kept under such security.

The warriors filed in, following Mason to the centre of the large room. None of them paid any attention to where they were going; their heads were too busy swivelling in wonder. It was like being in a library, but instead of books, shelves of weapons lined the walls and formed rows across the room.

Mason stopped the group and spread his arms out wide. "Welcome to the main armoury of the High Guardians." He smiled proudly while some of the warriors cheered.

"This particular room holds every state-of-the-art weapon that we have available," he said. "From crossbows to longbows, broadswords to daggers, and even shields to chainmail, everything you need for our next challenge is here, built with the finest material."

Kase took a quick peek around the room. Everything looked shiny and new. He was excited for the chance to browse for some new toys.

"For the next challenge, we're going hunting," Mason said with a grin. "Where we're headed, and what we're hunting for, will be revealed when we get there. Your task right now is to pick three items from the armoury in anticipation of what could come next."

A couple of the warriors hurried from the group towards a rack of swords, but Kase was unsure of what to do. A sword might be good in a fight, but he knew it wouldn't necessarily help him in a hunt.

A.J. walked in the opposite direction of the group. He remembered her talking about hunting with her brother, and figured that she would know where to start. He hoped she wouldn't forget about their alliance.

He followed her past a few racks of axes, and stood beside her as she admired the bows. She held one and gently caressed the string with her fingers. "Perfect," she said.

Kase decided to choose whatever A.J. did, so he grabbed a bow too. It was well crafted, but it didn't seem much different from the bows they practised with at The Academy. He wondered what made it state-of-the-art, by Mason's standards.

A.J. slung the bow over her shoulder and grabbed a quiver off the bottom shelf. She started counting the arrows inside. "Do you think each arrow counts as an item?"

"Good question," Mason said from behind them, making A.J. jump. Kase had seen him coming. "A bow, quiver and ten arrows count as one item. If you want more arrows, another ten would be considered extra. But if you don't want more, you can always use sticks instead." He patted Kase on the shoulder and walked away.

A.J. looked at Kase and raised her eyebrow. "Why would we use sticks?"

Kase shouldered his bow and grabbed a quiver. "When I faced Mason during my interview, I used two sticks to injure him enough to wrestle his morning star away." He quickly counted ten arrows. "How did you beat him?"

A.J. blinked a couple times and put her hand on Kase's arm. "You faced Mason in combat?"

"Yeah, during the …" Kase realized A.J.'s confusion. He slung the quiver over his shoulder too. "Didn't everyone have to battle him to prove they were worthy of the task force?"

A.J. laughed. "No, it was just an interview." She shook her head and let go of his arm. "You're clearly a part of this task force already; I don't even know why you have to go through with this hunt."

Kase liked A.J.'s confidence, but he still wasn't sure about the whole process. "Just think of it like I'm doubling your inventory; we now have twenty arrows together. What's next?"

A.J. tapped her chin. "Good point," she said. "Follow me."

They walked past a few more racks until they found one that held rope. A.J. slid her fingers along some of the strands, testing the different thicknesses available. She settled on one that wasn't too big.

"What do we need this for?" Kase asked.

"Rope has many uses," A.J. said. "It can be part of a trap, security for a shelter, or it could help us reach places we wouldn't be able to normally. It's tough to know exactly what we'll use it for, because we don't know where we're going. But ultimately, there is no substitute in the wilderness for a good rope. A hunter needs more than just weapons to be successful."

Kase nodded, although he didn't quite understand yet. He was happy to be learning from A.J. Perhaps the lessons would go beyond the task force.

They both threw a spool over their shoulders and went to find their final item. A.J. led him back to the sword racks, but instead of examining the broadswords that the other warriors were interested in, she stopped at the shorter ones. She picked up a war cleaver and studied it.

"I thought we needed more than just weapons," Kase said with a wink.

A.J. didn't laugh. "We're not using this as a weapon necessarily." She handed the knife to Kase. "We can use this for cutting the rope, clearing a path, and as a killing tool. You take this one; I'm going to grab a spear so we don't look identical."

Kase nodded. He studied the war cleaver she'd picked out. The blade was a foot and a half long, and only sharp on one side. It was tapered at the top, but he wouldn't use it to stab anything. It was more of a hacking tool.

"I'll meet you back with the others," A.J. said before taking off.

Kase made his way to the centre of the armoury and awaited further orders.

Once everyone had gathered, Mason led the group out of the castle and to the stables. They piled into the back of a horse-drawn cart and headed for the portal gateway. Mason sat up front with one-handed Derek, who awkwardly steered the horses.

The warriors sat in silence, but everyone's eyes darted around. As excited as they all were in the armoury, the seriousness of the competition was starting to take shape again.

Kase felt like he was getting sized up; he did the same to the others, trying to read their strategies. There were lots of warriors with spears and swords, but they were the only two with rope. Should they have taken more weapons? He was starting to worry that his decision to follow A.J. was a mistake.

He closed his eyes and tried to get some rest. He wanted to ensure that his mind was as ready as his body for the hunt. He wondered what the trophy was. Would it be an animal he could control? Would the environment be more dangerous than the hunt itself? He tried to prepare himself for everything.

The group travelled for a couple hours outside the portal gate and entered another valley. Tall brown cliffs surrounded the area, but instead of a dark forest covered in mist, it was a meadow of grassland, riverbeds, and short trees. The sun shone brilliantly, and the area smelled fresh from the morning dew. It reminded Kase of his aunt and uncle's farmland.

When the cart came to a full stop, the warriors exited and gathered around Mason and Derek. This time, Derek explained the challenge.

"Welcome to the playground of the minotaurs," Derek said. "Although they're one of the most dangerous animals in the realm, minotaurs tend to remain hidden, spending most of their time in the maze of caverns that line this particular valley. Their horns are extremely valuable, being a potent ingredient to some rare wizard potions."

Kase peered at the surrounding cliffs. There were multiple cave entrances scattered throughout the hillside, but he doubted that they were all connected.

"Facing a minotaur in the dark underground would be sure death, but out on the open plain, it's a little different," Derek said. "Although they're still dangerous, they're more vulnerable outside of their dens. This is where you will hunt them down."

Kase had never seen this side of Derek before. The friendly mask that he always wore was broken, and his killer instinct shone through.

Kase had long suspected he was more than the happy, perfect friend that he tried to be.

"Any warrior that can bring us the horn of a minotaur will move on to the next challenge," Mason added. "You have your weapons, and you have your goal, but there are no rules for the hunt. We'd advise that you don't venture into the caverns, but you're welcome to obtain a horn by any means necessary. Show no mercy." He put his fist over his heart.

"Dragoon," the warriors responded in unison.

All six warriors walked into the wilderness. This wasn't a race, so nobody was sprinting. There was an uncomfortable silence as everyone focused on the task. It was peaceful, but unnerving.

Kase slowed his pace as the rest of the crew spread out. He wanted to follow A.J. without making it look like he was. She was carefully surveying the scene, but he didn't get caught up in any of the sights or sounds of the valley; his only focus was on not losing her.

They walked for what seemed like hours until A.J. suddenly stopped. She waved her arm, gesturing for him to come forwards. He hadn't realized she knew he was still with her.

Kase stepped up to her side. "What is it?" he whispered.

"Minotaurs spend most of their time underground," A.J. said. "But if you were a cave dweller, what would make you come outside?"

She pointed to a beautiful pond at the base of a brown cliff. A small waterfall trickled down delicately, adding to the beauty. Kase made a mental note to bring Lenia back to this place—she loved waterfalls.

"I don't see any minotaurs though," Kase said. He wondered if they even cared about beautiful landscapes.

"There are cave entrances on either side of the waterfall," A.J. pointed out. "If the water flows underground, they won't necessarily need to come out for a drink, but we've got a better chance here than out in the open. It's a great spot."

Kase didn't know what a great spot looked like, so he was glad that A.J. had confidence in it. "So what's the plan?"

A.J. led Kase into the trees just beyond the edge of the pond. She used her rope to set a trap by tying the ends to two different trees. Kase didn't understand the logic of it, but A.J. assured him it would work.

They used Kase's rope to climb the tree and sat on a couple limbs that were well-concealed by leaves. They had a perfect birds-eye view of their hunting zone.

Kase rewrapped his rope around his shoulders. "So we're just going to sit here until a minotaur comes out?" he asked.

"Hunting is all about patience," A.J. replied. "We're out of view, the spatter of the waterfall should hide any noise we make, and the breeze is carrying our scent away. Now we wait."

A.J. leant back against the tree trunk, so Kase did the same. He didn't mind the break; he used the time to daydream about how much Lenia would enjoy the view. He even thought it would be a good site for their first kiss.

Over the next few hours, Kase and A.J. relaxed in the tree. They didn't talk. They didn't move. Kase was able to practise connecting to different animals around the meadow, including a hummingbird, a newt, and a ladybug. It wasn't that exciting, though.

Just as Kase was drifting off into another daydream, he noticed A.J. lean forwards. Her lips curled up. He checked the cave entrance next to the waterfall, and saw a minotaur walk towards the water.

Kase had never seen a minotaur in person before, although there had been an illusion of one in the WHOOP during his first year. The scavenger hunt for last year's Quest Series included the hair of a minotaur, but the Liberati had deemed the risk not worth the points reward.

This one's massive, bull-like head was covered in red fur with two long, gleaming white horns protruding from the top. Its arms, also hairy, were bulging, but its legs were short and slender, ending in cloven feet. Despite all the hair, it was clearly female. It looked around and then slowly crept towards the water. It walked with a waddle, shuffling its hind legs along like a satyr while its arms dangled at the sides.

The minotaur knelt down and stuck its hand in the water. It cupped the liquid and brought it up to its snout to smell, then started to slurp it down. It looked back towards the cave entrance and snorted.

A smaller, younger minotaur stepped into the light and wobbled towards the water.

Kase felt a tap on his arm. A.J. held her bow at the ready, and gestured for him to do the same. He carefully removed it from his shoulder, holding it straight with his left hand. He reached behind him with his right and slowly pulled an arrow from his quiver. He drew it back on the string, ready to fire.

The mother and baby looked so peaceful; he didn't want to hurt them for the sake of this task force. He thought about missing on purpose—perhaps A.J.'s shot wouldn't be good enough for a kill. He wondered if there was a way to connect with the minotaurs, perhaps force them to head back into the cave.

Something touched his backside, and he went tumbling to the ground.

The grass was coming up fast, but he turned his body so that he could roll on impact and avoid injury. His bow wasn't as lucky; it lay broken beside him. Arrows were scattered everywhere.

A loud roar came from behind him. It sounded like the low mooing sound that had been common on the farm, but angrier and sharper. He looked beyond the rope trap directly in front of him. The mother minotaur had her arms stretched out and stared right at him. She roared again and then charged.

Kase scrambled to his feet. He reached for his cleaver, but it was missing. He searched for it on the ground as he backed up. The minotaur was getting closer.

He stared into the black eyes of the beast. He thought about trying to connect with it, but he couldn't with A.J. watching so closely. The minotaur was stronger and faster than Kase, but if he could run far enough away from A.J., he could try to calm it down.

Even as he turned to run, he reached out to see if he could detect its presence and connect with it without disrupting its charge.

After several large strides, he heard a roar and a crash. He looked back to see the minotaur sprawled on the ground. It had tripped over A.J.'s rope. It looked up at him, and Kase suddenly felt the connection.

He felt enraged; his heart pumped wildly. Black spots of anger clouded his vision. A wave of dizziness overcame him as his body tried to adjust. Then he saw something fall from the tree.

A.J. dropped down, spear in hand, and landed on the minotaur. With the force of gravity and her added weight, the spearhead pierced through its tough exterior, past its ribcage, and into its heart.

Kase crumbled to the ground. It felt like the blade slashed through his own body. He screamed in pain, but was drowned out by the monstrous roar of the minotaur.

He clutched his heart, but in a second, the pain was gone. He felt a shortness of breath and a sudden, hollow emptiness inside. He knew the minotaur was dead. He looked up. Its mouth gaped, and its eyes were lifeless.

A.J. stepped off the minotaur and grabbed its horn with her left hand. Her right held Kase's cleaver. She hacked away at the back of the minotaur's neck, separating the head from its body. Blood spattered everywhere.

Kase stood. He felt like he had witnessed an injustice, and wanted to get back at A.J. somehow. He wanted her to pay for her murderous ways. He wanted to fight back for an innocent animal that had clearly lost. He resisted the urge to do something he'd regret.

"You used me," he muttered.

"You should be thanking me," A.J. said. She slashed again. "Minotaurs are territorial; it was only natural for it to chase you. I saved you from being torn apart."

With one final hack, A.J. slammed the edge of the cleaver into the ground. She lifted the minotaur's head to shoulder height and looked at it proudly. Blood dripped from its neckline.

"I'm taking this back to Mason." A.J. picked up the cleaver and pointed it at Kase. "I'm borrowing your war cleaver so no one steals it from me."

Kase nodded. "What am I supposed to do?"

"You have a trap and a spear," A.J. replied. "Go hunt a minotaur."

A.J. jogged away, and Kase didn't try to stop her. She had succeeded in her mission: she had followed orders and killed a helpless beast. As much as it hurt, she was only doing what she had to.

Kase glanced back at the carcass, and then beyond it. His heart melted as he locked eyes with the young minotaur, left at the edge of the pond. It quivered, making soft huffing sounds.

As if knowing it was spotted, it hustled back to the cave entrance. For a young, wobbling infant, it was pretty quick.

"Wait." Kase sprinted after it. He jumped over the rope hazard and kept running. He tried to connect with the little beast as it disappeared into the darkness of the cave. He wanted to help. He didn't know how, but he wanted to right a wrong.

He had been warned not to enter, but he ran in anyway. After a few steps, the darkness overwhelmed him. He couldn't see anything. He stopped before he hit a wall and resorted to searching for the pulse of the young minotaur, like he had with the puppy Anna-Bella.

He closed his eyes and slowed his breathing. He could feel the rushing heartbeat of the little one, but it wasn't in front of him. It was behind.

He walked back towards the light. Just inside the crest of the cave, the minotaur huddled in a crevice. Its fur blended well with the surrounding rock. It was scared, confused, and filled with sorrow.

Kase knelt down and offered his hand. "It's going to be okay," he lied. He slowed his breathing, and the minotaur became calmer. It reached its tiny arm out and gripped Kase's fingers. He guided it back out to the waterfall.

He let his emotions digress. He still wanted to keep the minotaur calm, but he was careful not to overpower it; he didn't want to control its actions. He sat down on the embankment as it waded into the shallow water.

The young one dipped its hand in and scooped up a sample from the pond. It sniffed the water, and then quickly lapped it up. It did that a few times and walked back to Kase. It sat down beside him and nestled its head under his arm.

Kase felt a sadness come over him. The feeling wasn't from the minotaur. He was reminded of his own mother's passing, and he wanted to push the memory down. He searched for an outlet, and saw something wonderful.

He grabbed his fire starter from his pocket, flicking it open to produce a small flame. He reached across the young minotaur and held it over a white dandelion. When he was close enough, the flower ignited, producing a small fireball.

The young minotaur made a short cooing sound. Kase could tell it had enjoyed the show; he felt its excitement. The minotaur reached towards another white dandelion and looked back at him.

Kase stared at the black eyes of the young beast. He saw beauty in them, even though it would grow up to become a recognizable monster. He couldn't help but notice the small horns already protruding from its skull. He suddenly had an idea.

Derek had told them to bring their trophy back by any means necessary. Hunters would assume that their prey had to be killed, but

Derek didn't specify whether the minotaur had to be dead or alive. All he needed was a horn.

Instead of hurting another relative of the little beast, Kase increased his power over the young minotaur and picked it up. Because he was in control, it was like handling a ragdoll. The minotaur was locked in a motionless state, unresponsive. It would be easy for him to race back through the meadow.

He started running, which was a good distraction from the events that had transpired. He jumped over the rope and raced past the carcass. His plan was sure to work. It had to.

He remembered the way, and since he wasn't cautiously tailing A.J. through the meadow, it didn't take him long to reach their starting point.

Before he was spotted by anyone, he used his rope to tie up the little minotaur as if it were his prisoner. He had enough rope to totally envelope the body of the little beast. He held it in his arms and made the final trek to Mason and Derek, releasing his power so that he wouldn't be caught using magic. To his surprise, the minotaur didn't squirm all that much.

He climbed the short hill and saw A.J. and another warrior sitting beside their commanders. The head of the minotaur was at their feet.

"Did you hunt down a baby minotaur?" Mason laughed. "You're even more ruthless than these two!"

Kase looked at A.J., and she put her head down.

"It's still alive," he replied.

Mason's smile disappeared. "You brought back a live specimen?"

"I brought you the horn of a minotaur, just like you asked." Kase held the infant so that its face was buried in his chest. He didn't want it to overreact or get scared. He tapped the small bud protruding from its head.

"That's not—" Mason started.

"Excellent work, Kase Garrick," Derek interjected. "You have successfully completed this challenge. I'm hoping that you're not going to kill that minotaur in front of us?" His sinister smile was hard to judge.

"No," Kase said.

"I don't think this counts," Mason said.

"Why not?" Derek snapped. "Those two came back with the head of one minotaur; it has two horns, so we let them both take credit for the kill. How is this different?"

Kase looked back at A.J., but her head was still down. The warrior beside her put his arm around her and rubbed it. Were they in an alliance? Kase felt like he had been played.

"Should we collect the horns?" Mason asked.

"This trial isn't about that; it's about their problem-solving skills and application," Derek replied. "Besides, they'll be more valuable when the young minotaur grows older."

"If it's okay with you, I'll take him back to where I found him," Kase said. "Releasing him to the same area should help him find his family easier."

"Of course," Derek said. "I wouldn't expect anything less."

"I still don't agree," Mason said. He pulled out his sage mirror and captured an image of Kase holding the young minotaur. "Congratulations on your victory, Kase Garrick."

Kase turned and walked back down the hill. As soon as he entered the cover of the meadow, he started to run. He wanted to run away from the task force entirely. He had made a mistake; he should have failed so that he wouldn't have to deal with it anymore. Using the young minotaur for his own personal gain felt just as bad as killing its mother.

The minotaur was getting restless, so Kase used his wizard power to control it again. The sadness in his heart strengthened. He could feel tears in his eyes, but he quickly blinked them away. His legs moved faster in a hopeless race to freedom.

He didn't remove the rope until he had delivered the minotaur back to the waterfall. When it was free, he released his control. The minotaur looked up at him, but didn't move. It just stared at him with sad eyes.

"Go on. Get out of here," he yelled, waving his arms at the young one.

The minotaur groaned. It sulked all the way to the cave entrance, but didn't look back. It disappeared into the darkness.

Kase slumped back down in front of the pond. He stared at the waterfall. It didn't look as beautiful anymore.

The Triple Thunder task force was worse than he had imagined. It wasn't testing his skills; it was breaking his morals. If this was what being a Guardian was all about, he didn't want to pursue it any longer.

He stood up and walked to the water's edge. He stared at his reflection in the water. Although he knew what he stood for, he didn't know what he was becoming anymore. All he wanted was to become a great warrior, but he felt like he was turning into something else. Something worse.

CHAPTER 11

It Was All A Dream

"You forgot it was your birthday?" Kase asked.

Cali slapped herself in the face and shook her head. It was something she did to stay awake. "I haven't slept in a while, so the days just blend together."

Her eyes looked bloodshot, and the purple circles under them were puffy. Kase thought there might be something growing in her hair. He didn't want to get too close to her, fearing he'd smell something he'd never be able to forget.

"You got the moving image from Uncle Eowin and Auntie Anna?" Kase covered his nose just to be safe.

Cali laughed. "Do they know they don't have to shout into their sage mirror?"

"I like how they both get really close to try and squeeze their faces into the frame," Kase said. "It's like they're fighting for position or something."

Cali laughed again. "So I guess you're here to make sure I go?"

Kase dropped his hand and smiled at his sister. "It will be a fun family dinner. Besides, when was the last time you had some scuffles?"

Cali closed her eyes and rubbed her belly, smacking her lips. "I can already taste them." She stood up. "Let's go!"

She made sure everything on her desk was in order. Her office mate, Sharaine, was still away on Triple Crown business, so the rest of the room was still tidy. Although Cali was in disarray, she still felt the need to ensure her surroundings were clean.

The duo left Cali's office. Kase was happy that his sister was able to escape her daily grind, but he was also relieved to get away from it all too. Days on the street with Curtis were disheartening, and he was still worried about what he'd have to do next with the task force. For the first time, he was unsure of what he really wanted.

Kase turned down the castle hallway towards the main entrance, but Cali stopped him. "Where are you going?" she asked.

"Umm, outside?" he said. "The faster we get out of here, the quicker the hike."

"Hike?" She yanked his arm, pulling him along after her. "It's my birthday, and I'm not walking all the way to the farm. The stables are this way."

Kase tried to stop her. "I don't have clearance for horses. I know it seems like I'm a big deal around here, but I don't get a lot of perks yet."

Cali smiled and tapped his arm. "Don't worry, little brother. I know a few people."

Kase realized he'd never walked around the castle with Cali before. As they wound their way through the halls, warriors, wizards, and scholars all acknowledged his sister with a nod or other pleasantries. When they arrived at the stables, it was easy for her to obtain a horse for their expedition—the hostler seemed to know her well.

Cali signed out two black stallions. They quickly mounted and trotted out of the castle. Cali led Kase down the streets of Kimroad to the closest portal gateway. The horses were used to the bustle and thrum of the portal gates, and took it without batting an eye.

On the other side, Cali trotted a little faster. "Want to race?"

Kase didn't have time to answer. Cali kicked her horse hard and took off in a gallop. He yelled, slammed his heels into his stallion's side, and lengthened the reins. He tried to lean forwards as they ran down the hillside and into the crooked tree forest.

The hostler must have really liked Cali, because both of their steeds were powerful. They were faster than any of the horses at the farm, and much stronger than Curtis' horse, Bojangles. Kase hoped that when he was ready to ride a horse as a Guardian, it would be as majestic as these two.

Cali didn't even look back; she was focused on winning. Kase tried to will his horse to go faster, but he couldn't seem to gain any ground on his sister's lead. They made a few turns, and sprinted down the main trails, but Cali was still ahead.

Kase thought about trying to connect with Cali's horse to slow it down. Then he realized that would be cheating. Since it was Cali's birthday, he thought it best to have a fair race. Then he started to think about all the times his uncle would play games with him, using his magic. Maybe it was his duty as a wizard to bend the rules in his favour.

While Kase wrestled with his moral dilemma, the two of them exited the crooked tree forest. They pushed on to their aunt and uncle's farm in the distance. Kase had to concede victory to Cali.

Cali pulled up on her reins to slow her horse down, and Kase followed suit. He trotted beside her and congratulated her on the win. Together, they guided the horses to the farm stable. They made sure there was enough hay and water, and left the horses in comfort.

Instead of knocking, they opened the door to the farmhouse and walked in—they were home.

Laughter was coming from the kitchen area, and Kase heard some friendly voices.

"You're doing such a good job, Talen," Anna said. "Those look beautiful."

"Talen?" Cali asked.

"There's more." Kase wrapped his arm around his sister's shoulders and led the way. They walked through the den, where a few logs burned in the fireplace to keep the house warm. He noticed it looked cleaner than usual, probably because it was a special occasion. But when they rounded the corner, the kitchen was a mess. Exactly as it should be.

"Cali's here!" Eowin said. He rushed over to give his niece a hug.

"Happy birthday, my dear," Anna added, rushing over as well. Instead of hugging Cali, she lifted up her knotted hair. "We weren't expecting you just yet. How about we clean you up a little before we sit down for dinner."

"I didn't think it was going to be a party," Cali admitted.

"Happy birthday, Cali," Lenia, Aura, and Talen said. They all stood at the table, helping prepare the meal. Talen was putting the last onion slice on a kebab stick, while Lenia and Aura rolled scuffles. There were potion bottles and spices all over the place, but that was usually how the kitchen looked when there was work to be done.

"Thanks, I really needed this." Cali let go of their uncle.

Anna wasted no time in leading her away. "Let me run you a hot bath and get you some clean clothes," Anna said. "It should give us time to get everything ready for you."

"See you in a bit," Cali said with a smile.

Kase wandered to the table and stood beside Lenia. He moved his face down to her cheek, hoping that she'd kiss him.

She giggled. "Not the right moment." She elbowed him in the side.

"You're both really good at rolling those," he replied. Aura and Lenia almost had the whole sheet covered with scuffles. The cinnamon tickled his nose.

"I don't even know what I'm doing," Aura admitted. "But it's been fun. Lenia ate one already."

Kase saw Lenia's blush. "Like, a raw piece of dough?"

She looked down and tried not to make eye contact. "Talen dared me to," she muttered.

"She asked what it tasted like, but I didn't know," Talen stated. "Therefore, I told her to try it. She liked it."

Kase reached over to the pan, grabbed an uncooked scuffle, and popped it in his mouth. He'd never eaten a raw one before, and it definitely wasn't as good. It was gooey and dry at the same time. He smiled anyway.

Lenia smirked at him. "Weirdo," she said with a laugh.

"Alright," Eowin said, "let's get all this food outside. It will taste better when it's cooked. Talen, grab your kebabs. Aura, the other tray of scuffles is on the counter; Lenia can take that one, provided Kase doesn't eat them all. Speaking of, Kase, there's a plate full of marinated steaks. Let's take those to the grill."

Kase sauntered over to the counter and grabbed the meat. They were thick-cut sirloins piled on top of each other. Some of the juices ran out on the plate, which made it look like a massacre. He froze as he stared at it.

He was watching A.J. attack the minotaur again. Blood squirted everywhere as she hacked its lifeless body. Its dangling tongue bounced. The dead eyes were blacker than night.

The minotaur was like the cow that had been butchered for their dinner. Although Kase enjoyed eating meat, and understood that his family raised cattle to feed themselves, he felt guilty. It was like he was holding a plate of murder.

Aura bumped into him as she carried the batch of scuffles.

"Sorry," he said. He wasn't sure why he apologized for being run into. She didn't even react.

He followed the group outside to the cooking area. There were two fire pits behind the old farmhouse. One was open, with a metal grill overtop that his aunt and uncle used to cook meats and veggies. The other was enclosed, used for baking breads and other goods.

The fire pits were already lit. Kase and Talen headed for the grill, while Aura and Lenia stood in front of the oven. Eowin pulled the door open on the enclosed pit, helped slide the trays in, and then closed it shut. He then walked over to Kase and Talen at the grill and placed the steaks in the centre; the skewers were loaded onto the edges.

"How long will you leave them on there for?" Talen asked. She had her hand on her chin, studying the layout. Her writing hand twitched for a quill.

"Well, I don't really know," Eowin said. "When we feel like they're ready to be flipped, we'll move them around. Then we'll pull them off after the other side cooks."

"Judging by the thickness of the cut and the heat coming from the fire"—Talen tapped her chin—"I'd say, four and a half, maybe four-point-six minutes per side?"

Eowin raised an eyebrow. "Maybe even four-point-seven," he said.

"I could see that as a real possibility," Talen said.

"Who wants some lemonade?" Anna shouted from behind them.

Talen left the pit and headed to the table, but Kase didn't even turn to look. He stared at the slabs of meat being tickled by the flames. The scent of the marinade hit his nostrils. It made him sick, but he couldn't look away.

"Are you okay?" Eowin patted Kase on the shoulder.

Kase kept staring at the fire. "I'm fine," he said.

Eowin leant down and tried to meet Kase's gaze, tilting his head awkwardly to do so. "Are you sure?"

Kase closed his eyes and sighed. He couldn't get the image of the headless minotaur out of his mind. "I just don't know what I'm supposed to do anymore," he admitted.

Eowin tapped him on the shoulder. "Want to talk about it? I have four-point-six minutes to listen before I have to flip these steaks."

Kase chuckled. He looked at his uncle and then the rest of the group. Anna was just finishing pouring a glass of lemonade for Talen. Lenia caught his eye and gestured for him to come over, but he wasn't ready to join them just yet.

"Some time has gone by, so I think you may have four-point-two minutes left," he said.

He told his uncle about the latest event in the task force. He didn't mention his wizard ability, but he talked about the hunt, the trap that A.J. had set for him, how hurt he'd been when the minotaur had died, and how bittersweet it felt when he'd found an alternate solution.

"I know the point of the exercise was to show no mercy," Kase said, "but it felt like the minotaur died for no reason. It was a waste of life."

Eowin finished turning the kebab skewers and stood tall. He put his hand on his chin and stared at the fire. "That's quite a challenge," he said. "What do you feel you should do?"

"I want justice for the minotaur," Kase admitted, "but it's too late now; what's done is done. But I don't know how I'm supposed to keep competing for a spot on a task force that I'm not sure I want to be a part of anymore."

"You want to quit?" Eowin asked. "That's not like you."

"I don't know what's like me anymore," Kase said. The words felt heavy, but saying them made him feel better. "I don't want to be on the task force, but I still want to be the greatest warrior in the realm. I don't know how I can do one without the other. If I quit, then my dream is basically over."

Eowin put his arm around Kase. "I know it's always been your dream to be like your grandfather. He was a strong warrior, and admired by everyone. But you don't have to be like him to be success-ful. All you have to be is you."

Kase wasn't impressed. "That's too simple," he said. "All I can be is me. I can't be anyone else."

"Exactly." Eowin tapped Kase's shoulder. "Everyone grows and changes in different ways. There are some situations that will push you through boundaries in a good way, but others that will challenge you in a negative way. The minute you start drifting away from who you truly are is the minute you see yourself as unsuccessful."

Eowin paused a moment to let that sink in. "If the task force is making you do things that challenge who you are as a person, it might be a sign that it isn't for you. Are there other groups that will support you, and still challenge you to be the best?"

Eowin turned Kase back towards his friends. Cali stood at the head of the table in some clean clothes. Her hair was damp, but she looked refreshed. She was hugging everyone and laughing. Lenia looked over at Kase and smiled. She waved her hand again for him to join them.

"I don't think there's a person over there that would test how great you are as a warrior," Eowin said. "They already know that you're the best. It doesn't matter if you're part of a task force, patrolling the streets of Kimroad, or crowned as the High Warrior of the realm. They'll grow with you no matter what, because they know you."

Kase waved back at Lenia this time. His uncle was right: there were more important things in life than a warrior task force. "I just want to do so much more, you know?" he said.

"It's okay if you want to apply for a challenging position within the Guardianship," Eowin said. "But there are many different ways to get to where you want to go. If you don't like the task force, that's okay. There will be other opportunities for you, as long as you stay true to who you are. Keep being the best version of yourself, and keep living your best life. If you do that, then I've no doubt that you'll be a great warrior."

"The greatest warrior," Kase corrected. He put his arm around his uncle and smiled. "Thanks, Uncle Eowin."

"Go have some lemonade." Eowin tapped Kase on the back. "Or don't. Just do you."

Kase took a deep breath and walked to the table. He felt better about himself thanks to his uncle's advice. He wasn't worried about the future, or regretting the past; he was in the moment.

He sat down beside Lenia, put his arm around her, and gave her a peck on the cheek. He grabbed a full glass of lemonade and took a sip. When he put it down, he realized that everyone was staring at him.

"What?" he asked. "This lemonade is really good."

Anna smiled at him. "Thank you, Kase." She turned her attention back to Cali. "Tell me what else you'd like for your birthday."

Kase felt something wet brush his cheek. He turned to a blushing Lenia. She moved her eyes to the left and giggled. Then she placed her head on his shoulder. He pulled her close and took another sip of his lemonade.

The group mingled and enjoyed their drinks. Cali talked about her work at the Triple Crown, and made some jokes about being 'off the record' with Talen. Aura told a story about how she'd delivered a baby on the streets of Flonkertown, and Lenia shared some Soup-a-loop recipes.

Eowin joined the table with the cooked meat and veggies, and they all started dinner. Kase had forgotten how good his Aunt's steak marinade was, and delightfully enjoyed seconds. When the meal was finished, they all devoured some freshly-baked scuffles. Everyone had enough to take some home with them.

The Liberati helped Eowin and Anna clean up after dinner. The dinnerware was taken to the wash basin, the fire pits were put out, and the potion bottles used for baking and marinade were placed back in the cupboards in the kitchen.

Lenia was standing on a stool, helping organize the potions in the cabinet above the cauldron. She pulled out a dusty blue bottle shaped like a star. "What's this one?" she asked Anna. "It's in such a beautiful container."

Anna laughed. "That's not even mine." She took the bottle from Lenia and held it in her hands. "It's a potion that Kase and Cali's mother created so that she could write secret notes to their father. She called it Hidden Speak."

Cali, Talen, Kase, and Lenia all froze and looked at each other.

"Sounds romantic," Aura said. She finished drying the final plate and placed it on the stack.

Cali had been washing the dinnerware, but turned to face her Aunt. Water dripped from her fingertips onto the floor. "How does it work?" she asked.

Anna pulled the cork off the bottle and sniffed it. She raised her eyebrows in satisfaction and smiled. "The liquid is blue when it's wet and clear when it dries. But when the dried solution is heated, it turns blue again. All you have to do is hold the note over a candle, and the writing will be revealed."

Anna put the cork back and laughed. "Your father was so slow at writing, so careful with his letters, that the invisible ink would dry. So he used to draw ones and zeros as a guide. He'd then use them to write his Hidden Speak message legibly."

Cali walked over to her aunt and caressed the bottle. "Can I try it?"

"You can have the whole thing," Anna said. "I forgot it was even up there. Thanks for de-cluttering my cupboards, Lenia. If you see anything else out of place, we'll try to get rid of that too!"

"This is the best birthday gift you could have ever given me." Cali wrapped her arms around her aunt, startling Anna in the process.

"You're welcome, dear," Anna replied. "Do you have any paper here? Why don't you run to your old room; I'll finish washing for you."

Cali raced out of the kitchen, and quickly returned with a piece of paper and a fresh quill. The table was empty, so she carefully dabbed her quill in the Hidden Speak and wrote a short message.

"Wow, this does dry really fast." She held up the paper.

Kase stared at the blank page. "Did you even write anything on it?" he asked.

"Do you have a fire starter?" she said, disregarding his question. She was breathing heavily, and her hands were shaking. Kase wondered if she was nervous or exhilarated. It was probably nexhilaration.

"I've got you covered," Lenia said. She touched her trident and the head burst into flames above her head.

"Woah," Anna shouted. "That's too much, Lenia. Here, let's use …" She opened another cupboard and grabbed a candle. "This will do."

Anna held the candle under the trident head until it caught. She passed the candle to Cali, who put it on the table.

"Now, just hold the paper slightly above the flame," Anna instructed. "It needs a bit of heat to work, but you don't want to burn the paper."

The group gathered around the candle and the paper Cali held over it. After a few seconds, the message reappeared: 'Now we know'.

CHAPTER 12

Key By The Three

K ase couldn't stop staring at his new gauntlets. They were so shiny he could see his reflection in them. He still couldn't believe he was wearing the armour of the High Guardians. Even though it was in the same colours, the material was glamorous compared to his regular uniform. It was also incredibly lightweight and comfortable.

He moved his hand closer to his face. He was able to see the outline of his head in the reflection, but nothing detailed. Suddenly, his palm was forced into his nose. He closed his eyes in discomfort.

"Did you get a close enough look?" A.J. said.

He turned away from her, trying to hide the water building up in his eyes. He wasn't hurt, but she had gotten him square. He started chewing the air to try and ease the irritation. "I hate you so much," he said with a chuckle. He felt her punch him in the arm.

After the last event, A.J. had confessed what had happened when she'd returned from the hunt. She'd been ambushed by Neil, and was forced to give up her minotaur trophy. She was able to convince him to team up with her rather than just steal the horns for himself.

She admitted that in hindsight, she would have rather teamed up with the person that had actually helped her with the hunt. Kase appreciated her honesty, but still felt a little betrayed. He decided that a continued alliance with A.J. would be better than giving her the cold shoulder, but he was careful not to trust her completely.

"Dragoon," Mason said sternly to get their attention.

There were only four warriors left in the trial for the task force: Kase, A.J., Neil, and Ash. They all stood at attention in a line facing the road that ran in front of the castle of the Triple Crown. They hadn't been given any instructions for their third event yet, but it was obvious that their next challenge was about to start. They all leant forwards to get a better look at the impressive spectacle approaching them.

Eight beautiful black horses pulled the most extravagant carriage Kase had ever seen. Everything looked like it was made of gold or silver. There were three doors on each side of the long midsection; the roof was flat with decorative moulding around the edge, and the solid chassis was lower than normal. Even the four wheel spokes were shiny and pristine. It was the kind of carriage that represented luxury and power.

When the stretch vehicle came to a stop, Mason opened the door closest to the back end. The warriors stood tall, waiting for somebody to come out, but no one exited the gold chariot.

"Get in," he instructed.

Neil pumped his fist and led the way. A.J. and Ash followed close behind. Kase hesitated before entering. He had prepared himself for another rough trial full of danger, and now didn't know what to expect from such a fancy façade. He took a deep breath and jumped into the carriage before Mason could shut the door.

When he saw who was waiting for them inside, he wanted to escape right back out.

Along one side of the interior, High Wizard Zuke sat with Derek and two others that Kase had never met before. Zuke wore his usual extravagant robes and golden leather gloves. The others were dressed in different robes, but they still looked fancy. Kase wondered if that meant they were all high-ranking wizards from the Triple Crown.

"Welcome to your third trial," High Wizard Zuke said warmly. "This time, we're going to take a break from the challenges to get to know each other a little better. Would anyone like a beverage?"

The warriors relaxed their guard and gladly accepted the drinks that Zuke's helpers passed out. Kase held his cup, but was too mesmerized by the interior of the carriage to take a sip.

The inside walls were lined with mirrors, which made the area seem bigger. The ceiling was gold, but the floor was covered with a thick, purple carpet. The matching purple seats that lined the front and back of the carriage were cushioned with a material so soft that he felt like taking a nap. The ride itself was so smooth it didn't even feel like they were moving.

"This drink is delicious, High Wizard Zuke," A.J. said politely. "What's in it?"

"I call it a Mali-mali-boo-yah," Zuke said proudly. "It's my own personal mix; I wanted a cocktail that tasted like a vacation. Relaxation, stress release, and pampering are all mixed together in a beautiful concoction."

Kase had never tasted a vacation before. He lifted the glass to his lips and took a sip. There were hints of pineapple and coconut, which made him think of Aura's Slurp-a-lurp contribution last year. The blend was similar, but she had used small bits of ice to make it cooler. He thought hers tasted much better.

"What do you think, Kase?" Zuke asked, singling him out.

Kase cradled the cup in his hands. It was short and had intricate designs blown into it somehow. Even the weight of it felt fancy. "It's one of the best drinks I've ever had," he lied.

Zuke stroked his chin, as if deep in thought. He'd caught Kase lying before, so it was possible it could happen again. Kase met the High Wizard's gaze, took another sip of his drink, and smiled politely.

"It really feels like I'm in a dream," Neil said.

Zuke kept studying Kase. It felt uncomfortable, but he wasn't going to let up on their staring contest. Finally, Zuke broke it off.

"I'm glad you all enjoy it." Zuke tilted his head and slammed back his entire drink. "Finish up; we're here."

Kase didn't want to have any more of the Mali-mali-boo-yah, but he drank it anyway. He was surprised that they had already arrived at their destination. It was either close to the castle, or the horses were as fast as unicorns.

The driver, who was also dressed in the armour of the High Guardians, opened the door. She helped everyone exit the grandiose carriage.

They had arrived at one of the main portals in Kimroad. A giant triangular stone door stood directly in front of them. Derek went to the keystone, while Zuke led the team in front of the giant doorway.

A light pulsed twelve times as the portal calibrated to the desired destination. The two panels slid open, stone grinding on stone into the edges of the doorframe.

The landscape through the portal glimmered. Kase could see a short, grassy hill leading to a beach, where the sunshine bounced off the water. It was midday, but it looked like the sun was setting in this region. The lake looked rosy.

When they stepped through the portal, Kase realized that the sun wasn't setting at all. Zuke had taken them to the Pink Lakes, the scene of his grandfather's final battle.

Although he knew the history behind Roman Garrick's heroic efforts against Mardious Hood—Grand Master Carter had even given him a personal account that was more detailed than any history book—Kase had never actually been to the battleground itself. He had never seen the site where his grandparents were slain. He felt his heart drop.

Zuke extended his arms and basked in the sunshine. "This is one of my favourite places in the realm," he said.

Kase wondered why Zuke had brought them to the Pink Lakes. Was it really an afternoon of 'getting to know each other'? Was Zuke aware of his connection to the historical site? Was it really a group excursion, or was he getting singled out again? He didn't know what to think, and the churn of emotions was smothering him. He closed his eyes and tried to take a deep breath.

The group walked away from the circle of black stones that surrounded the portal gateway and up one of the rolling hills of the beachfront. There were a few open, grassy fields with patches of forest in the area. Even though they could have walked to any hillside, Kase couldn't help but wonder if they were on the exact spot of his grandfather's infamous battle with Mardious Hood.

Zuke stopped again when he reached the apex. He took a deep breath. "Sometimes I like to come out here and just stare at the open water," he said. "It's so peaceful: a good escape from the hectic life at the Triple Crown." He turned and faced the warriors. "Does anyone else have a spot they like to go to unwind?"

Kase felt the world close in on him. The air was heavy, and the sun too hot. All he could think about was the death of his family members. It was as if he could feel their pain.

"I like to take my dog for a walk," Neil said, taking the lead again. "We usually go to the parks around Kimroad, but I'm sure he'd enjoy it here too. There's lots of open land for him to run on."

Kase thought about dogs trampling the grass on the land his grandparents had fought to protect; grass their life's blood was spilled on. It felt like Neil was disrespecting him.

"I like to go rock climbing," Ash said. Her voice was a little louder than Neil's, as if she were trying to make it sound more important. "There are some good cliffs on Mount—"

"I like to stay inside and sharpen my weapons," A.J. interrupted. The relaxing questions had turned into a competition. "Some people find the process boring, but it's soothing to me."

"Excellent answers." Zuke smiled and nodded respectfully to the group. "Kase?"

The breeze was humid, and the sun felt scorching. Kase could feel the sweat bead down his neck. He wanted to run away from this hillside and never look back. He stood his ground, but refused to share anything personal with the group.

He thought of something to say, and remembered Cali's favourite relaxation technique. "I like to unwind in a hot bath with lots of bubbles," he said. "Light some candles, maybe a little incense, and then read a book."

The group looked at him as if he'd sprouted a second head. He didn't care.

Zuke stroked his chin again. "Read a book," he said softly. "Like a scholar. Is that something you learned from your sister?"

Kase felt his heart stutter. Was High Wizard Zuke a mind reader? Was that something that powerful wizards could do? Either way, Zuke was definitely trying to get under his skin. He refused to react to the prodding. He nodded respectfully.

"Interesting," Zuke said. "Seems like you have more skills than the average warrior."

Kase froze. In his attempt to remain discreet, he had said something too wild. The other warriors glared at him, as if he were a threat. He felt like he didn't belong; he needed to get away before he said something worse. He didn't need anyone finding out his truths.

"Let's head down to the water, shall we?" Zuke said. "There's a boat on the shore that we can use to get to this lake's little island. There we can eat, drink, and share some more stories."

"Dragoon," the warriors said.

Zuke appeared to shudder a bit, but smoothly turned and led the way to the lakefront. Kase hadn't noticed before, but there was a boat on shore that looked like it could fit twenty people. Two warriors already stood in it. Like the task force recruits, they also wore their High Guardian armour.

When the group reached the sand, Kase noticed his boots felt infinitely heavier. The warriors slowly trudged over the beach, but the wizards danced across. Zuke even lightly flicked his fingers as he skipped towards the boat.

A horn sounded from behind them.

Kase turned. Around twenty men, all dressed in rags, waved swords in the air, screaming in response to the charge. They all had black hair, full beards, and dark glares.

"It's the Brotherhood!" exclaimed Zuke. "Get to the boat!"

The warriors sprinted through the sand, but Kase stared at the threatening thugs. They all crept forwards through the grassland, not moving very swiftly. He searched the crowd to see if he recognized J.R., D'Angello, or any of the other gang members he'd met on his trips to the Badlands.

"Hurry, Kase," A.J. called.

The boat was still twenty yards away. Beyond it, he could see more members of the Brotherhood running down the beach. These ones must have been lying in wait, for it seemed like they had come out of nowhere.

The wizards reached the boat. The two High Guardians stepped off to help and got them safely aboard. They drew their swords and stepped towards the running warriors.

"We need to buy them some time." One of the High Guardians put a closed fist over his chest.

"Dragoon!" Kase said with his comrades. He drew his sword and turned back to the crowd.

The initial twenty members of the Brotherhood had reached the edge of the grassland, but didn't pursue any further. They had bows drawn and were about to fire.

Down the beach, on both sides now, more members of the Brotherhood sprinted towards them. Kase focused on their feet; they were incredibly fast compared to his run through the sand. There wasn't even any dust floating from their steps.

Arrows rained down upon the warriors, but none of them landed even close. They all stuck out of the sand in an oddly-symmetrical design.

Kase felt a sharp pain in his neck. There was no way one of the arrows had hit him. He brought his hand up, but there was nothing there. He instantly felt woozy, and turned to face the rest of the group.

One of the High Guardians that had gotten off the boat was smiling and holding a dart. "Goodnight," he whispered.

Kase closed his eyes and fell to the ground.

The air smelled like a wet blanket. The walls were black, except for the cracks, which were covered in moss. There were no windows, but a single, barred gate stood in the corner of the room. It was the only way out.

Kase tried to get his feet under him, but he could barely touch the floor. His arms were stretched above his head, and his wrists were locked in shackles that dangled from the ceiling. He didn't have much energy; it was really tough to focus. It felt similar to when he had inhaled Rosebud during the attack by the Money Jane impersonator.

"What is your name?" The High Guardian that had poisoned him was standing with a torch in his right hand. In his left was a sickle.

Kase tried to remember how he had gotten here. He had been with the task force, and they had been … ambushed by the Brotherhood? He could remember seeing the gang members, but for some reason he wasn't too sure. If that was the case, then that must mean his captors were part of the gang.

Kase looked up at the man. He wondered why someone from the Badlands would be holding a curved blade made for farming. The terrain was too rough in the Badlands; a sickle would be useless. Maybe that's why it was so shiny, like it had never been used.

He remained silent.

The other guard in the room crossed his arms impatiently. He wasn't wearing armour or rags, just a clean undershirt and trousers. The fresh clothes were also inconsistent with what Kase had noticed on his trip to the Badlands. He had seen J.R. wear fancier ones, though.

"How about we move to trivia instead," the sickle holder said. He leant his head in close to Kase's. "How long do you think your small intestine is?"

Kase could smell the man's breath. It was minty and pleasant. Even the man's teeth were pretty clean. Something didn't seem right. He was starting to get the feeling that his captors were only pretending to be with the Brotherhood, but he didn't know why.

"I bet yours is around twenty-two feet," the man added.

Kase felt like shouting the word 'twos.'

The sickle moved across Kase's belly. His armour had been taken off, and the blade scratched his exposed skin. But he didn't feel threatened; he was convinced that his torturer was bluffing.

The other captor moved his fist up to his mouth and coughed. "Can we not do this right now?" he asked. "I'm starving, and it's almost lunchtime. Let's just move to plan B and get it over with."

The man dropped his arm and sickle away from Kase's abdomen. "Yeah, I'm hungry too," he agreed. "This one is tougher than the others. He doesn't seem scared at all."

Kase almost smiled, but reminded himself last-minute that he didn't want to show any emotion. There was a chance that he had only escaped minor pain, and would have to save his energy for something more challenging.

The man with the torch and the sickle moved away from Kase, while the other captor came close. He pulled a small sac from his beltline, opened it, and carefully dumped some of the contents on his hand.

"Not too much," the other warned.

The powder looked orange, but there wasn't enough light for Kase to be sure. He didn't recognize what it could be, but he knew he would be able to control it. All of his secret practising with Lenia moving sand particles was about to pay off.

The captor blew the small pile of orange dust towards Kase.

As soon as the particles were airborne, Kase took control. He remained calm and focused, and was able to disperse the cloud. Even though it appeared to have been blown towards him, he spread it throughout the room.

"How long does it take?" the sickle holder asked.

"Just count to ten." The captor backed away and reattached the sac to his beltline. "Then the powder will take effect, and we'll get the truth out of him."

Kase split the invisible cloud of powder in two and moved it towards the guards. The sickle holder breathed in half, and the other captor took in the rest. This time, Kase couldn't help but smile.

"Are you sure you didn't use too much?" the sickle holder asked. "It smells like vanilla in here now."

Kase tapped his toes where they brushed the ground and counted to ten. He wondered how long the truth powder would last. He tried to think of as many questions as possible, in case they fell asleep or freaked out.

Ten seconds passed, and the guards stood frozen. To test if it was working, Kase asked them their names. The guards pivoted and answered at the same time.

"Jake," said one.

"Arthur," said the other.

The torch flickered, and Kase could see the colour of the guard's eyes. They were both pitch-black, like Lenia and Aura's had been when they were under the effects of The X last year.

"Jake, can you release me from these chains?" he asked. He needed to escape before their attention was drawn elsewhere, or they grew tired.

"No," Jake replied. "Our orders are to keep you locked up until all questions have been answered."

Kase sighed. He'd have to think of another way to get free. "Arthur, who gave you your orders?"

"High Wizard Zuke," Arthur replied.

Kase raised his eyebrow. So it wasn't a day to get to know each other after all. It was a test wrapped up in lies and misdirection. At least he knew now that he wasn't in danger.

"Send moving image," Derek said from behind Kase.

This time, Kase froze. Did Derek know that he'd used his wizard abilities to control the orange powder? Was the entire interrogation on his sage mirror? Who did he send it to? He felt like his world was about to crash. He'd finally been caught by someone he didn't trust to keep his wizard power a secret.

Derek walked in front of Kase and took the torch from the guard. "Jake, Arthur, your work here is complete. Go upstairs and help yourselves to the snack bar."

Jake and Arthur didn't acknowledge Derek, but they left through the barred gate. They didn't even close it behind them.

"Where are we?" Kase asked.

Derek moved closer to Kase, holding out the torch. He kept turning his head, as if to study Kase from different angles.

"I couldn't really tell before why she likes you," Derek said. "You're ugly, arrogant, and a little selfish." He turned his head again. "But now I know. You're quite remarkable."

Kase stared back. He didn't know whether to be insulted or flattered. "Are you going to release me now?"

"I wish I could," Derek said with a smile. He took a few steps back and waited.

Moments later, High Wizard Zuke rushed into the room, followed by High Guardian Mason. The warrior held a large club. The weapon was smooth, but looked heavy. Kase was relieved that it didn't have any spikes on it.

Zuke shook his head. "I should have known better," he said. "You don't accept things for what they are, and push things a little too hard. You ruined a perfectly good plan."

Kase was confused. He'd bested the guards. If this was a test of survival, he should have passed. "What do you mean?"

"I told you," Zuke said with a sneer. "We're trying to get to know you. Fear is a powerful motivator; all you had to do was answer the questions honestly. You would have made it through this trial, and become a member of the Triple Thunder task force."

Kase didn't accept that explanation. It seemed like too elaborate a plan to have such a simple outcome. He felt like the High Wizard was hiding something.

Zuke stroked his beard and sighed. "I really had high hopes for you, Kase Garrick. I thought that our fates were going to be intertwined. You could have been a part of history with our mission: on the forefront of changing the realm for the better. Now, we're going to have to make you forget."

Kase felt a little guilty. Even though he had been caught in a trap of lies and deceit, he felt like he'd ruined his chance to become a great warrior. He had been dismissed because he'd used his wizard power; he had failed because he had been himself.

Zuke pulled a small sac from his waistline. He had a collection of five or six tied around his belt, but the one he chose looked similar to the one Jake had used earlier.

"More powder?" Kase asked. "It didn't really work last time."

Zuke smiled. His dark eyes looked sinister in the minimal light. "This one is different. It's going to ensure that you don't remember anything that happened today."

Mason sauntered beside Kase, but he wasn't the threatening one. His club rested on his shoulder, and his grip was loose and relaxed.

Kase was more concerned about Zuke, and the sac that he tossed back and forth between his pristine leather gloves. If it opened, he was ready to disperse the powder throughout the room. He just needed the string to loosen a little bit more.

"Before we go any further, I'm going to ask you one thing." Zuke stopped juggling his potion and crossed his arms. "I don't expect you to tell the truth, but I want to see your reaction."

Kase hung silently in his chains, intent on Zuke and the powder he held.

"There was a time, not long ago, that you had to explain how you killed a dragon," Zuke said. "In single combat, you were supposedly able to defeat one of the realm's most dangerous creatures. Do you remember what you told me, High Scholar Sheese, and High Warrior Mac?"

Kase had tried to forget about that day; it marked the beginning of his torment at The Academy. He had unwillingly slain a dragon during the Quest Series, and had to share the story with the leaders of the Triple Crown. They had asked him to admit to a different story: that he hadn't killed the dragon at all, but merely found it. Instead of a dragon slayer, he became known as the 'Dragon's Liar' among his classmates.

He nodded. "The dragon choked on my sword."

Zuke laughed. It was a little overdramatic, but if he was trying to look like a madman, he was succeeding. "Right, your sword killed the dragon." He abruptly stopped and stared at Kase with a wicked smile. "Or was it a magical black trident?"

Kase stared straight back at the High Wizard, careful not to show anything in his expression. He had used Lenia's trident to defeat the dragon, but felt he had to protect her secret when he faced the leaders of the Triple Crown. He had to protect her again, but he wondered how Zuke had figured it out. He didn't think Lenia would have told Derek just how powerful her trident really was.

Before he could answer, Zuke nodded in the direction of Mason. With a swift swing, the butt end of Mason's club connected with the back of Kase's head.

CHAPTER 13

Seen A Lot Of Pain In The Game

"Scholar beats warrior," Curtis mumbled. He sighed in frustration. "You win again. That's three in a row! How did you get so good all of a sudden?"

Kase didn't care; he wasn't even paying that much attention. His head had been aching for two days, ever since he had been kicked off the task force.

"Are you using your wizard powers somehow?" Curtis asked.

Kase chuckled. "You figured it out," he said. "I've been training so hard lately, working on my craft, just to beat you at Warrior-Scholar-Wizard. My secret's out!"

He swiped the apple from Curtis, but couldn't move it to his lips yet. His superior's hand gripped his wrist.

"It's nice to see you laugh again, Too Good." Curtis smiled and let go of Kase's arm.

Kase had been disappointed in himself the last couple days. After the last trial, Mason had pulled him aside to let him know that he wouldn't be chosen for Triple Thunder. Even though he was a little relieved that he wasn't going to be forced into something like the task force, he felt like he'd failed. The worst part was, he didn't even know what he had done wrong.

Every time he tried to remember what happened, his head seemed to hurt more. They had started with a ride in an extravagant gold chariot. There were a few questions from High Wizard Zuke as they drank some mediocre Mali-mali-boo-yahs. Then they'd returned to the castle of the Triple Crown. Time had passed quickly during the carriage ride: the trip hadn't seemed that long, but they'd left in the morning and returned in the afternoon.

Had he offended the group of wizards? Were the other warriors really that much better than he was? How was he going to be the greatest warrior of all time if he couldn't even get a spot on Triple Thunder? If he didn't belong on the task force, then where did he belong?

He took a bite of his apple. He'd thought it would taste sweeter.

Curtis pulled out his sage mirror and leant against the wall. Light flashed on its face as he checked his moving images.

Kase looked down the street. They were standing in the shade of an alley entrance. People walked around, going about their business as usual. It was just another normal day.

Kase pulled out his own sage mirror and checked it. He didn't even try to hide it from his superior. He took another bite of his apple as the light flashed before his eyes.

"Hey, you!" Lenia danced in her moving image, smiling brightly. "I'm officially done with the research group, and Brie is giving me the afternoon off. Tell me where you are so we can celebrate!"

Messages from Lenia were usually something that excited him, but this one made him feel worse. He was proud of her accomplishments, but it only amplified his own failure. He slid the sage mirror back into his pocket.

"Aren't you going to respond?" Curtis asked.

Kase had to back up a step. He was surprised at how close Curtis had gotten without him noticing. Curtis' steps were usually loud and clunky. "Not while I'm on duty," he said, trying to dodge the question.

Curtis smiled. "Then as your commanding officer, I order you to be done your shift for the day. There's only one condition: invite Lenia here so I can finally meet her."

Kase slid his hand into his pocket. His shift with Curtis was a nice distraction from everything that had happened to him recently. The grind was comfortable: no big decisions to make or emotions to face. But it didn't seem like he had a choice anymore.

"I'm still going to get credit for today though, right?" he asked.

Curtis put a reassuring hand on Kase's shoulder. "As far as anyone is concerned, you were with me all day."

Kase pulled his sage mirror back out of his pocket. "Mirror, mirror, capture moving image."

A cloud appeared on the mirror face, but Kase soon saw his reflection. "Hey, you," he said with a smile. "I just finished my shift too! I'm beside that novelty store where you made me laugh so hard, I thought I had whipped cream coming out of my nose. Send moving image to Lenia Rie."

Curtis gave Kase a weird look. "You laughed so hard, cream came out your nose?" he repeated.

"Yeah, the storeowner looked at us like we were crazy, so we ran out. It was embarrassing, but hilarious." Just telling the story made Kase feel better.

Curtis shook his head. "You're a funny kid sometimes, Too Good. I can't wait to meet your girl." He stuck out his fist. "Ready for another match?"

"Oh, she'll be here any second now," Kase said.

"What do you mean?" Curtis said. "She has to see your message, travel to a portal ..."

Curtis kept rambling, but Kase already felt Lenia's arms wrap around his waist as she hugged him tightly from behind. He tried to return the hug backwards. Her giggle was muffled as she pressed her face against him.

"Wait," Curtis said. "She's already here?"

Lenia peeked around Kase's shoulder and then moved into view. "Hi, Curtis."

Curtis put his hand on top of his helmet in disbelief. "I knew you were better than Too Good here, but that's amazing."

Kase patted Lenia in the ribs playfully. "I guess that means we're ready to go."

Curtis stood, awestruck, as Kase and Lenia exited the alley.

Kase put his arm around her shoulder and pulled her tight. He received another hug in return. He looked back, and Curtis gave him a wink.

"What should we do?" he asked once they were out in the street. "What's an appropriate way to celebrate being a successful Triple Crown consultant, Professor Next Level?"

"How about a sugar crawl?" Lenia said. "We'll just walk down the street, enter whatever shops catch our eye, and eat a few treats at each." She hugged him tight. "They'll all add up to a perfect day!"

"Let's start here." Kase grabbed her hand and raced across the street. They ducked into a coffee shop and started their afternoon together with a tasty drink.

The aroma in the coffee shops around Kimroad always made Kase feel relaxed. Although this one only had a few tables and a small counter at the back, it was packed with deliciousness. A display rack flaunted some baked goods, but they focused on the menu above it instead.

There was no line up, so they were able to order quickly. They both decided on an extra small hot chocolate, so they could guzzle it faster. They didn't even grab a table, but stood off to the side and sipped their cocoa.

"Tell me everything," Kase said, raising his drink.

"Okay," Lenia said after taking another sip. She was already halfway finished, so Kase tried to keep pace. "First, we finished the large-scale levitation platform. It's so cool! It's like twenty feet long and wider than you are tall, with waist-high walls around the outside to keep anything from spilling off. There are four quadrants, each with their own lever, so it takes a few wizards to operate. But by controlling the quadrants separately, the container can move in any direction."

"Done!" Kase placed his mug in the dish bin beside the counter. "Next stop, here we come."

Lenia giggled, tilted her head, and put back the rest of her drink. "I think I feel a sugar rush already."

Kase grabbed her hand again and yanked her out of the shop. He raced down the street, weaving in and out of the residents going about their business. They bumped into a few people, but Kase was quick to apologize. They didn't stop until they reached a favourite shop of theirs that sold jellybeans.

The candy store looked like the inside of a rainbow: jars of different-coloured jellybeans lined all the perimeter walls. Kase liked the fruity ones, but Lenia loved taking different flavours and mashing them together. Her favourite mash-up was peach and vanilla, but every time they visited she was excited to try something new.

They didn't want to spend time sampling different flavours, so they went straight to the counter and ordered a multi-bag. It was a game of chance; they didn't know what each bean was, so it was perfect for guessing and mash-ups.

After their purchase, they stood under the eaves just outside the shop instead of returning to their trip. Kase opened the bag and popped a couple in his mouth. "Blueberry and lime," he said. "Pretty good."

Lenia made a face after chewing two of her own. "Lemon and chocolate. It's bittersweet."

"What else did you guys finish today?" he said. He grabbed a couple more. Corn and cinnamon. He was not a fan of that combination.

"We were able to test the levitation container to see how much weight it could handle," she said. "We got it all the way up to twenty tons!"

"That's a lot of rocks," Kase admitted. He grabbed a handful and shoved it all into his mouth. He tried to ask another question, but his voice came out muffled.

Lenia laughed. "Mr. Zeller was excited about it; he congratulated me on how innovative our project was. The invention eliminates the need for horses, so there's no downtime for taking care of the animals. He's convinced it will change the world of mining, and help the community do great things."

Kase finally chewed all the jellybeans and swallowed. He couldn't pinpoint the exact flavours, but he knew it was a mistake to try and eat as many as he did.

"I'm really proud of you," he said. He smiled with his mouth closed, because he could feel the candy sticking to his teeth. He noticed the braid running down the side of her head was a little crooked, so he adjusted it.

Lenia moved her eyes to the left and shrugged. She grabbed his hand and pulled him away from the jellybean shop, three stores down to a bakery. Kase loved the smell of fresh bread, but they weren't there for anything wholesome. Lenia led him to a display case of cupcakes.

They picked out two shaped like unicorns. The vanilla icing had colouring to show the eyes and a golden, spiral horn. One had a pink mane, while the other had a blue one.

Kase carefully peeled the paper on his pink unicorn and held it out, while Lenia did the same for her blue one. They tilted them together, like they were clinking glasses in Slurp-a-lurp. It was impossible to eat them carefully; although they tried, they had to wipe away the icing from the corners of their mouths.

"Have you seen Luna or Turanus lately?" Lenia asked.

"No," Kase replied. "I haven't even been back to The Academy stables recently. Some days I kind of expect to see Turanus in an alleyway, ready to take me on a special unicorn flight, but it hasn't happened yet. Have you?"

Lenia shook her head. "Should we visit them now?" She reached back and touched her trident.

"Maybe in a little bit," Kase replied. "We're still celebrating your accomplishments! Where to next?"

"Trust in the path of destiny." Lenia grabbed his hand and led him away.

They didn't see any more sugar shops right away, so they slowed their pace. "What about the potion you were working on with Derek?"

Lenia shrugged. "I haven't really seen him lately. It's almost like he's been working on his own. He brought in a special powder one day that he'd gotten from High Wizard Zuke. He called it 'The Mushroom Cloud.' Even a little bit of it created a huge explosion of light and dust when we tested it with The Firefly mix. He was so convinced that it was the missing ingredient, the experiment kind of stopped." Lenia looked down at the ground and scuffed the cobbles.

"Do you wish you could have been a bigger part of it, like with the levitation platform?" Kase asked.

"Not really." Lenia shrugged. "I just thought we were becoming friends. He was always really nice to me and interested in my work. I was going to try and set him up with Aura; she's been bugging me about him since the beginning of my tenure. Then all of a sudden, he just kind of disappeared. Like a ghost."

Derek was pretty shady. The more Kase thought about it, the more his head hurt. His mind felt foggy, but he thought that it might have been a side effect of all the jellybeans he'd shoved in his mouth.

"Have you noticed anything odd about him during your trials?" she asked.

Kase stopped walking and looked down. He hadn't told Lenia that he had failed. It felt like he had let her down, and he didn't want to ruin her day. But he also didn't want to lie to her. "I got kicked off the task force," he admitted.

"Oh no." Lenia reached both hands around him and held him tightly. "I know it meant a lot to you."

Kase felt her hands dig into his back with the fierceness of her hug. It made him feel better. "Thanks, but today isn't about me. It's about you." He kissed the top of her head.

Lenia pulled back and looked up at him. "There's something that could make this day special for the both of us." She puckered her lips and stood on her tiptoes.

Kase wanted to lean in and kiss her, but something didn't feel right. He didn't feel at his best, and couldn't help but wonder if she was offering the kiss out of pity. It wasn't the moment he'd been hoping for.

People continued to walk by them on the street; Kase didn't care about them until a glimmer caught his eye. He instinctively looked to his right, and recognized the glittery blue robes.

He leant down and angled his head into Lenia's shoulder, trying to hide his face. "Can you teleport us to an alley close to here?" he whispered.

Lenia reached back and touched her trident. In an instant, they stood in the safety of a side road around the corner. "Are you embarrassed by a public display of affection?" she asked, amusement colouring her voice.

"I, more than anything, want to kiss you so hard right now," Kase said seriously. "But J.R. passed us on the street. There's a possibility that the Brotherhood is here."

Lenia let go of Kase and tiptoed towards the alley entrance. They peeked around the corner, Lenia looking left, Kase looking right. He pointed across the street. "There."

"Is that Robyn with him?" she asked. "She looks so pretty."

J.R. was wearing his blue shiny robes, while a girl with a bright green dress strolled beside him. Her hair was beautifully combed, and her skin was clean. She blended in well with the locals of Kimroad, and it took Kase a moment to recognize her as J.R.'s sister.

"You're right," he said.

"So what do we do now?" Lenia asked. "Can we report them to anyone?"

Kase had a better idea. "Would you be up for following them? I know it's not as much fun as a sugar crawl."

"As long as you call me a super warrior." Lenia giggled.

"Dragoon," Kase said, putting his fist over his chest. Lenia did the same.

They left the alley, but kept a fair distance from J.R. and his sister. They decided they would only teleport again if absolutely necessary; they didn't want to draw attention to themselves. The average person would think it weird to see a couple disappear and reappear out of nowhere, and may cause a scene.

J.R. swung his arms as he waddled down the street, while Robyn kept checking her small sac. She was an avid feather collector, and Kase wondered if she had come to town in search of more. No one else seemed to be walking with them, so the Brotherhood wasn't around.

They turned another corner, and J.R. and Robyn stopped in front of a glamorous, gold carriage. Kase pulled Lenia back and huddled at the edge of the building, out of view of their quarry.

"Those were some pretty nice wheels," Lenia whispered.

"That's High Wizard Zuke's carriage," Kase said. He peeked around the corner carefully. J.R. and Robyn entered the carriage and closed the door.

"Why would they be going for a ride with Creepshow Zuke?" Lenia gripped his shoulder as she looked too.

The carriage pulled away. "Let's keep following them, super warrior," Kase said.

They kept to their plan; the horses stayed at a walking pace, so they were able to follow on foot without looking foolish. The carriage driver didn't look back. She took a few turns, but kept to the main roads.

When the carriage reached one of Kimroad's main portal gateways, it stopped.

Lenia put her hand on Kase's shoulder again. "Let's get closer," she whispered.

Before he had a chance to respond, they were huddled against the back of the carriage. The door opened.

"See you, Uncle Emjay," Robyn said. She landed on the ground with both feet, creating a little dust cloud as she hopped around. "I hope you're able to come over for dinner again soon."

"Maybe in a few weeks," Zuke said from inside the carriage. His voice lowered. "Make sure you get this list to your dad. I needed these items yesterday."

"I understand," J.R. replied. Another set of feet hopped onto the ground; a bigger dust cloud formed.

J.R. and Robyn stepped towards the back of the carriage. Before Kase had a chance to tell Lenia they should go, they had already teleported back to their previous vantage point. They hugged the wall of the building, safely out of view.

"Is Zuke Porkchop's brother?" Lenia asked.

"And is Zuke his first or last name?" Kase said. "Could Zuke's last name be Porkchop? Or is his first name Emjay?"

Lenia giggled. "Creepshow Zuke Porkchop. I like it."

Kase peeked around the corner. J.R. and Robyn were heading to the last portal gate, which had access to one special location: the Badlands. The carriage pulled away from the gateway, its gold wheels clacking against the cobblestones.

"Maybe Talen or Cali would know," he said.

"Let's get the O.G. Liberati back together." Lenia wrapped her arm around his waist, and they disappeared.

CHAPTER 14

Shake It Cali

Sharaine tapped the pile of papers on her desk to ensure the stack was tight. She placed her quill horizontally over them, as she did every night before she left. "You're staying late again?" she asked.

Cali pretended to scribble something in her notebook. "High Scholar Sheese returns tomorrow, and I have to get this proposal finished," she said. She had already finished that work, but wanted to stay late to work on her secret project. "I won't be too much longer."

"Well, a bunch of us are going to Shark Alley tonight for drinks," Sharaine said, running a hand through her hair. "You should come."

Cali looked up and faked a smile. "I'll try."

Sharaine stood, pushed her chair back in neatly, and left their office.

As soon as the door closed, Cali quickly organized the sheets on her desk. When everything was neat and orderly, she reached into her drawer and pulled out a notebook. She wanted to study its instructions once more before implementing her plan.

For the past couple weeks, she had been monitoring the halls on the tenth floor. She made notes of who frequented the hallways, what the patrol was like at night, and how much time she'd have for her personal mission. She needed to get into the secret room outlined in her father's notebook.

Although she'd had some success deciphering three sections—with Talen's help—she still felt like she was lost. The cipher that utilized her mother's Hidden Speak potion told of a portal door on Skyland. There was a map with instructions on how to get from the Skyland Grind to a cave hidden deep within a dragon's den. From there, one had to dig to uncover the portal entrance. To top it off, the door needed to be covered in dragon fire before it could be opened.

Coupled with the details of Jenim Island and Eidolan portal in the desert, it felt like she was making progress towards solving the entire notebook. On the other hand, it felt as if she were piecing together a puzzle without knowing what it looked like. Small sections fit in place, but she still didn't understand the bigger picture.

For instance, she didn't know how her father fit into it, or how the Triple Crown was involved. She needed more. She knew—she just knew—that Dominic Garrick's life depended on it.

As dangerous as it may be to find a secret passage within the castle of the Triple Crown itself, she was convinced that she had to at least try. She had considered all the risks involved, but not acting was driving her crazy. She couldn't predict what conspiracy lay ahead at the Triple Crown, but she tried to remain focused on her goals. Whatever might happen, it was a chance to fill in the missing pieces.

She closed her notebook and tapped her pocket to ensure that her sage mirror was in it. She slid her quill beside her mirror, hugged the notebook to her with both arms, and took a deep breath. She was ready.

Her plan was pretty simple, in theory. She needed to make it to the secret room without being seen. She'd give herself about an hour to collect data, and to take as many images as possible. Finally, she needed an alibi for the evening. Sharaine's invitation for drinks was perfect, as long as she could get there in time for everyone to verify that she'd made it.

She exited her office, latching the door behind her. A few people still walked down the hallway. She said hello politely, and tried to look as casual as possible. After another deep breath, she started her journey.

She kept her head down. At the main stairway at the end of the hall, she went down instead of up. She didn't want to go straight to her target, in case someone was following her. On the floor below, she walked to another stairwell at the side of the castle, which she knew was used less frequently.

Instead of heading up the steps, she curled around the entryway; there was enough of a nook there to hide from view. She peeked around the corner. The hallway was empty; no one had followed her. "Go, Cali," she whispered. She turned and hurried up the stairs, all the way until she reached the top floor.

She tiptoed down the empty halls, her head on a swivel. She had done enough research to know that there was no patrol at this time, but she still wanted to be careful. She took a quick left, walked past a few offices and a flypen for homing pigeons, and then turned right. The lone, innocuous door at the end of the hall made her extra nervous. She took one last look over her shoulder. No one there. She hustled to the door.

Cali wiped her sweaty palm on her shirt. Before she could lose her nerve, she turned the handle, pulling the door open slowly enough that it wouldn't make a sound. She left it open to study the bricks behind the brooms and cobwebs. It looked just like any other rarely-used broom cupboard. But when she found what she was looking for, she froze.

A pentagram was etched into a brick on the bottom left side of the closet. It was the mark of The Chosen. From what she had read in her dad's notes, that was how she had to open the secret door: count three blocks to the right of the mark, and then up six. She had to push both bricks at the same time to bypass the first lock.

She steadied her hands on the correct bricks, but paused to take one more look back. Still alone. She took a deep breath and applied pressure to the wall.

The two bricks slid in half an inch and then stopped. Cali pulled her hands back and counted to five. She heard a snap from the other side, and then proceeded to the next level of the locking mechanism.

She counted two bricks to the right of the top indentation, and then one down. She applied pressure until it, too, moved into the wall and stopped. She counted to five again. Instead of a snap, the entire wall drifted up.

Cali's hands shook as she peered into the darkness. There were no windows, and no candles burning, so she couldn't see what lay ahead. All she could do was follow the careful instructions laid out by her dad, trusting in her heart that it would work.

First, though, she pulled the closet door shut. She stepped into the dark, open area and pulled out her sage mirror. "Mirror, mirror, show me the moving image of the sun," she whispered. She held the mirror up to shine light on her surroundings.

She wanted to look around, but she had to close the entrance. There was a metal lever on the wall to the left of the opening that looked promising. She pulled it down, and the wall returned to normal. She let out a sigh of relief; the hard part was over.

She lifted her illuminated sage mirror over her head to get a better view of the room. She had captured enough sunlight to last a while, but she was a little disappointed that it didn't shine across the whole room. There were too many shadows, which made the space feel eerie.

A large table rested in front of her, with chairs on all sides. The mess of papers scattered about made her cringe. Shelves lined the wall beside her, so she decided to walk around the edge of the room first to check them out.

She expected to see books, but potion bottles rested there instead. It reminded her of her aunt and uncle's kitchen, but on a much bigger scale. It was a rainbow of powders, liquids, and even some animal parts. She shuddered when she saw one filled with tiny eyeballs.

The shelves spanned the entirety of that wall, so she continued down the next one. A mixture of potions and old artefacts filled those shelves, but nothing of interest. She moved the light to her other side, still disgusted by the mess of papers on the table. The handwriting on them wasn't even legible.

She couldn't help but look beyond the table to the wall opposite. A giant map of the realm hung there, fit inside a gold frame. Beside the map were two large, black, drawn curtains. What were they hiding?

The one closest to her wasn't wrapped as tightly as the other; green stone peeked from behind the curtain. She couldn't make out the details, but her heart beat faster. Ignoring everything else, she raced across the room, giving up on trying to tiptoe.

Her fingers caressed the edge of the curtain's black material. It was secure at the top, but loose at the bottom. As she peeled it back, she noticed the beautiful designs that were etched into the stone artefact beneath. It was similar to the portal doors throughout the realm, but much more elaborate. The light from her sage mirror shook with her excitement.

The stone was about six inches wide and six inches deep. Pulling back more of the curtain, she could see that it formed an oblong column that stretched almost ten feet high. It came to a right angle at the bottom, and continued almost six feet along the floor before stopping at a jagged edge. It was clearly part of something much bigger.

It was exactly what she was looking for: a piece of the doorway of life.

Her dad's notebook was true. The relic existed! It wasn't just a wild goose chase to find a legendary item; it outlined the steps of a successful plan. She couldn't help wonder where her dad was now, after having discovered this much about it.

A loud snap broke her thought process. Someone was unlocking the secret door to the room.

Cali scanned the area for somewhere to hide, but there were only shelves on the wall and the large table in the room. A black cloak was draped over one of the chairs, but it wouldn't be big enough to hide under. The only option seemed to be under her hand.

She stepped onto the bottom edge of the doorway and pulled the curtain closed behind her. She didn't want anyone to hear her give the command to stop her sage mirror image, so she hid it under her shirt instead. She was back in the comfort of darkness, but her mind was anything but calm. She heard the door open.

"Mirror, mirror, illuminate," High Wizard Zuke commanded.

More questions flooded her mind the instant Cali recognized his voice. Why was the most powerful wizard in the realm there? Was High Scholar Sheese aware? If it involved someone at the top, how long had this conspiracy been around for?

There was a small slit between the curtain and the edge of the stone frame. It was paper-thin, but enough for Cali to realize that the room had brightened. She thought about peeking through the crack, but it was too risky. She kept her head down, her sage mirror tight against her stomach, and remained as still as possible. All of her practice playing hide and seek with Kase when they were young was about to pay off.

"Here it is," Zuke said. Cali heard something hit the table. "This is the last of my personal stash, but it should give you enough to get started. When my order is delivered, it will be more than enough to finish."

"Do you want me to focus on the small flyers, or the destroyer?" a male voice asked. Cali didn't recognize who it was, but it made her wonder how many others were in the room.

"The small flyers will take more time, so start with them,"

Zuke replied. "The delivery will come in four days, which will give you enough time to finalize everything before next Thursday. Understood?"

"Yes, High Wizard Zuke," the man said unenthusiastically. "That matches my schedule."

There must have only been two of them. Cali didn't hear anyone walking around, and no one else spoke. She closed her eyes and tried to concentrate harder.

"Is something wrong?" Zuke asked. "You look concerned."

"I'm not confident in both the warriors on our task force," the man said. "I don't think we picked the strongest applicants."

"You think we should have taken the Garrick boy," Zuke said in an accusatory tone.

Cali opened her eyes. What did they want with Kase? Was his task force mixed up in the search for the doorway of life? She wondered how much he knew. Was he still not telling her everything?

"I saw him move that dust with my own eyes," the man said. "He's a powerful wizard, and would be a useful ally. If he already killed a dragon with the trident, he'd be perfect for this mission. We might not even need the—"

"He's not ready," Zuke interrupted. "I don't care how powerful he is; I don't trust him."

"He's noble," the man said. "He's fearless. He's kind. I'm confident he would take our secrets to the grave, if needed. He would die for the cause."

"We don't need him to keep quiet or give his life in battle," Zuke said, anger creeping into his voice. "We need him to die when we *tell* him to."

Cali's stomach churned. Kase was in danger, and from the sounds of it, he didn't even know it. She started to tremble at the thought of anything happening to her little brother, but forced herself to remain calm. If she freaked out, she'd give away her position, and maybe beat her brother to the grave.

"I understand," the man replied. There was sadness in his voice.

"We don't need his talents yet, but we might be able to use him for the Leviathan Triangle." Zuke seemed a little calmer. "We have a lot riding on this mission and the next. Don't you want to get that hand back?"

Cali realized who Zuke must be talking to, but couldn't remember his name. He was the annoying, blond intern with a missing limb. She'd only met him once, but he'd felt fake to her. He reminded her of her ex-boyfriend, Niveous.

"I want it as much as you want your friend back," the one-handed man said. "I trust you."

"Trust the process," Zuke said in return. "Wait. There's something ..."

Cali heard someone hustle across the room. Their footsteps were light, but the rustle of robes made it sound like they were running. A shadow crossed the slit of light between the curtain and the stone, and then stopped. Cali froze.

Zuke's voice was much closer now. "You little ..."

Cali closed her eyes. She'd been caught. She was so frozen that she couldn't make a sound. It felt like she was shrinking in on herself.

A loud bang made Cali shudder, but she didn't scream. She cracked one eye open, expecting to see Zuke with the curtain pulled back, letting the light of judgment shine down on her. But she was still encompassed in the safety of darkness.

"I don't know how these spiders keep getting in here," Zuke said. The papers on the table rustled. "You need to clean this place."

"Yes, High Wizard Zuke," the one-handed man replied. "After we complete our quest."

"Of course," Zuke said. "Then let's get back to work."

Light once more slipped between the curtain and stone edge. The rustle of robes grew softer; High Wizard Zuke must have returned to the entrance. A clicking sound followed.

"Mirror, mirror, eclipse," he commanded. The light went out, and Cali heard the secret door close.

Cali wanted to escape her curtain shroud for a breath of fresh air, but she was still cautious. She waited a few minutes, just in case Zuke or his partner had stayed in the room. It remained quiet, so she decided to step out.

She pulled out her sage mirror and shone it around the room. She didn't see anyone: just the mess of papers on the table and the library of potion bottles. She finally let herself gasp for air. Her heart was pounding, but she couldn't tell if it was fear or exhilaration.

She wanted to take a moving image so she could remember everything, but her sage mirror wouldn't be able to do that and act as a light at the same time. Since she was the only one in the room, and it took a few seconds for the door to open, she didn't see any harm in using the lighting that Zuke had activated.

"Mirror, mirror, illuminate," she commanded. Nothing happened. The sage mirrors in the room must have been calibrated for Zuke's voice only. She would have to gather information the slow, diligent way.

She didn't want to touch anything; she was paranoid that someone would notice a paper out of place, a smudge on a dusty bottle, or another dead insect, so she kept her hands to herself. She didn't have anywhere to put her sage mirror, so she bit the corner of it and held it in her mouth. She opened her notebook, pulled the quill out of her pocket, and went to work.

She spent just over an hour sketching the room, reviewing the material on the table, and describing the doorway pieces. She even tried to guess the names of the potions, since some of them looked similar to ones at the farm. However, time pressed in on her: she had to get to Shark Alley and meet Sharaine. She needed to make sure she had an alibi for the night, just in case.

When she was satisfied, she pulled the lever beside the entrance. The stone wall smoothly lifted. She cracked open the broom closet door to ensure the hallway was clear before leaving. She heard a click from behind her as the entrance wall automatically dropped.

Even though there was no one in the hallway, she hustled back to the stairwell. She didn't even realize she was holding her breath until she was halfway down the steps. She leant against the wall and took a few gasping breaths before she kept going.

Her planned exit was through a back door on the main level of the castle. All the entrances were guarded, but she wanted to avoid being seen by too many Guardians in case they noted the time that she left. The door she picked was patrolled by an old, sleepy warrior named Geoffrey, and was the perfect escape. It was an emergency exit, leading out to a back road, so he usually slept on shift because of the minimal traffic.

As expected, Geoffrey was laid back in his chair, eyes closed. Cali tiptoed to the door, opened it as quietly as possible, and then closed it tight. She hugged the wall of the castle; the shadows provided some cover. The empty street was peaceful. She was almost free.

Luckily, Sharaine's usual watering hole was only a few blocks away. When she got to the pub, it was packed. She bumped into cheery people swaying from drinks and good times. She saw Sharaine and her friends in the corner, and headed straight for them.

"Cali, you made it!" Sharaine said when she saw her.

"I sure did." Cali hugged her notebook tight and smiled as she greeted her other friends. "High Scholar Sheese will be pleased with my hard work," she lied.

"That's a good reason to celebrate." Sharaine raised her drink high.

Cali was in the mood for celebration, but not because of her daily paperwork. Not only had she successfully implemented her plan, she was still alive to tell about it. She even felt a little dangerous for being such a sneak.

She needed to analyze the data further, but she was confident it would not only help decipher the rest of her dad's notes, but also reveal what High Wizard Zuke was up to. She knew that she couldn't do it alone, though.

She needed to get the O.G. Liberati back together.

CHAPTER 15

Hold Up

A firefly hovered above Lenia's finger. She moved her hand up to touch it, and the illusion disappeared. "You've been practising," she said happily. "It's so bright!"

"I've been getting better at creating creatures that I've seen before," Kase admitted. "But the ones I've connected with are easier. Is that common?"

"I'm not sure." Lenia shrugged. "I've never had much trouble with illusions."

Kase laughed. "Oh, because you're naturally so gifted, you're good at everything?"

"Well ..." Lenia touched her finger to her chin as she thought about it. She looked up at Kase and chuckled. "I couldn't keep a straight face!" She hugged his arm and buried her face into his shoulder. "I was going to say people used to call me Student Next Level."

Kase tapped her leg and looked back out across the lake. "I love that, but you can't make up your own nickname."

"Well, if you say so, Hawk-eye." She laughed again and took his hand.

They were sitting high up in Kase's favourite tree, enjoying tea and each other's company. It was the place he'd gone when he was young to escape the farm and clear his mind. It wasn't just his place now, though; it was theirs.

He leant his head on top of hers. It felt like nothing else in the world mattered. He wished he could stay up here forever. It was simple, safe, and peaceful.

Lenia checked her sage mirror, and a new moving image appeared on its face.

"Hi, Lenia," Talen said. "I'm finished with work and can meet with you and Kase now. I'm at Co Co. in Kimroad. See you soon."

The image disappeared, and Lenia returned the sage mirror to her pocket. "It's time to go." Her voice sounded sad.

"Can I try teleporting this time?" Kase asked. He hadn't attempted to on his own, even though he'd had accidental success before. He didn't know exactly what the process was, but he was confident he could replicate the feeling. He wasn't sure he had enough power to travel the entire realm, but going from the treetop to the lakefront seemed reasonable.

"As long as you take me with you." Lenia wrapped her arms around his torso and clutched him tight.

Kase held her close and touched her trident. He closed his eyes and tried to imagine where he wanted to go. He thought about the gentle water, the warm sun, and the cozy sand.

"I like to relive a specific moment, and feel my emotions at that time," Lenia advised. "The more intense the emotion, the easier it is to reach the destination."

Kase smiled. The last time they were on the lake, he had tried to kiss her. Feeling her in his arms now was similar to that experience, and he remembered the rush of emotion stirring within. He felt solid ground beneath his feet.

He opened his eyes, but had to squint at the light bouncing off the lake. "We did it." He hugged Lenia tighter.

She leant back and smiled. "You did it, Student Next Level."

Kase moved his head in closer. He still felt elated from his accomplishment, and his emotions stirred with the memory of the last time they were here. It felt like the perfect time to kiss her.

Lenia looked up and past him. She cowered against his shoulder, eyes on the sky. Kase stopped. Eyes wide, her head twisted around and down until a loon glided into view and took a spot on the water.

Kase leant back. It wasn't the right time. At least she wasn't blatantly pushing him away, but he was still a little disappointed.

Lenia reached behind her back. She disappeared without saying good-bye.

Kase turned and walked back to the blanket they had set up. There wasn't anything on it, because they had taken the tea up into their tree perch. He didn't feel like climbing back up to get it, so he decided to enjoy the sunshine instead. Lying on the blanket, he spread his arms and legs out like a starfish and took in the warmth.

A few minutes later, Lenia returned with Talen. They both held cups oozing with whipped cream. Kase sat up, excited for the tasty treat. "Slurp-a-lurp!" he said.

Talen looked around while Lenia handed Kase a drink. "Where's Cali?" she asked.

Kase opened his mouth, but he was too focused on the cup he swivelled in his hands to answer, trying to figure out how to attack the drink with the least amount of mess.

"I haven't heard from her yet," Lenia said. "Should we wait for her?"

Kase felt the sweet, warm cocoa slide down his throat, but his upper lip stayed moist. He licked away the excess whipped cream and smiled. "Too late."

"How long do you think she'll be?" Talen asked.

"She didn't give us a timeline," Lenia said. "Why?"

"I want to tell you what I found out." Talen sipped her drink. "I just don't want to have to repeat myself too much."

"We'll catch her up," Kase said. He licked his lips again, savouring the sweet taste.

Talen and Lenia sat down on the blanket, and Talen pulled a notebook out of her sac. "I was able to look up all the public information on Brothers' Inc." She flipped quickly through the pages to the one she needed. "It's a legitimate company. They report their earnings, file their taxes, and abide by all the laws governed within the realm of real estate. They have a number of registered shareholders, but three of them have the same last name, which I noted as irregular."

Talen placed her open notebook on the blanket. Three names were circled on the paper: Pollock Tamworth, John Ross Tamworth, and Robyn Tamworth. Kase scanned the rest of the names and recognized D'Angello on there too.

"I can't prove it for sure, but I think it's Porkchop, J.R., and Robyn," Talen said confidently. "If I'm right, that means that our enemies from the Badlands own part of Kimroad."

Kase felt proud that his hunch was correct, but he worried about what it meant. "How much of Kimroad do they own?"

"About forty-one point three seven percent," Talen said.

"So if they own almost half of Kimroad, why do they live in the Badlands?" Lenia asked.

"It's barely two fifths …" Talen started. She cleared her throat. "That's a good question, but I don't have an answer. The Badlands is tricky when it comes to property ownership."

"What do you mean?" Kase took another sip of his drink, but it wasn't as sweet this time.

"There aren't really any ownership laws there, so a person owns any property that they can claim. If you and I wanted to, we could move to Camptown and take any of the houses there for ourselves. We might have to fight for it, but it would be ours. Therefore, I doubt that Brothers' Inc. owns any property in the Badlands; it does, however, allow them to invest elsewhere."

"How many other places do they own property in?" Lenia leant forwards. "Anything in Flonkertown?"

Kase was also worried about his family; he wondered if there was any farmland around his aunt and uncle's that was Brothers' Inc. property.

"That's one of the peculiarities," Talen said. "Brothers' Inc. only owns property in Kimroad. It's the biggest city in the realm, and likely brings in value for the company, but most property ownership enterprises diversify their portfolio. My hunch is that they're doing it for a reason, but I don't understand what it is yet."

Kase thought about how friendly J.R. and Robyn were with Zuke. He wondered if the High Wizard was an investor. "Is it possible that they use a different name for other businesses?"

"No," Talen said plainly. "I ran Polluck, John Ross, and Robyn through the system, but nothing else turned up."

"What about an Emjay Tamworth?" he asked.

"Good one," Lenia agreed. She checked her sage mirror again for Cali, but no new messages waited for her.

"I wasn't looking for another Tamworth," Talen admitted. "Why Emjay?"

Lenia and Kase explained their last adventure in Kimroad. They left out the sugar crawl, but they told Talen about J.R. and Robyn riding in High Wizard Zuke's private carriage and what they'd overheard.

Talen tapped her chin. "Are you sure she was talking to Zuke when she said 'Uncle Emjay' and not someone else?"

"Positive," Kase said. "Is High Wizard Zuke's first name Emjay?"

"No, Zuke is his first name," Talen said, still tapping her chin. "His last name is Hagen. He's from the mountain region of

Snowsmoke. He graduated from The Academy with a major in illusions, and got an internship with the Triple Crown shortly thereafter. He worked there for years before High Scholar Sheese appointed him High Wizard."

"So he's not related to Robyn," Kase said.

"I took a modern history class at The Academy," Talen said. "Trust me, Zuke is not from the Badlands. But it's interesting that he would have a relationship with people from there."

"Why?" Lenia asked. Her sage mirror flashed, and Cali appeared on it. "I'm ready," was all that she said.

"The Badlands is so disconnected from the rest of the realm that it's unlikely—exponentially unlikely—for one of the most powerful people to be coincidentally associated with anyone from there," Talen explained before Lenia could leave. "If he does have relations with the Tamworths, there must be a reason for it."

"Maybe Cali knows," Kase said. He nodded to Lenia, and she disappeared.

Kase took another sip of his cocoa. He was going to ask Talen another question, but she appeared deep in thought, busy scribbling down some notes.

Moments later, Lenia reappeared with Cali, who clutched a book of her own. This time, she wasn't distraught by the teleportation. Instead, she was engaged and focused—the best Kase had seen her since her birthday. Her hair was neat, but her eyes showed that she was still sleep-deprived. Kase knew she was serious.

"Sorry, I don't have much time." Cali flopped down on the blanket, almost spilling the two drinks saved for her and Lenia. "High Scholar Sheese has returned to the castle, and he dropped a whole new stack of work on my desk. I need to tell you what I found, though."

After Cali was caught up on the rest of the Liberati's information, she described her own excursion into the secret room at the castle of the Triple Crown, and what she'd overheard with High Wizard Zuke and Derek.

"They're going after the third piece this Thursday," she said. "I'm sure of it. But I still don't know why High Wizard Zuke is involved. Derek said he wanted to bring back a friend, but who is it?"

"You don't think …" Talen flipped through her notebook, and then scanned the page she was looking for.

"What is it, Talen?" Cali asked. "Was there something I missed in my dad's notes?"

"No." Talen looked up, her eyes wide. "Worse. I think High Wizard Zuke could be trying to bring back Mardious Hood."

Cali nodded slowly, accepting Talen's revelation, but Kase was still confused.

"Why?" he asked.

"Zuke and Mardious were coworkers at the Triple Crown, but they were also great friends." Talen tapped her notes. "So much so, that when Mardious Hood died, Zuke made special burial arrangements for the notorious criminal. It caused quite a stir among the public, but Zuke was granted the right to do so because he paid for the services out of his own pocket."

"It caused quite a debate in one of our history classes," Cali said, supporting Talen's claim.

"So if we know that High Wizard Zuke is planning on using the doorway of life to bring back Mardious Hood, what can we do about it?" Lenia asked.

"We need to report them," Kase said, dropping a fist into his palm. "If they're putting people in danger, and wanting to bring back the most notorious criminal of all time, then we have an obligation to speak the truth."

"No way," Cali said. "I'm not going to say anything until we figure out who else is involved, and how our dad is mixed up in it. The more information I find, the more I worry about how much danger he's in."

Kase wasn't holding onto the same false hopes that his sister was about their dad. He was more concerned about what was right. If Zuke were willing to sacrifice him and the rest of the Triple Thunder task force in order to bring back a madman, he had to be stopped.

"This … this is my levitation container." Lenia pointed to an open page in Cali's notebook: a rough sketch of some plans opposite her list of potions. "Except that this one's twice the size and is more of a box than an open cargo container."

The sketch looked like a carriage with no wheels, complete with a set of doors on the side. At the front there were only two holes at eye level. The roof had scribbles all over it, with a label that read 'Black Rock.' It didn't look that impressive to Kase.

"I was wondering about that one. I think it's how they're going to transport the doorway piece away from the dragon's den," Cali said. "They're going to try and camouflage it with the shale of the terrain, so they're not seen from the sky."

"It's brilliant," Talen noted.

"A dragon's eyesight is better than you might think," Lenia said. "They're true Hawk-eyes."

"Like me," Kase and Talen said at the same time.

"Either way, we know what they're attempting to do, and when," Cali said. "This might sound crazy, but I think we're the ones who will have to try and stop them; we can't bring it to anyone else without proof. We're all connected to this in one way or another, and it gives us the best chance to gather some hard evidence against them. Once we can prove their intentions beyond a shadow of a doubt, then we can turn them over to a higher authority."

Kase, Lenia, and Talen all nodded. Lenia looked at Kase and smiled. "Looks like the Liberati are getting back together."

"The O.G. Liberati Task Force?" Kase chuckled.

"The Liberati Next Level," Lenia said.

"I love it," Talen agreed. "Does that mean we're going back to do research at The Academy library? I haven't been there since graduation."

"No, we can't be seen together," Cali said. "Well, I can't be seen with you. We'll have to divide and conquer."

"What do you need us to do?" Kase asked.

"We have a lot of the pieces, but we still need to be certain about how their plan fits together. Let's start with their end goal, and work our way back to the beginning."

Talen already held a quill over an open page in her notebook. Kase and Lenia leant forwards and listened intently.

"We know from dad's notes that the doorway pieces are located behind special portals hidden throughout the realm. We've all seen the black portal in the desert, which led to the treasure of the Eidola. I found a gold doorway piece, part of the frame, in the Triple Crown secret room. It matches what was written in dad's notebook about the relic that the Eidola were protecting."

Kase nodded. He hadn't read the notebook himself, but Cali had been talking non-stop about it.

"The second relic that I found there is from the portal door on Jenim Island; Dad described it as the green piece of the doorway of life. It's hard to be certain, since we haven't decoded the rest of his book, but that matches the other portal piece that I found in the castle of the Triple Crown."

"We'll figure it out soon enough," Talen said reassuringly.

"The third relic is located in the heart of a dragon's den. It's protected by the beasts that inhabit the area. Like the others, the portal to get to the door is also in the ground. We have a map that leads to the exact spot, but the black shale of that terrain covers the entrance. I'm suspecting that the Triple Thunder task force will have to dig in order to access it."

"Oh no." Lenia leant back and covered her mouth.

"Your project," Talen added. "Do you think they'll use the potion that you helped develop?"

Lenia nodded. "I don't know what the final composition was; Derek figured that part out. But since he has been involved in both, they must be using it. It'll put a hole in the earth faster than anyone can dig. It's so powerful they would have to be careful not to destroy the portal door."

"The portal doors are indestructible, so they don't have to worry about that when they're removing the rock around it." Cali said. "Can you go back to The Academy and see if you can find out how they're using it? There must be others like you who aren't part of the Task Force, but still know something because they were involved."

"Dragoon," Lenia said, accepting her orders.

"If they're moving an explosive potion through Skyland on an armoured levitation board, they must also know the way to the dragon's den," Cali said. "Although we have a map, we should probably walk the path before we follow them, so we also know what to expect."

"I'm on it," Kase said. "As long as someone can show me the way."

"I'll go with you," Lenia said. "That way I can teleport around once I've seen it all."

"That's a good idea," Cali said. "Plus, you'll be able to save Kase from any dragons."

Kase elbowed Lenia again and smiled. He appreciated her help, and knew that no dragon would stand a chance against her. "Maybe we can visit our satyr friends while we're there," he said. "Taste some of their popcorn."

"Talen, can you make them a map?" Cali asked. She didn't laugh at Kase's joke.

"Dragoon," Talen said. She made a note in her book.

"And since we know most of the members of their team," Cali said, "I want you to do a background check on each of them. I have the names listed in my notebook."

Talen nodded while she scribbled on her paper.

"If we're outnumbered, should we try and recruit more people to help?" Kase asked. "I could ask Curtis, so we have just as many warriors as Triple Thunder."

"And I could ask Aura, since she's also part of the Liberati," Lenia said.

"I don't think we need to match their numbers," Cali said. "Besides, we don't want to put anyone else in harm's way. As much as we joke around as friends, this is a serious assignment."

Talen, Lenia, and Kase all nodded.

"I have to go now," Cali said, "but we'll meet back here on Wednesday. I'm going to try and find Zuke's schedule. If he's taking time away from the castle for a secret excursion, I should be able to figure out if anyone outside the task force is joining him, or at least covering for him."

Lenia nodded and stood up with Cali. She reached for her trident.

Cali grabbed her hand. "Before we go, I just want to say thank you," she said. "To you, Talen, and Kase. I know I've been a wreck lately, and what I'm asking is extremely dangerous, but I really appreciate your help."

Lenia squeezed her hand. "We always have your back."

"We're your friends," Talen said.

"We're the Liberati Next Level," Kase added. He loved his new task force.

CHAPTER 16

Not Trying To Be Rude

K ase leant beside Professor Rie's door, waiting for her class to end. He held a bouquet of white dandelions, and tried to remain as still as he could so that the seeds wouldn't float away.

Today was the day of their reconnaissance on Skyland. He had been able to get the afternoon off from his Guardian duties. Curtis didn't even need to know the reasons behind his requested absence; he trusted Kase, and granted him what he needed. Kase felt like their friendship was evolving, and was grateful to have such a good partner. He never would have guessed that during the beginning of his practicum.

Footsteps echoed towards him. He put his head down, hoping he wouldn't be recognized.

"Mr. Garrick," Grand Master Carter said cordially.

Kase looked up and fake smiled. He didn't know if he should come up with an excuse for missing his shift, or if he should just stay quiet. He didn't want the Grand Master to be suspicious.

"It's so good to see you," Carter said. "I've been meaning to talk to you ever since your application for the task force was rejected."

Kase looked down again; he didn't want the Grand Master to see his embarrassment. "I'm sorry I failed you."

Carter placed his hand on Kase's shoulder. "You didn't," he said. "I'm actually quite pleased that you didn't make it in."

Kase was confused. Was the Grand Master rubbing it in? He hadn't thought his failure would bring anyone pleasure, especially someone who had helped foster his career. The Grand Master had once stressed that if he wanted to be a great warrior, he had to start today: that doing all the little things great would add up to a successful path of greatness.

"What do you mean?" he asked.

"Being a member of a Triple Crown task force is a dangerous job," Carter explained. "The higher the ranking officer, the more deadly the mission. When High Wizard Zuke told me he was overseeing your interview, I immediately thought it might cost you the ultimate price. I'm glad you're alive and well."

Kase understood the Grand Master's concern, but he felt a little disrespected. He could handle danger. And now his secret task force was about to attempt the same mission. He gave another fake smile. "Thank you," he said politely.

The Grand Master tapped him on the shoulder before he walked away. As Kase watched him head down the hall, he wondered how much Carter knew about the Triple Crown and Zuke's true reason for the mission. He thought about asking, but he didn't know how trustworthy the Grand Master was anymore.

The door beside him finally opened, and students bustled out into the hallway. Kase waited for the majority of the group to leave the class before he entered. He didn't want anyone to bump him and ruin his perfect gift.

Lenia was at the front, putting her potion bottles away. When she saw the dandelions, she stopped and smiled. "Are those for me?" she asked.

"It's how we started each Quest Series," Kase said. "I thought it would be a perfect start to our new quest too."

"A next level bouquet for our next level adventure," Lenia said, clapping her hands together. "I love it."

She reached back and the head of her trident ignited. The flame smoothly transferred from the trident to her open palm. She moved the fire to the edge of the bouquet, and it flashed beautifully. Kase could feel the warmth from the short blaze.

"Thank you." Lenia put her hand on Kase's and smiled. "Now, help me put these potions away, and we'll get going."

It didn't take long for the two of them to clean up her demonstration and ensure that everything was tidy for Professor Bright's next class. The last of the students filtered out, so they were finally ready to teleport away.

"I have to go to the lab first," Lenia said. "Mr. Zeller came looking for me before my class, and I promised I'd talk to him afterwards."

"Is it anything serious?" Kase asked. "Are Derek and the others going to be there?"

"No, the group finished a couple weeks ago," Lenia said. "Mr. Zeller just wants to show me the results of the field test. He seemed really excited about it, and since Cali didn't mention him in her notes, I think it's safe for us to visit. Besides, he might be the one that inadvertently gives us information on the task force."

Kase nodded. He was a little excited to see where Lenia had been working, and witness first-hand the results of her special wizard project. "Let's go," he said.

Lenia wrapped her arms around his waist, and then reached back. A second later, they were in front of a closed, wooden door in a hallway that Kase didn't recognize.

"Are we still at The Academy?" Kase whispered.

"Yes, we're in the basement of the wizard castle." Lenia whispered back. "A secret wall with an illusion covers this door."

Kase looked around mockingly.

"We're behind the illusion now, silly! It blocks off the whole end of the hallway."

End of a hall in the basement of the wizard's tower. Now why did that sound familiar?

"Only exclusive people know about it, so make sure you keep it a secret, or else." Lenia elbowed him playfully.

Kase pointed at his heart and made an X with his index finger.

Lenia turned her attention back to the task at hand. She knocked on the door before entering carefully. "Mr. Zeller," she said curiously.

"Lenia, over here!" Mr. Zeller said.

The room they entered was four times the size of Lenia's classroom. There were short bookcases filled with different potions, multiple cauldrons above tiny fire pits, and sage mirrors that covered entire tables. Mr. Zeller was in the corner of the room, staring down at a colourful, flashing table.

"I hope it's okay that I brought a friend with me," Lenia said as they approached.

Mr. Zeller looked up and smiled. "Yes, of course. We've met before, correct? You were at Professor Rie's first classroom presentation."

Kase shook Mr. Zeller's hand, appreciating his good memory. "Kase," he added.

"Stanley." He looked down at his table again. "I'll start this from the beginning. Mirror, mirror, show moving image one thirty-seven."

The cloud that formed on the table mirror cleared to reveal the base of a mountain with a cavern entrance the size of a portal door. A giant levitation container, overflowing with rocks, floated away from it. Two wizards walked alongside it to control its speed and trajectory.

"Look how many samples there are," Stanley said, gesturing to it excitedly. "We're able to move exponentially more than we used to by hand."

A second levitation container followed the first, carrying just as much rock.

"It's all thanks to your invention!" Stanley patted Lenia's shoulder proudly.

"How do they get all those rocks inside the container?" Lenia asked. She didn't seem too impressed.

"Those do have to be loaded by hand," Stanley said. "But first, we use the dragonmite to blast the earth to a more manageable size."

"What's dragonmite?" Kase asked. It sounded pretty dangerous.

"It's the term Derek came up with for the magma mixture that was created." Stanley waved a hand. "He made many different sizes, but we really only need the one. I don't particularly care for the name, but as long as it works, I'm happy."

"How many different sizes did he make?" Lenia shared a worried look with Kase.

"I'm not sure exactly," Stanley said. "The others took their supplies a few days ago, leaving me with just enough to continue with the mining operation. They must have another assignment to complete, because I haven't seen any of the group since."

Stanley turned to Lenia and smiled. "Speaking of, I have another project coming up soon, and I wanted to ask if you'd join me for it. You were my favourite partner, and because of the success we've had, I know our next project will be even better. What do you say?"

Lenia glanced at Kase and smiled. "Unfortunately, I'm already on another team, but maybe next time."

"Of course you are," Stanley said. "You're a wonderful wizard, Lenia. I hope you don't mind, but I'm going to keep asking whenever something new comes up."

Lenia thanked him, and then left the room with Kase. As soon as they closed the door behind them, she reached around and gave him a huge hug.

Kase closed his eyes and held her tight. She felt warm, even when the cool breeze touched his skin. He looked around to find they were already at the top of the Skyland Grind.

The sun shone brightly on the island, perched as it was above the clouds. The field they stood in had fresh grass and budding roots. When they had been here before, the terrain was freshly burnt and smelled like bacon. Kase was a little disappointed with the ordinary freshness of the landscape.

"Cali will be happy with what we found out about the dragon-mite," Lenia said.

"We're crushing our adventure so far," Kase said with a smile.

"On to the next one," Lenia said. "Do you have the map?"

Kase reached into his pocket and produced the folded paper that Talen had given him. It had their starting point, goal, and path marked clearly. The different types of terrain were labelled with a colour scheme that made it easier to read. It even had estimated times for each leg of the journey.

"Looks like we have a two hour and thirty-three minute hike," he said.

"Threes!" Lenia laughed and clutched his arm.

It didn't take them long to make it through the grassy field to the tree line. There, they followed a clear and open trail. According to Talen's guide, they had a forty-two minute trek until they reached the black terrain of the dragon's den.

Kase clutched Lenia's hand and rested his head on her shoulder. "Tell me a story," he said in his most polite tone.

"I've been waiting for you to ask me that." She giggled. "Once upon a time—"

"Oh good, a classic." Kase clutched her hand tighter.

"Once upon a time," she repeated, "there lived a dashing young prince. He was so good at everything he did that his people didn't even call him by name. Instead he was known as Prince Next Level."

Kase laughed. "This story is next level."

Lenia smiled, but held back her laughter. "One day, on one of his many quests, the prince was prancing along a trail when he came across a young wizard."

"Next level princes prance?" Kase asked.

"She was guarding a bridge that led to the Isle of Dragonmite. As good as Prince Next Level was, his magic was not as powerful as the wizard's. Luckily for him, she was kind and gentle."

He squeezed her hand again. She squeezed back.

"She challenged him to a game of Warrior-Scholar-Wizard," Lenia continued. "If he won, he could pass. If he didn't, he'd get a consolation prize: he could ask her one question that she would answer truthfully."

"Curtis would like this story too," Kase admitted.

"Their first match was a disaster for the prince," Lenia said, "but he didn't give up that easily. He returned the next day, and the day after that, even though the wizard kept winning."

"Sounds like a next, next level wizard," Kase said.

Lenia giggled. "All was not lost, though. After a while, he started to get to know the young wizard. When he lost, he asked her about her life, what she enjoyed, and where her dreams took her at night. He answered her questions, even though he didn't have to. He realized that he enjoyed spending time with her more than his quest for dragonmite."

"Sounds about right," Kase agreed.

"One day, she finally let him win," Lenia said.

"What a lucky guy," Kase said, rolling his eyes.

Lenia stopped walking and looked up at Kase. "Instead of crossing the bridge, Prince Next Level asked one final question of the wizard."

She wrapped her arms around him and held him close. He felt his heart beat a little faster.

"Can I kiss you?" she said.

He pulled her closer, and this time she didn't shy away. He leant his forehead on hers, embracing the beautiful moment. He moved his chin forwards, closer to her lips.

"Dragon Slayer!" someone yelled from a distance.

Kase startled, and he felt Lenia shudder. "So close," she whispered. She put her hand on his chest and pushed him away.

He glared down the path, wanting to hurt the latest person to ruin his chances of kissing Lenia. He relaxed when he noticed three satyr kids running towards them.

"What are you doing here, Dragon Slayer?" one of the kids asked.

"He's probably here to slay a dragon," another scoffed.

"We're not here to hurt anything or anyone," Kase assured them. "We've just come to see what the dragons' dens are like."

The three kids looked at Kase and Lenia in awe. "You're just going to walk around with the dragons, and not even hide your scent?" the third one asked.

"Good luck," the second kid quipped.

"Hide our scent?" Lenia said. "Why would we do that?"

The kids laughed, but Kase and Lenia didn't get the joke. They shared a look of confusion.

"Everybody knows that dragons can smell you from miles away," the first kid said. "That's why you have to carry dragon repellent with you wherever you go. We're good—we brought ours. See?" She took a pouch from around her waist and handed it to them. "Just in case we have to get somewhere that doesn't have safe tree cover."

Lenia untied the knot and opened the pouch. She threw back her head when the smell hit her. "What's in here?" she asked, pinching her nose with her free hand.

Kase took a whiff, but didn't have the same reaction. It reminded him of the farm.

"It's mostly pig manure, but there's a little bit of butter mixed in so that it's easier to put on," the first kid answered proudly.

"You put this on your skin? No thanks." Lenia handed the pouch back to the satyrs.

"You'll get used to it pretty fast." The third kid showed them his pouch and the second kid's. "Besides, it's better than getting eaten by a dragon."

"We'll take our chances," Lenia said. She touched her trident and winked at Kase.

"Thanks for your help," Kase said. When Lenia turned to continue their trek, he reached back for the pouch of manure. He brought his finger up to his lips for the kids to keep his secret.

They giggled and handed over a pouch of dragon repellent. "Dragon Slayer," the first kid whispered. She patted her heart with her fist.

Kase tucked the pouch into his pocket and caught up to Lenia, putting his arm around her. They only passed a couple other satyrs in their walk through the forest, but they weren't as excited to see them as the kids were. Before they knew it, they had reached the part of the island where the dragons made their dens.

There didn't appear to be any life on this part of Skyland. The black, rocky terrain wasn't soft enough to sprout growth, and the pools of lava in the distance proved that there was no water available for the soil. It was like being on the top of a volcano, but without the giant cliffs. There was only an unending horizon of caverns, fire, and darkness.

"It's beautiful," Lenia said.

Kase checked the map and led her across the rugged terrain. Talen's notes advised them to stay as close to large boulders as possible, and to remain as quiet as mice. They both focused on not drawing attention to themselves.

Climbing one of the area's many hills, Kase thought he heard a sound from the other side. He pulled Lenia close to a rock, and they waited. She pulled out a bottle of water from her pocket and took a sip. She offered him some, but he refused.

When they risked moving again, they only made it a few steps before they heard a crash further up the hill. Rocks slid down and bounced across their trail. A dragon perched on top of the hill, staring down at them. It didn't make a sound, but sniffed at the air intently.

"What should we do?" Lenia whispered.

Kase stared back at the curious beast. Its torso was patterned with dark green scales and a few orange stripes. It reminded him of the cat he and Curtis had rescued at The Juice Moose.

"Keep one hand on your trident," Kase said, clutching her other. "Let's see how far we can get before it attacks us."

They continued on their path, keeping one eye on the dragon. When they passed the hill, they heard the dragon bark twice, but it still didn't move.

"Do you think—" A crash in front of them made Lenia stop.

A dark blue dragon had landed to block their path. Its snarl wasn't nearly as curious as its partner. It was angry and serious.

Kase heard other growls from the sky. A shadow crossed the soft clouds above them. "We're about to get ambushed," he said calmly. "We should go."

The blue dragon reared its head back, and an orange glow appeared in its throat. Kase looked back at the green one, which flapped its wings as if to take off.

In an instant, they were back where they had begun their journey, at the top of the Skyland Grind.

"We could have taken them," Lenia said confidently. She rubbed Kase's hand gently.

"Oh, probably," he said sarcastically. "Should we go back?"

Lenia moved her eyes to the left and smiled. "In a bit."

"Are you seriously not afraid of dragons?" he asked. "They're basically birds, but with gigantic teeth and claws."

She looked up at him. Her smile had disappeared. "Birds are way worse. At least you know what you're getting with a dragon. Birds are unpredictable and crazy."

Kase smiled proudly. He liked her fearlessness when it came to monsters, even if it was misguided on harmless creatures. "Can I take you somewhere, before we head back to the dragon's den?" he asked.

"What did you have in mind?" she said.

Instead of answering, he wrapped his arms around her and grabbed the trident. He closed his eyes, and remembered his exhilaration the last time he had faced a dragon. When he opened them, they stood on an island of the Skyland Grind just below cloud level.

He stared into her beautiful green eyes. "The first time I teleported," he said, "I thought I was saying goodbye to you. I was falling through the air towards my death, and all I could think of was how I wanted to see you one last time."

He leant his forehead against hers. He pulled her in close, and their noses brushed. "You were already in my mind and, more importantly, in my heart." He closed his eyes, and tilted his head until he could feel her soft breath. He nudged his lips further, and gently pressed them against hers.

This time Lenia didn't disappear. Her lips were soft and gentle, but fiery and passionate. She squeezed him tighter, her fingers clutching his back. She tilted her head and kissed him harder.

He held her in his arms and pulled her tight. He could feel her quickened heartbeat. Everything else around him disappeared.

Lenia put her palm against his chest and broke the kiss. He didn't want to stop, but he was glad to breathe again.

They stared at each other, not worrying about what came next. No one interrupted them, or even mattered at that point.

"Was that a good moment?" he asked.

Lenia smiled. "It was perfect, because it was ours." She pulled him down by his shirt and kissed him again.

CHAPTER 17

Let's Take Them Back

"We have to put this on our face?" Cali clutched the pouch of dragon repellent and shook her head.

"We have to put it on everywhere," Kase said. "It's the reason we were able to scout the entire trail and not run into any more dragons."

After their scouting mission, he and Lenia had gone to the village of the satyrs and picked up some more stock, along with some homemade satyr popcorn. They'd also taken the opportunity to spend some more time with the satyr kids, and sign up for future volunteer work. Since the satyrs had helped them with their quest, it was their duty to repay the kind gesture.

There was enough repellent for all four of the Liberati Next Level, plus a little extra. It lasted for hours, but they didn't want to be caught without it. They knew how quickly the dragons could find them, and it was crucial for them to remain hidden if their plan was to succeed.

"It's not that bad," Talen said. She'd already lathered her cheeks, and was applying the rest to her neck, arms, clothes, and hair.

Lenia shook her head at Talen. "It's pretty bad," she said. "They said you get used to it, but it's just too gross. I plugged my nose with some straw and breathed through my mouth."

"And you're sure it will work." Cali didn't seem convinced.

"We still have to sneak around," Lenia said. "But it will ensure that we won't get any surprises. When we weren't wearing the repellent, the dragons were on us in a flash."

"This is so cool," Talen said. She was covered in a thick, brown layer of manure, but her smile was dazzling. "I even have enough to show off to Harlow."

"You want to take manure to your girlfriend?" Kase asked. He was confused by the gesture, since Lenia was clearly disgusted.

"She's always bringing me gifts from her trips, so this time I get to do the same," Talen said. "I know she hasn't seen this stuff before, so she'll think it's cool."

"It's not a classic gift, but I think it's cute" Lenia looked at Kase and smiled. "You have something on your ..." she pointed at his lips, and then snuck a kiss.

"How dare you," Kase said in an affronted air. His smile disappeared when he noticed the blank stare from Cali and Talen's whimsical one. He waited for one of them to make a clever remark.

"Now we can cross that one off our list." Lenia said. She put some straw into her nose. It was a dorky look, but she was still beautiful.

"You have a list?" Talen asked.

"It's personal." Kase looked at his sister again, thinking she would make fun of his kissing list with Lenia.

Cali grinned, and then turned her attention back to her pouch. "I guess I'll use the straw method if it gets too pungent," she said. She dipped her hand in and started lathering herself up. "Tell me about our hiding spot."

"There's a cave that overlooks the entire area where the gate is supposed to be," Lenia said. She started to get ready with manure too. "A river of lava surrounds that single cavern. A rock bridge grants access from the south, but we'll be perched up on the east side, well out of sight."

Cali crinkled her nose. "And hopefully scent."

"We'll be too far from Triple Thunder to be noticed, but we'll also be covered against any dragon interference," Kase said. He was proud of the nesting spot that he and Lenia had found.

"You still think the task force is going to use the bridge?" Cali asked. "If they have a levitation board, won't they just fly through the air and land wherever they want to?"

"I don't think their design is strong enough to withstand a dragon attack," Lenia said confidently.

"I agree," Talen said. "From the plans, they're using it for transport only. They're likely carrying dragonmite inside, and then using the device to haul the doorway of life piece away. They camouflaged it for a reason: to keep it hidden."

Kase finished lathering himself up with dragon repellent, and Talen, Cali, and Lenia soon followed. They were ready for their mission.

"From this point on, we don't make a sound," Cali said. "We wait for the task force to make their move, and we capture them on our sage mirrors. It will give us the proof we need to show the rest of the Triple Crown what High Wizard Zuke is doing."

The Liberati Next Level nodded. Cali and Talen put the extra repellent in their sacs. Kase checked to make sure he had a sword and shield ready. Lenia ensured that the straps around her trident were tight, and then, one by one, she teleported them to them to their perch.

By Talen's calculations, they had enough time to get comfortable and set up their sage mirrors before the Triple Thunder task force would arrive. Lenia had spotted them earlier at the beginning of the Skyland Grind, confirming they were on schedule.

Kase didn't have anything to do, except keep an eye out for dragons. The darkness of the den was more eerie at night. The glow of the lava lit up the area, but the sky remained pitch-black. Clouds covered the starlight, which meant that anything flying overhead would be invisible.

The entrance to the lone cavern where the portal was buried faced the bridge. They were unable to see directly in, but a yellow tail dangled outside of it. They hadn't seen a dragon occupying the cavern during their research time. Kase wondered if it would leave soon, or if it would be a surprise to the task force too.

The tail rocked back and forth slowly, which made Kase think that its owner was relaxing. He hoped it would stay that way—at least, while they were in their hiding spot. They didn't need an alarmed dragon to tip off the task force to their presence.

Talen and Cali had their notebooks open and their quills ready. They both lay with their stomachs on the ground and their sage mirrors perched in front of them. Cali wanted to make sure they captured a moving image of the entire event, and two sage mirrors were more reliable than one.

They all waited in silence. It was boring, but they understood the seriousness of their mission and remained focused. A short while later, their patience was rewarded.

The enclosed levitation board crept into sight. When it reached the base of the bridge, the doors slowly opened, and four members dressed in black, hooded garments swiftly exited. They hustled to a small cave with the same instincts as the Liberati: they had pre-picked a hiding spot to elude any unwanted enemies.

A smaller platform coasted out of the levitation container. It carried a glass box the size of a horse. Most of it contained a bright green liquid that glowed in the night, but there was a smaller section above it that held a dark, round object.

Kase felt a little jab to his midsection. Lenia had her hands together, and then spread them apart. "Boom," she mouthed.

He stared at the giant dragonmite box. It glided across the terrain at a steady pace, but he wasn't the only one who had noticed it. The dangling dragon tail had slipped inside. Moments later, a golden dragon head extended from the cave. It was quickly followed by two more. Kase could see that all three necks connected to a single body.

One of the heads sniffed, while another gave a warning growl. The glowing liquid never slowed. The dragon heads started barking, but not at the threat. It was as if one would speak, and the other would reply. It must have been discussing its strategy.

A small explosion in the sky grabbed its attention. All three heads watched as smaller balls of dragonmite were launched into the air. While the dragon was distracted, the large glass cube picked up speed.

One of the dragon heads noticed the charging threat. It roared, leaning back as an orange glow appeared in its mouth. The dragonmite disappeared into the cave as all three heads readied for attack.

It was too late.

A huge bang echoed through the dragon's den, and a light shone so brilliantly that Kase had to shut his eyes. He turned and held his shield in front of him and Lenia. What followed was a rush of wind, the pitter-patter of falling rock, and then eerie silence.

Kase opened his eyes and turned back to the scene. Talen and Cali were both steady, each capturing a moving image through the dust that settled. The lone cavern was gone, along with the ground underneath it. The dragon was in pieces. Only a white, glowing portal door was left unaffected by the blast.

He heard quiet sobbing, and felt Lenia's shoulders shake under his protective arm. He held her tight, and thought about getting her somewhere safe. He touched her trident, and teleported them away.

They were back at their spot on the Skyland Grind. Although he was proud for teleporting them farther than he ever had before, his focus was on her. "Are you okay?" He rubbed her back gently. "Did some of the debris hit you?"

"It's all my fault." Lenia looked up at Kase with pools in her eyes.

"No, it's not," he said. He hoped her tears wouldn't drip down her face and mix with the manure.

"I helped invent the dragonmite," she said. Her voice was stronger, but still sad. "They used it to murder an innocent animal. I'm a killer."

"*They* used it," Kase said. "They're the ones who took something of yours and applied it irresponsibly. It doesn't define who you are."

Lenia shook her head, unimpressed. "I shouldn't have joined the Triple Crown project. Everything would be easier if I had just stayed a professor, or even become a healer like my family wanted."

Kase put both his hands on her shoulders. "You can still do that stuff, but they don't define you either. You'll still be you no matter what career you have or what invention you create. You're a multi-talented, next level, super wizard warrior, and I'm proud to be beside you. No matter what."

Lenia's eyes darted to the left, but she still didn't smile. "So even if I create a device that destroys the world, you'd still be with me?"

"I'd be there with some satyr popcorn, ready to watch everything burn," he said.

Lenia giggled. She looked back up at Kase and kissed him quickly. He tried to ignore the manure on her lips.

"But let's not destroy everything today," he said. "We still have an opportunity to stop the task force and make things right. Are you ready to teach them a lesson, Professor Next Level?"

"As long as you're with me, Boyfriend Next Level," she said with a smile.

Kase's mouth opened in shock. It was the first time she had called him that. Before he could respond, she touched her trident and teleported them back to their hiding spot.

Lenia held Kase's hand as they both looked over the destruction. In the time they were gone, a small moving platform had been brought out to hover above the white portal door. On top was a giant hog, but it wasn't moving.

Cali and Talen didn't even look up with their reappearance, so

218

Kase tapped Cali on the shoulder. He pointed at her, then himself and Lenia. He made a gesture with his hand like a quacking duck. Cali nodded and gave her sage mirror to Talen.

Lenia touched Cali, and they both disappeared. A moment later, Kase was also transported back to their lake by the farm. It was the meeting place they had agreed upon as the only spot safe enough to talk about their plan.

"What?" Cali's arms were crossed, and she tapped her foot.

"Lenia and I want to do more," Kase said firmly.

"We want to stop them from using the dragonmite on anything else," Lenia added.

Cali looked across the water, and her head swayed back and forth. "I don't want to put you in any danger, but I agree. We have to find a way to expose High Wizard Zuke and his team. The images we have now won't be of any use; the task force can't be identified. We have to unmask the villains."

"So how do we do that?" Lenia looked at Kase for a suggestion.

"We'll have to draw them out of their cave," he said.

"Hmm. Is it possible for you to use the levitation board that the hog is on?" Cali asked.

"Yes," Lenia and Kase answered in unison.

"Okay." Cali raised her eyebrows and shook her head. "Their second phase seems to involve using the hog as bait. The portal door needs dragon fire to open, so if we remove their lure, they'll have to come up with an alternative."

"They'll be vulnerable when their plans are disrupted," Kase agreed.

"Let's do this." Lenia put her hand on Cali.

"Wait," Cali said before they teleported. "I just want to say I'm really happy for you two. But promise me that you won't get hurt by the task force or by dragons."

"We'll be fine, Cali," Kase said with a smile.

"Thank you," Lenia added. She and Cali disappeared.

Moments later, Kase was staring at the sleepy eyes of the giant hog. It snorted while it slept. He didn't know that hogs could snore.

A circular ridge surrounded the portal door from the dragonmite blast. Kase stood about a foot under the level ground. The white glow of the portal door was a little distracting, but it wasn't as magical as Lenia's quick work.

The levitation board sat idle beside the hog, which the task force had dumped on the portal door. Kase assumed they were hoping that a dragon would torch its prey before consuming it, thereby energizing the door.

Lenia teleported to the board and activated the solution inside. With her finite control of the burning effect, she turned the board so that its surface faced the hog. Then she wiped the giant bait off the portal door, as if she were swatting a fly with a rolled-up piece of paper.

When she was done, she placed the levitation board back on the ground, moved the levers so that no more solution could mix, and teleported back to Kase's side. "Now what?" she asked.

"Now we take them to class," he answered. He drew his sword and took a few steps to clear the ridge, but stopped. Lenia was laughing.

"I know what you're trying to do," Lenia said, "but I don't think it came out as tough as you thought."

Kase looked back at her and made a sweeping gesture with his sword. "Do you have something better?"

She teleported beside him and stared ahead. Her face was expressionless, but her voice got lower. "Now we roast them."

Kase sighed. He appreciated her quip, but he didn't think it was that great. "Here they come."

Three small levitation boards, the size of Lenia's original design, headed towards them. Each of the outside boards held two members of the task force, while the middle one had a single rider. They were all dressed in black. They landed a few yards away from Kase and Lenia, but remained nonthreatening.

The lone rider removed his hood. "What are you two doing?" Derek yelled.

"Your mission is over," Kase said. "You've failed. Go home, and never return to this den again."

Derek rubbed his forehead. He looked exhausted. "Look, Kase. I'm sorry we didn't choose you to be a part of this, but there will be other opportunities. You're still an important part of the Triple Crown, and will be on the right side of history."

"Kase doesn't need you," Lenia said. "He's already chosen which side he wants to be on." She grabbed his hand and stood strong.

Derek rolled his eyes. "We're all on the same team here. Do you even know what we're trying to do?"

"You're going to erect the doorway of life and create a world of evil," Kase said.

"Whoa," Derek said, holding his only hand out. "The relic on the other side of that portal is powerful, yes. But it will give us an opportunity to change the world for the better. We can bring back those who have been lost too early, like your parents. Don't you want that?"

Kase never even thought about bringing his mom and dad back to life. Having his grandparents around would be better, though.

"So your plan is to kill living creatures in order to bring already dead people back to life?" Lenia asked. "You don't understand what kind of mess you're making."

Derek laughed, and his crew followed. "You mean the man-eating, fire-breathing, three-headed dragon? Are you serious?"

"Some of us like dragons," Kase said. "And some dragons like us."

He pointed up to the sky. A purple dragon descended from the cloud cover. It landed in the wreckage behind Kase and Lenia, on top of the portal door. It spread its wings out wide and roared menacingly. Its one remaining eye glared at the task force.

"I'd like you to meet my friend, Billy Do-Dance," Kase said. "If you're not going to leave this place, then Billy will make you."

Derek looked at the dragon in terror. "That's impossible," he said. "Retreat!"

The three levitation boards floated up into the air and raced back towards their hiding place. As they sped away, Kase made the illusory dragon flap its wings and chase after its prey. He didn't want them to make it back to their cave, so he used the illusion to chase them around for a bit. He even made the dragon blow fire for effect.

"It's perfect," Lenia said. "You even got all the sounds right. It's terrifyingly accurate."

"Thanks," Kase said proudly.

"But 'Billy Do-Dance'? Did you just make that up?"

"I like to think that Billy comes from a long line of dancers," Kase said. "His father was a dancer, and his father before that."

While the three levitation boards were being chased around, a single hooded figure walked steadily towards them. Although his head was down, his golden leather gloves stood out clearly in the darkness.

"It looks like someone isn't afraid of Billy," Kase said.

"If he's leaving his post, then there's no one left to guard the rest of their dragonmite," Lenia said. "If you can keep everyone occupied, I'll see what else they're hiding in that container."

"Go roast them," he said.

Lenia giggled. "Nice try, but it sounds better when I say it." She touched her trident and disappeared.

Kase kept his focus on Billy Do-Dance, but he watched High Wizard Zuke. Did the most powerful wizard in the realm see through his illusion? How desperate was he to obtain the doorway of life? Would he show mercy, or was he as evil as his old friend Mardious Hood?

When Zuke was about twenty feet away, he stopped. Grinning, he slowly removed his golden leather gloves. He held out his palms, and Kase lost focus of Billy. The illusion disappeared. Zuke had the same scar as Money Jane.

"It was you," Kase said.

Zuke was the one who'd stolen Lenia's trident. He'd poisoned her to get it, and taunted them as they tried to recover it. He'd been with Porkchop when they were ambushed in the Badlands. He was the Money Jane impersonator.

"Impressive illusion," Zuke said. "You're becoming quite the wizard. How would you like to be even more powerful?"

Kase was both confused and insulted. But he knew he needed to stall Zuke to give Lenia time. "What do you mean?" he asked.

"I'm only going to offer this once." Zuke fluttered his fingers, as if he were tickling the air. Kase had seen this move before, and knew that it was how the Money Jane impersonator focused his magic. "Join me, and I will show you more power than you've ever dreamed of."

The three levitation boards had returned, and landed behind Zuke. The two extra members were the ones to jump off this time. Both drew their swords. A.J. and Neil even pulled their hoods back, revealing a pair of worried looks. Kase didn't know if they were scared of him or concerned for him.

"Never," he said.

Zuke laughed. "I knew you'd say that." He looked over his shoulder. "Get him."

A.J. looked across at Neil, who was already moving forwards. She kept her united front with her partner. Her sword was shaking, but she wasn't going to back down. She was a true Guardian.

Kase gripped his own weapon and studied their movements. He wished he had his shield, but he'd have to make do. Zuke was still wiggling his fingers, which meant that he was probably going to get attacked by both magic and metal. He tried to search his emotions, to feel what Zuke was up to, but he felt nothing.

A crash to his left disrupted everything.

The dark blue dragon that Kase and Lenia had seen earlier glared at the entire group. It spread its wings wide, and kept its head low to the ground. It let out a skin-tingling roar that made Kase flinch, but the rest of the group laughed.

"Another illusion?" Derek said. "We're not going to fall for that again."

Kase looked back at Zuke, whose eyes were wide with shock. They both knew the dragon was real.

Another crash to their right added to the chaos.

A red dragon with two heads stood tall after its sudden landing. One of the heads sniffed the air, while the other one barked. Other draconic roars could be heard throughout the night sky. Kase wondered if the green and orange striped dragon was lurking around somewhere.

Zuke turned to his group. "Go get the dragonmite," he yelled.

An explosion added to the mayhem. Its bright light, followed by a beautiful flash of fire and a thick, grey cloud, surged from the task force's hiding spot. Lenia had succeeded in her mission and obliterated their stock. He hoped she'd return to his side soon.

"What now?" Derek was panicking, and already moving away from the dragons.

"Retreat!" High Wizard Zuke yelled.

The task force took off, riding their levitation boards away from the dangerous beasts, but Zuke remained behind, glaring at Kase. He stretched out his arms. Dust started to circle at his feet.

The blue dragon barked, and the red dragon barked back. The two-headed dragon flapped its wings and chased after the fleeing members, just as Billy Do-Dance had.

Another roar moved Kase's attention to the blue dragon, but he didn't run. It wasn't that he thought his repellent would work; he might not be appetizing, but the dragon would still defend its territory. It was that he was more worried about what Zuke was up to. He had a feeling that the Money Jane imposter had other plans.

Suddenly, Kase was surrounded by dozens of Zuke look-alikes. They all had black hoods and golden gloves. He couldn't see their faces, which must have been the key. It was an incredible illusion that didn't fool Kase, but the dragon wasn't as perceptive.

The blue dragon roared, and orange flame filled its mouth. The illusions tried to attack the dragon, but were drowned in fire as soon as they approached the great beast. When the flame touched their robes, they ignited. The burning Zuke illusions ran around and screamed in pain.

Kase wondered how Zuke was able to control multiple illusions at the same time, and have them all act in different ways. So much concentration would be needed in order to make each one believable in its own right. He could appreciate the power required for such a spectacle.

As impressive as it was, he had to stop Zuke. He focused on the swirling dust, knowing that the wizard was hiding within. His emotions stirred along with the wind as he connected with it, and he used his power to create a hole in the middle. To his surprise, there was no one there.

A sharp pain in the back of his right knee made him lose focus.

He crumbled to the ground. His entire leg throbbed. All of the illusions around him laughed. He swung his sword, but it only hit air. He tried looking for the figure without golden gloves, but the real Zuke had escaped.

He checked his knee: the gold hilt of a dagger stuck out the back of it. He thought about pulling it out, but worried about the blood loss and possibly slicing a tendon. He'd stabbed Mason in the same spot. Zuke had gotten him with his own move.

He wished he could heal himself, or that Lenia was close. He stood on his good leg to try and make himself more visible.

There was a crowd of Zukes standing on the white portal door. The dragon moved towards it, perfectly guided. Kase yelled and swung his sword to take out as many illusions as he could, but he was already too late. The dragon blew fire directly at the crowd.

The glowing white light of the portal door turned black when the flame hit it. It was absorbing the heat, and changing colour in the process. Once the darkness encompassed the entire door, a light pulsated once: exactly like how portal gateways calibrated themselves.

The crowd of Zukes dispersed, leading the dragon in the opposite direction. Like a moth chasing a flame, the beast followed curiously. It roared and blew fire at the fleeing illusions.

Meanwhile, the inner panels of the portal triangle slid into the outer edges, opening an entrance in the ground. Instead of a glimmer of where the portal led to, there was only blackness.

Kase hobbled towards it as fast as he could. He had made it past the circular ridge of the blast radius just as the giant levitation board floated over to the portal. The real Zuke hopped on. When he dove down into the darkness, all the illusions disappeared.

Kase kept hobbling. He heard the dragon roar again, and knew it was directed at him this time. He didn't turn back to see how far away it was; his focus was on the portal door.

His leg hurt more and more with every step. He felt the edge of the blade scraping bone, but he pushed on. He wanted Lenia to appear and take him to safety, but he knew he couldn't rely on that option.

When he was close enough to the gateway, he launched himself forwards. He cleared the edge of the doorway and fell head first into the portal.

CHAPTER 18

Searching For Euphoria

K ase lifted his upper body off the stone floor. In front of him was a wide, deep staircase that led down to a treasure trove, much like the one he and the Liberati had discovered behind the desert portal hidden by the Eidola. The room was like that of a castle's, but there weren't any windows. Instead, ten rings of fire surrounded the perimeter of the room, lighting the way.

Three flights of stairs led down to the open arena. Piles of gold and old artefacts were dispersed throughout. Shelves of books lined one side, and rolled-up parchments piled on the other. Unlike the fourth hidden castle of the Eidola, the treasure here wasn't a prop.

Zuke was at the back of the room, already unravelling a silver chain that wrapped a red, oblong artefact. It was being held at six points between two gold pillars. The levitation board was at its base, ready to move the artefact away.

Kase dragged his injured leg to the top of the staircase and pivoted. He slid down like a toddler, trying to save his energy for a standoff with Zuke. He didn't have his shield, and must have dropped his sword in the dragon's den. He didn't know what he was going to do, but he was determined to stop the evil wizard.

"I'm glad to see you made it," Zuke shouted. He didn't turn around.

Kase stopped sliding. He looked around, but he was the only one in the room with Zuke. It wasn't that he was trying to be quiet; he was just a little shocked to hear Zuke sound so friendly. He opted not to say anything, and continued sliding instead.

"Your persistence is admirable," Zuke said. "It reminds me of someone I used to know."

Kase had reached the bottom of the first flight of stairs. There was a short landing before the next section. He hobbled forwards, putting most of his weight on his good leg. He tried not to wince, but he couldn't help it.

Zuke still had his back turned, holding two lengths of chain. He crisscrossed his arms, and then switched his grip. It looked like he was trying to untangle a difficult knot.

Kase decided to engage the High Wizard. Perhaps he could slow him down long enough for Lenia to arrive. "Who?"

"Your father," Zuke said.

Kase was a little surprised that the High Wizard had known Dominic Garrick, but considering his father's notes, it wasn't too shocking to know that the two of them were connected. He wondered how much of a relationship they'd had.

"Did you stab him in the leg too?" he asked.

Zuke laughed. "I wanted to," he admitted, "but Dom was too valuable. His research efforts were unmatched; but you already know that. You've clearly deciphered his journal, or at least the part about this piece of the doorway."

Kase sat on the edge of the second flight of stairs and slid down. "How do you know about the journal?" he asked.

The top ring of fire that lit the room went out. It didn't become noticeably darker in the arena, but Kase wondered what it meant. He turned his head around, thinking that maybe someone else had joined them, but he didn't see anyone.

"I know you're the one who took it from my trap when I decided to give Lenia her trident back," Zuke said. "I was hoping you might find a new clue, or discover something that I've overlooked. But I can tell you don't have a plan. I doubt you two really know what you're capable of."

Zuke pulled his arms apart triumphantly, and the chain pieces dangled to the sides. The artefact tilted forwards, now supported at only four points instead of six.

"She's more powerful than you." Kase hobbled to the third set of stairs. "I've felt it."

"Maybe," Zuke said. "But what good is power if you don't use it?"

He pulled on another piece of chain, but it wasn't wrapped as well as the others. It quickly dangled to the side, leaving only three more to go. "She's not like you and me," he said. "She's not a fighter. She's not willing to sacrifice for the greater good. She's not willing to break the rules in order to get what she wants. She only runs away."

Kase shook his head as he slid down the steps. Zuke's reasoning was unjustified. He was posturing like he knew everything, but Kase knew Lenia better than that.

"I hope she didn't get hurt in that blast," Zuke added. He finally looked back in Kase's direction.

Kase glared at Zuke. He remembered when they had met in the Badlands, and he'd used Lenia's trident to overpower him as the Money Jane imposter. He knew he had the strength to do it again, even without his partner. He could feel the anger inside give him energy.

Zuke let go of the chain in his right hand, and the artefact fell a little further. There were only two points connecting it to the pillars. Zuke bent down to untangle the final two.

Kase finally made it to floor level. Before he could stand, Lenia appeared in front of him. She bent down and touched his leg, but he clutched her arm and put his finger to his lips.

Cali stood beside them, holding her sage mirror. She pointed it at Zuke, capturing him with the piece of the doorway of life.

As happy as he was to see them, Kase had an idea that could help them all. "Hide," he mouthed.

Lenia nodded. She looked back at Zuke, but he didn't seem to notice her presence. She put her arm on Cali's shoulder and touched her trident. They disappeared—Kase didn't know where. All the better.

He needed to keep Zuke talking. "Were you partners with my father?" He stood up and instantly regretted sending Lenia away before she could heal him.

"We never worked together directly, but I'm grateful for what he did," Zuke said. "Not only did he figure out all the locations of the doorway, he was able to get the second piece from Jenim Island. Too bad it cost him his life."

Zuke leant to the right and swivelled away from his treasure. The final chains swung to the side, and the red door piece landed on the levitation board with an echoing thud.

Kase noticed another ring of fire disappear. The room was still bright, but he felt like it wouldn't last long. He stepped forwards, dragging his leg with him.

"What happened to him?" Kase asked. He thought about Cali, and how she needed to hear the truth. She also needed to capture Zuke's face to verify his identity.

Zuke stood, brushed himself off, and stepped onto the levitation board. He made sure his treasure was secured, and then walked around to the front. "I wasn't there, so I don't know all the details," Zuke said. "But he gave his life fighting for what mattered most to him. He was trying to find a way to bring back your mother, I believe; he wasn't going to give up on her. It's the one thing that made me respect him." Zuke spread his arms and tickled the air again.

Kase was too far to reach the High Wizard, so he stopped. He focused on the levitation board instead, to control its burning effect.

He could feel Zuke's influence, and tried to stop him. It felt like he was in an arm wrestling match, pushing for power over the element.

"You can't stop me." Zuke stepped off the levitation board and walked to a treasure pile. He picked up a gold sword, all while still challenging Kase's control of the device.

Kase looked around for a weapon of his own to counter the wizard. All he saw were gold coins and statues. He reached down and wrapped his fingers around the dagger in the back of his knee. He yanked it out, and a rush of pain swept through his body.

He pointed the bloody tip towards Zuke and got in a ready stance. "I'm not going to let you obtain the doorway of life," he said.

"Why not?" Zuke asked. "You seem to be misguided. It was hidden long ago out of fear, but fear can be enlightening. It can push us to do remarkable things, and change the realm for the better. The doorway of life will help everyone recover losses in their life, so they can be free and happy."

"I know you're not using it for good," Kase said. "You're going to resurrect Mardious Hood."

Zuke laughed. "That might be an impossible task." He lowered his sword and raised a hand to his face, framing his evil grin. "I *am* Mardious Hood."

"What?" Kase's control over the levitation board wavered as he tried to accept Zuke's statement. Was it a trick? Mardious Hood died years ago. How could he pretend to be someone else? How could such a tyrant live among the highest authorities and reach the top of their political chain?

"After I killed your murderous grandparents, I was able to switch places with Zuke," Mardious said. "It's been the greatest illusion of all, working at the castle of the Triple Crown while he rests in the great beyond. He served his purpose, much like your father did."

Kase felt heat rise up his throat as he looked at the man who had eliminated his grandparents. Blood pounded in his ears. "I'm going to expose you," Kase said. "You're going to get the justice you deserve."

Mardious laughed again. "You can't stop me; Lenia can't stop me. You couldn't put together an army to end my pursuit of ultimate power. The world is mine, and you should be grateful that I see a use for you. I am not the enemy you think I am."

"I'll tell everyone who you are," Kase threatened. "Then we'll see what the world thinks of you."

"Tell anyone you want," Mardious said. "No one will believe you."

"They will when they hear it from your mouth," Cali said. She stood on the levitation board with the doorway piece, holding her sage mirror high.

Mardious turned. Kase was ready to throw his dagger to take the evil wizard down, but Lenia appeared. She jammed something into Mardious' neck, and then disappeared again.

Mardious was stunned. He yanked the dart out, and held it in his open palm. He swayed a little, and then looked back at Kase. "You don't know what you're …" He fell to the ground awkwardly.

"Stop moving image," Cali said. She tucked her sage mirror into her pocket and jumped down from the levitation board.

Lenia appeared beside Kase and touched his knee again. "Are you okay?" she asked.

Kase was busy studying his sister. She didn't look upset at what Mardious had said. She was strong and composed as she surveyed the scene.

He had so many questions to ask her. He felt his knee stop hurting; there was someone stronger helping him out. "Are you okay?" he asked Lenia.

Lenia stood and smiled. It was as if she had absorbed the pain that transferred from his body to hers without feeling anything. She was truly the most powerful wizard he had ever seen.

Instead of responding, she grabbed him around the waist and kissed him deeply. He closed his eyes, and the rest of the world disappeared for a moment.

She pulled back. "Now we can cross this place off our list," she whispered.

Kase laughed. "I didn't know the secret portal in a dragon's den was even on it."

"It's not on anyone's kiss list," Lenia replied. "But it's on ours."

"How long does this last?" Cali said, interrupting them. She stood over the collapsed wizard.

Lenia walked over to Mardious and knelt down. "If they were used to magically sedate a giant hog for a few hours, I'm guessing he'll be out even longer. I have extras if we want to give him an even bigger dose." She reached into her pocket and showed Cali five more darts. Cali picked one out and held it at eye level.

Kase joined the group. It felt good to move his legs again. "What are we going to do now?" he asked. He watched as another ring of fire around the room disappeared.

Cali had noticed the fire too. "We don't have much time left here," she said. "Once the light goes out in this room, the portal door will close. We should get out of here soon, but I'm not entirely sure what our next move is."

"Should I get Talen?" Lenia asked.

"Good idea," Cali said. "Grab her, but tell her she can stop her sage mirror before you come back. We have enough evidence already."

Lenia touched her trident and disappeared again.

Kase tried to make eye contact with Cali, but she wouldn't look at him. "Did you believe what he said?" he asked softly.

She closed her eyes. "I never wanted to accept that he was dead," she admitted. "But now I don't know what to believe. I understand how much he wanted mom back, but I can't imagine him working with Mardious Hood to get her. Maybe I didn't really know him at all."

Kase put his arm around his sister. "It's okay," he said, rubbing her shoulder. "We don't have to explain it all right now. We've done a lot today; we'll figure out the rest together."

"Thank you, brother." She forced a smile, and then jammed the dart she got from Lenia into the limp body of Mardious Hood. She sighed. "That makes me feel better."

Lenia reappeared with Talen. Instead of staring at Mardious, Talen scanned the room. She stopped and stared at the bookshelves on the sidewall.

"Here's what I'm thinking," Cali said. "The first thing we need to do is get us, the levitation board, and this piece of the doorway of life out of this cave."

"Why don't we just leave it here?" Kase asked. "It's well-guarded, and the room needs dragon fire for entry."

"If they got in here once, they'll be able to do it again," Cali said. "It's easier now, with the portal exposed. We have to protect it, at least until we can figure out how everything is connected. We still don't know who else is aware of Zuke's true identity."

"True identity?" Talen said.

"Talen, meet Mardious Hood," Kase said, pointing to their prisoner.

"No way." Talen knelt down and studied his face. She picked up his hand and checked his scar. "What a mystery. It does have the possibility to fill in six—no, eight—gaps in my research, but I have so many new questions."

"Once we get the artefact out of here, how do we get it past the dragons?" Lenia asked. "It's too big for me to teleport away."

"If we're just transporting the artefact on the levitation board, we can control it from afar," Kase said. "We can even put it in the levitation container, so that it's covered."

"The container is kind of ..." Lenia moved her eyes to the left. "Occupied."

"How?' Kase asked.

"I removed all of the dragonmite from the container before igniting it all," Lenia said. "I found the darts in there and guessed that they were used to put the hog to sleep because they reeked of valerian root extract—it's the main ingredient in most sleep potions. I used them on the task force. I was able to teleport to each one, inject them with the sleeping potion, and then transport them to the container."

"It really was a genius move," Cali said.

"After I had them all inside, I didn't want the dragons to notice their scent, so I covered them with hog manure. It ... smells pretty bad."

"You can transport a pile of manure?" Kase was impressed.

"I remembered where the satyrs kept their stash, so I just made a bunch of little trips," Lenia answered. "It took a little longer than I wanted, but it worked."

"What are we going to do with the task force?" Talen asked. She looked at Cali. Kase and Lenia followed her gaze.

Cali had her chin in her hand. "I think we have to turn them in to the Triple Crown," Cali said. "To High Scholar Sheese and High Warrior Mac."

"Are you sure we can trust them?" Talen asked. "If Zuke is Mardious Hood, would he have been able to keep that a secret without their help?"

"That's a good question," Cali said. "I don't know who else we can trust, though. We can't go to anyone the High Wizard outranks, so they're the only ones who have the power to make a decision about his claims. I've worked with High Scholar Sheese, and I trust him more than High Warrior Mac. We'll show them what we've found, and hope that they'll do the right thing."

"I'll go with you," Kase said. "We can put Mardious Hood in the levitation container, and I can move it back to the castle of the Triple Crown. We'll stay there and refuse to open it until the High Authority comes to claim it."

"That leaves Lenia to move the artefact to a safe place," Cali said. "I don't want to present it to the Triple Crown until we know it will remain out of Mardious Hood's hands. Do you know where you can hide it?"

Lenia turned to Kase and smiled. "I have a secret place," she said with a wink.

"What about me?" Talen asked. "How can I help?"

Cali put her hand on Talen's shoulder. "You have the most important job, Tal. You're our fail-safe. I'll send you my moving image, which includes Zuke's admission that he's Mardious Hood. That way, you'll have both images. Since no one saw you with us, no one will know you have them. If things go wrong, and you don't hear from us by tomorrow, I want you to send it to everyone you know."

Talen put a hand over her heart. "Dragoon," she said, like a true warrior.

Another ring of fire went out, but it didn't matter. Lenia teleported Talen to safety, and then came back to get Mardious Hood, Cali, and Kase. She put them into the stinky container, and then returned again to move the artefact with the levitation board.

Kase watched the portal door from the entrance of the container. He was surprised at how calm the dragon's den was now. The red, two-headed dragon was eating the hog that had been used as bait, but the other dragons had disappeared. No beasts were flying around or watching from a perch.

Lenia emerged from the portal. She moved the levitation board to rest beside the triangular portal frame, opposite the hungry dragon. Once she was on level ground, she teleported away, joining them in the container. The dragon didn't even seem to notice, and just kept eating.

As Kase used his power to move the large container, Lenia used hers from afar to control the board with the artefact. Cali adjusted the levers to a position where Kase felt comfortable controlling the burning potion, and then stood guard with their prisoners. She had a handful of darts that Lenia had saved, just in case any of them decided to wake up. They were a perfect team.

They moved slowly through the terrain, but didn't get bothered by any more dragons. The camouflage of the container and the cloak of night, along with the smell of manure, was the ideal cover.

They made it all the way to the top of the Skyland Grind before initiating the second half of their plan. Lenia took the levitation board with the artefact to a safe place, while Kase directed the container to the castle of the Triple Crown. Lenia would teleport back to them once they reached their destination.

Instead of using the gateway portal system, Kase flew the container through the air like a dragon. They were much lighter than the tons of rock the container was designed to carry, so they had enough levitation potion to last for days. Since they didn't need to stick to any roads, they took the most direct route from Skyland to Kimroad and enjoyed the peaceful night sky.

When they were close to Kimroad, Cali used her sage mirror to send High Scholar Sheese a personal message. She didn't tell him that they had stopped the task force and captured Mardious Hood, but she mentioned that they had subdued some high-profile criminals, and stressed the importance of a meeting with him. She urged him to be present in the central courtyard with High Warrior Mac and a few High Guardians. She staked her entire reputation on it in order to convey her seriousness.

When they finally reached the castle of the Triple Crown, Kase couldn't see where he was supposed to land—the portholes in the side of the container didn't give him a view of the ground beneath them. He slowly moved the container from the sky to the ground, hoping that no one would get crushed underneath it.

When he was just above the ground, Lenia appeared beside him and held his hand. She'd waited for them outside the castle before teleporting inside to the rest of the group. "You're a next level wizard," she said encouragingly.

Kase felt the container touch down and finally relaxed. He and Lenia pulled the levers so that the potion would desist. It had been a long trip, but he was glad it was over.

He heard rustling outside the container and peered through the openings. A half-dozen High Guardians stood by the entrance of the castle, but only High Warrior Mac and High Scholar Sheese waited beside the container.

"Are you in there, Cali?" High Scholar Sheese asked. "Are you okay?"

"Yes, sir," Cali replied. "Before we open the doors, I want you to look at the moving image on my sage mirror," she said. "It explains everything."

She handed the High Scholar her mirror through the opening. High Scholar Sheese raised his eyebrows, but gestured for High Warrior Mac to huddle in close, so the two of them could watch it together. Flashes of light accompanied the low sounds of the moving image, but it was hard to hear through the walls of the container.

While the highest-ranking leaders in the realm evaluated the evidence, Cali, Kase, and Lenia all waited in silence. Cali had warned them that there were two possible outcomes.

The first was Mardious Hood and his task force being arrested. They would be taken out of the container and properly imprisoned until they woke up. After that, they could be processed and questioned accordingly, and then prosecuted to the full extent of the laws of the realm.

The other would involve the Liberati getting arrested, should Sheese and Mac side with the High Wizard. If they didn't want to be locked up, they'd have to disappear quickly. Lenia could handle that, but then they'd be on the run until they could get more evidence to support their claims. It would be up to them to expose the conspiracy to the rest of the world.

"Oh, my." High Warrior Mac's rumbling voice carried to them in the container.

Kase could hear the dragons barking from the moving image. They had reached his and Zuke's standoff, and he wondered if they could see him get stabbed in the leg. He wanted to watch Cali's image himself, to see how Zuke had managed to slide out of the swirling dust and surprise him with a crippling blow.

They all waited anxiously as the moving image continued. It was quiet for a few moments until Cali was teleported through the portal. Kase heard Zuke's voice as he made his threats and unveiled his identity. Then there was nothing.

"Open the door, Cali," Sheese commanded. "I want to check your prisoners."

Cali nodded to Kase. "Moment of truth," she whispered. She grabbed Lenia's hand. Lenia tightly held the shaft of her trident. They stood against the wall, a few steps from the entrance. Kase opened the door and put his arm around Lenia.

High Scholar Sheese stood strong, but the stench made High Warrior Mac turn in disgust. Mac took a few steps back, while Sheese carefully entered the container. He walked past the Liberati, and knelt beside Mardious Hood. He turned the High Wizard's palm over and stared at the scar.

"I don't believe it." High Scholar Sheese sighed. "The mark of the madman. How could I have been so oblivious to such a fiendish ruse?"

The High Scholar looked distraught, but Kase didn't know what they were supposed to do. He checked Cali's reaction, hoping that she knew what was going on. He waited for her cue to either run away, or relax because everything would be all right.

Sheese stood up and handed the sage mirror back to Cali. "I'm sorry you had to go to such elaborate lengths to uncover the plot of this criminal, but I'm grateful that you were brave enough to do so. Let's go inside, and we can try to make sense of this—together."

"Of course, High Scholar Sheese," Cali said politely. She accepted the sage mirror and let go of Lenia's hand.

Her smile was relieving, but Kase was still a little unsure if this was part of her plan.

Sheese left the container. Cali was about to follow, but Kase tugged on her sleeve. "What now?" he whispered.

Sheese went over to Mac. He turned away from the Liberati. Mac listened and nodded. Sheese pointed to the Guardians at the entrance of the castle, but then looked back at the Liberati.

"I trust them," Cali said with a smile. "I've worked with High Scholar Sheese long enough to know when he's puzzled. I'm confident that he wasn't aware of the High Wizard's true identity, and needs us to help resolve everything."

They exited the container. Kase took a moment to breathe in some fresh air. The Guardians rushed past them and entered the container. There were no complaints about the smell, but they did drag the bodies out as quickly as possible.

High Scholar Sheese led Cali, Lenia, and Kase into the castle of the Triple Crown. Sheese talked to Cali privately while Kase and Lenia followed behind. Kase gripped Lenia's hand, but kept his head on a swivel. He still didn't know what to expect; even though Sheese was on their side, he knew there could still be enemies lurking in the shadows.

They walked down long stretches of hallways and up a few flights of stairs until they reached the High Scholar's office. It made Cali's look like a closet. There were cushioned chairs around a fireplace on one side of the room and tall windows on the other. A long table was stationed beside the windows, with an old oak desk along the back wall. A few tapestries and statues decorated the meticulously organized room, making it look both historic and pristine.

The High Scholar gestured for the Liberati to sit at the table. He grabbed a notebook and quill from his desk and then joined them. He opened his book to a fresh page, flattening it with a gentle touch. He fiddled with his quill, but hesitated before writing anything down.

"I have to be honest with you," Sheese said. "I knew that the High Wizard was on an excursion to Skyland, but I wasn't aware of his intentions. It's not the first time he's taken a special team to that area of the realm."

The Liberati listened intently. The information the High Scholar shared was classified, and not widely known nor recorded.

Apparently, Zuke and Mardious had been tasked with doing research on dragons and their habitat when they both started working for the Triple Crown years ago. There was always a concern that, if the dragons' sanctuary were disrupted, the beasts would seek refuge in another part of the realm. Since their movement would jeopardise the safety of anyone occupying the dragons' preferred territory, the leaders of the Triple Crown wanted as much information as possible to create a plan of action in case of disaster.

When Mardious Hood had turned against the Triple Crown, and was seemingly brought down by Roman Garrick, Zuke was left alone in his quests. He started putting new teams together in order to continue his research. Even when Zuke was promoted to High

Wizard of the realm, he wanted to remain in charge of his passion project.

"If I had known of the other secrets of the area, I would have been more suspicious," Sheese admitted. "Magic, beasts, and ancient portals are not within my interests, but that's not an excuse for ignorance. I guess we all have our secrets though, right Cali?"

Cali sighed. "I'm sorry I didn't come to you earlier," she said. "I didn't understand it all, and I needed proof before we could say anything."

The door to the High Scholar's office opened, and High Warrior Mac entered. He closed the door firmly and sat down at the table.

"Report?" High Scholar Sheese asked.

"The prisoners are locked up, but still asleep," Mac said. "We'll have to wait until they wake before we can interrogate them."

"What happens to them now?" Cali asked.

"We'll let them each share their accounts. Our wizards have ways to ensure it's truthful," Sheese said. "If they refuse to cooperate, we'll officially charge them. They'll have the right to a fair trial, as per the laws of the realm."

The High Scholar picked up his quill once more. "In the meantime, I need all the facts that you can give me so that we can build a strong case. Although your sage mirror shows what happened, I need to know everything that led up to the event, along with any details that aren't shown as clearly. Such as how Kase"—Sheese turned his full attention to him—"was able to combat Mardious Hood's magic?"

Kase looked to Cali, who gave him a reassuring nod. He felt Lenia's hand grip his, and he relaxed. Even though he had used his wizard power against the High Wizard in front of the task force, he was still nervous to admit it to the other authorities of the Triple Crown.

Kase, Lenia, and Cali took turns explaining their story. Kase talked about his showdown with Mardious and his manipulation of the levitation board, illusions, and elements. Lenia shared her teleporting ability with the trident, and what she knew of the contents of dragon-mite. Cali described the notes from her father's journal, the relic that Mardious was after, and the secret room behind the broom closet of the tenth floor. They admitted that they knew where three parts of the doorway of life were, but the fourth was still a mystery.

When they were finished, High Scholar Sheese closed his note-book and set his quill down. "There are things about this castle that surprise me every day," he said. "I thought I knew about all the special rooms and relics that we kept here. It looks like I have a lot of work to do if I want to continue leading this realm."

"I suggest that we gather up everything in that room and secure it as evidence against our prisoners," Cali said.

"I agree," Sheese said. "You and I can go there now, but it's already been a long night for all of you." He looked at Kase and Lenia. "I think I have all the information I need from you two, so you're welcome to go home, clean up, and get some rest. Tomorrow, I'll be interrogating the task force. We'll revisit the events of tonight once we get their stories. We can also make a plan to secure all the pieces of the doorway of life, and maybe speak some more about your father."

"They're not going to stay here?" High Warrior Mac asked.

"They're not under arrest, and it's not like we can force them to remain here," Sheese said. "Seeing as they're heroes that can teleport at any time."

Kase clutched Lenia's hand again. He gave her a wink, to which she blushed.

"Again, I want to thank you for your bravery in this matter," Sheese said with a smile. "We've uncovered a lot tonight. I hope you know to keep everything you've experienced to yourselves. We don't need the public finding out about true identities, special task forces, and powerful relics."

"We understand," Kase said. Sheese's words reminded him of his last encounter with the High Authority, when he had been forced to keep his dragon slaying a secret from students at The Academy. This time, he felt proud instead of ashamed.

"Of course." Lenia smiled and nodded politely to the High Scholar and High Warrior.

Mac stood and put his fist over his chest. "I also want to congratulate you in your victory tonight. You all have skills and knowledge that are worthy of the highest recognition. Uncovering this plot and to bring down a known criminal is a great feat."

He looked directly at Kase. "I know you're still a recruit, Kase Garrick. Last time we met, I promised you a position with the High Guardians once you graduated. However, you have shown even more skill and honour in your latest pursuits. You are one of the greatest warriors I've ever met, and I like to keep talent like that close. I want to invite you to be part of my personal staff as you continue with your program at The Academy, and then beyond."

Kase tried not to smile. Working directly with the High Warrior was the greatest position he could have hoped for. He took a few deep breaths so that his excitement wouldn't make him say something embarrassing.

He stood up proudly and put a fist over his heart. "Dragoon," he said.

They all left the office. Sheese and Cali went to gather the evidence, and Mac went back to the holding cells. Lenia touched her trident, to teleport her and Kase away. They appeared on the lake near his aunt and uncle's house.

They waded into the water and scrubbed the dragon repellent from their clothes, hair, and skin. Once they were clean, they moved to their secret tree house. They had warm tea, heavy blankets, and a surprisingly comfortable red stone seat.

"Are you happy to be a Triple Crown recognized wizard hero?" Kase took a sip of his drink and enjoyed the moonlight.

"It's just something more to add to my name," Lenia said. "I'm a next level professor, a super wizard warrior, an advanced healer with two Quest Series medals, and now I have the recognition of the highest authorities in the realm."

"I mean ..." Kase moved his eyes to the left, mimicking her. "What else can you add to that name? What's next for Lenia Rie?"

"Everything," she said with a smile. "I want it all."

Kase put his arm around her. "I want it all with you."

"I wouldn't have it any other way," she said.

He leant his head forwards and kissed her.

He wasn't thinking about their kiss list, and how their tree house was now a part of it. He wasn't worried about the incredible night they'd had together, stopping the most historic villain in their lifetime. He wasn't even thinking about his future as a recognized great warrior of the realm.

He was enjoying the moment. He was happy, safe, and where he needed to be.

He was with his next level girlfriend.

About the Author

T.K. RIGGINS started writing because of a dare. His friend was searching for something new to read, and after coming up empty-handed, challenged Riggins to take action. Instead of recommending a book, Riggins decided to pen a story of his own.

He shared an experience from his past, where he'd witnessed a cattle farmer help a cow give birth to a calf that had become turned around inside the womb. With a little bit of tugging, some questionable language, and a healthy dose of faith, the calf entered the world and took its first breath with ease.

Growing up in the city, Riggins thought he'd witnessed a miracle. On its own, the calf would have surely been dead, but with the help of the farmer it was alive and well. Riggins turned this day on the farm into a fantasy story with a flying lion and a tale of magic, because the experience was magical to him.

His audience loved the story, so Riggins was obligated to make more. Instead of focusing on just the farm, he used other aspects of his life to create a world with the physical strength of a warrior, the intellectual prowess of a scholar, and the passionate magic of a wizard. After a while, he'd created his own book series.

Although he doesn't have a typical writer's background in Literature or Education, his BSc in Mechanical Engineering helps him innovate, problem solve, and attack his series with a fresh perspective. He's able to take a classic fantasy setting and add a modern twist, creating a world and story all his own.

T.K. Riggins is the author of the fantasy series *How To Set The World On Fire*. Originally from the Midwest, he now lives on the Canadian west coast, where he enjoys hiking the path less travelled, swimming against the current, and continuously pushing the boundaries.